MW00975114

At Last!

∞

Tracy~
The original "Bev" is
Thank you SO MUCH for
your love & support! It's
only uphill from here!

God Bless
Today Tomorrow & Always
Your Friend
Lisa Harrison
Jackson

At Last!

Lisa Harrison Jackson

Writers Club Press
New York Lincoln Shanghai

At Last!

All Rights Reserved © 2001 by Lisa Harrison-Jackson

No part of this book may be reproduced or transmitted in any form or by any means, graphic, electronic, or mechanical, including photocopying, recording, taping, or by any information storage retrieval system, without the written permission of the publisher.

Writers Club Press
an imprint of iUniverse, Inc.

For information address:
iUniverse, Inc.
2021 Pine Lake Road, Suite 100
Lincoln, NE 68512
www.iuniverse.com

This is a work of fiction. Names, characters, places and incidents either are the product of the author's imagination or are used ficticiously. Any resemblance to actual events, locales, organizations, or persons, living or dead, is entirely coincidental and beyond the intent of either the author or the publisher.

ISBN: 0-595-20869-X

Printed in the United States of America

Especially for my parents,
L.G. & Shirley Harrison

ACKNOWLEDGMENTS

First and foremost, I would like to give honor to The Almighty God for blessing me with a passion for the written word. I love touching people's lives through my works. I believe it to be a sincere privilege to be a vessel in His plan.

I'd like to thank two important people in my life, my parents, L.G. and Shirley Harrison for allowing me to express my creativity in various art forms. Your encouragement was appreciated while your foundation gave me the determination to press toward my dream.

To my husband Nate and daughters, Chandler and McKinley. Your support and understanding were endless especially when I had to spend a lot of nights on the computer writing and re-writing. I love you all very much!

I'd like to also acknowledge the following people who helped to make this book come to life: Kim Whiteside without your persistence and encouragement, this book never would have been; Tia Harrison thank you for the long distance creative sessions, beautiful cover design and helpful marketing tips; Professor Ojay Johnson, thank you for taking the time to edit my book while in the middle of completing your dissertation. Joyce Parker, thank you for your friendship and for encouraging me to get out of the cage to pursue my dreams. Last but not least I want to say thank you to EVERYBODY in Omaha, Nebraska who read the first print of this book and gave me such helpful feedback, comments and encouragement—God Bless!

LOVE UNCONDITIONAL

The magnificence of the evening sun

at days end, stretching across the indigo sky

like arms, reaching wide, touching the green horizon

brings to my mind what your embrace feels like.

The soft summer breeze, drifting in an open window,

ruffling curtains and cooling tempered skin

brings to my mind what your kiss feels like.

Fond memories of youthful days gone by

laughter, tears, hopes, dreams and tender hugs easing fears

brings to my mind what having you in my life is like.

thank you Lord for loving me.

Lisa Harrison Jackson

CHAPTER 1

The tears clouding Alexa's eyes made it difficult to see the winding road ahead. Headlights from the approaching cars began to resemble starbursts in the distance, causing her to periodically slam on the brakes out of uncertainty of their precise distance. The day easing into the night, only further impaired her vision.

With one hand on the wheel, Alexa used the other to wipe the tears from her eyes. Lord, she wished she could stop crying, but she could not. Memories from the past, which had lain dormant over the years, haunted her like a recurring nightmare. The pain was so real like it was just yesterday.

A delivery truck turned off of a side street and right into the path of Alexa's car, jolting her from her thoughts. The headlights were so bright that they temporarily blinded her, causing them both to swerve to avoid a collision. Blood rushed to her head and her heart pounded wildly in her chest as she slammed on the brakes spinning the car into a complete stop in the middle of the road. Adrenaline from her close encounter with death paralyzed her with emotion and caused a sudden outburst of sobs to spring forth, tearing through her body. With tear glistened eyes, Alexa glanced over her shoulder at the truck retreating into the darkness. Her hands shook as she fumbled with the gear shift. Somehow she managed to maneuver the car to the side of the road where she collapsed against the wheel, sobbing. She remained there for a few minutes, letting it all out before attempting to get back on the road.

When she felt another tear could not fall, she searched through her purse for a tissue and came across a wadded piece stuffed in one of the side pockets. Unfolding it carefully she wiped her eyes and blew her nose. When she was done, she lowered the mirror above her head to survey the damage her emotional state had caused. Obvious trails of tears streaked her foundation like rain on a windowpane and her mouth was stained with the remnants of lipstick.

She pulled out her makeup case and began the process of restoring her once flawless image. Before returning the bag to her purse, she pulled out a small bottle of eye solution to remove the redness. She squeezed a drop in each eye and turned her head from side to side, examining her reflection. The results were remarkable that if she was on the outside looking in at herself, she would swear that the episode just moments earlier had never taken place.

Over the years, Alexa got good at concealing her feelings. In her line of work, it paid to be polite, pleasant and professional at all times. This usually meant keeping one's personal business, whether good or bad, away from her interactions with clients. If her peers could see her now, they would be stunned by her outward display of emotion as they never witnessed such.

Alexa prided herself on being in control of every aspect of her life, leaving others with a vote of confidence in her abilities as well. In their eyes, she embodied a strength that they admired while at the same time envied. She was more than physically attractive; she was confident, intelligent and most deserving as the managing editor of a prosperous magazine. She lived in a beautiful home, drove a nice car, and had a hefty nest egg in the bank, thanks to wise investments.

Sure the accolades felt good, but they did not say who Alexa Denise Kirkwood really was. Beneath her tough exterior, there was a passionate woman who had a zeal for life. A woman who adored the written word, especially poetry, watching old black and white movies, mixing buttery popcorn with M&Ms and laughing with children. At one time, she believed in the power of love and even had the opportunity, but her life's path did not journey in that direction.

In fact it was this absence of a relationship in her life that triggered her tears. Earlier that morning her friend and co-worker Teressa Brantley floated into the office, flashing a new engagement ring. Her announcement came as a shock to the whole office, especially Alexa who could recall a discussion the two had shared just two months prior.

The setting was at a colleague's baby shower. Both she and Teressa were nursing virgin daiquiris, wishing they had some alcohol to add. To her, the shower was a step above boring. All evening the conversation stemmed on having babies, children and husbands. Pictures were passed around with everyone cooing over the precious images. Alexa wondered if her present outlook would have been different had she been married with children too. Teressa confessed that although she been with her boyfriend Lewis for three years, she didn't think their union would lead to marriage. She remembered thinking that Teressa's on-again-off-again relationship may appear unstable, but at least she had a prospect, unlike herself.

Mixed feelings of joy and envy swirled inside her stomach like a tornado. The single sisters club was slowly dwindling. Only she and Teressa held posts after their good friends Gina Miller and Angela Winslow sailed off into marital bliss the past summer and fall respectively.

What upset Alexa most was the fact that she had been there, not once but twice. Both proposals occurred at times in her life when her views and aspirations opposed that of her intended. The more profound relationship of the two came while she was in college. That one left a stain so deep that she could identify with the statement, *"first loves always hurt the most."*

Alexa loved Darius, but felt she was too young to commit to someone for the rest of her life. She was barely out on her own and hadn't accomplished anything that resembled success in life.

At Last!

Thinking about something as simple as their first kiss, the way her heart pounded while in his presence, and how she sank totally under his submission from a mere hug were all intricately etched in her mind. Even after nine years of being separated, thinking of Darius still brought forth feelings of great loss.

Her second failed attempt at matrimony departed on the heels of Sean Hardaway. Alexa met Sean at a Black Business Leaders Networking Social. Not only was he educated, handsome and successful he was also cultured, sitting on the board of the local Museum and Cultural Arts Council. The two spent the whole evening huddled in a quiet corner flirting while comparing personal stories of their experiences in corporate America.

It didn't come as a surprise when the successful singles united as a power couple. At the end of their second year together, they decided to take their relationship to the next level. Getting married seemed like the natural step to take since they were already cohabitating in Sean's townhouse. Both were settled in their careers, making handsome salaries. Since they were approaching their thirties, they thought it was a good time to get married, considering that they wanted a family.

Alexa knew from the beginning that marriage was a big step, but got caught up in the idea of being engaged and having the *perfect* wedding. She daydreamed about her big day often. She even went as far as to imagine herself in the future, reflecting back on her special day with her own children. Spreading the word that she had a fiancé delighted her as well as receiving attention from friends and family alike for her soon-to-be bride status.

Alexa believed that their success was due in part to carefully calculating each step of their relationship. They dated for two months before sleeping together and an additional six before they agreed that it was time to meet their respective families. Five months later, they found a town house together. Exactly two years to the date of their meeting, they became engaged.

She was proud at how they mapped things out: career, marriage and family in that order and actually got a rush from the envious looks that she got from other women who listened with envy to her self centered rattling. They may not have verbalized their feelings, but she could see the wanting in their eyes whenever she talked about her fiancé and their elaborate wedding plans.

So, everything, down to selecting the *perfect* ring, was done with great care. They browsed three different jewelry boutiques before Alexa's eye caught the ring of her dreams—a 2 ½-carat, pear-cut solitaire encircled by a complimentary band of baguettes. She imagined peoples' eyes widening in awe at the exquisite piece when she showed it off.

"*This* is gorgeous, Sean," she cooed, slipping the ring on her finger.

"Yes it is," he agreed.

Alexa gently cupped his strong jaw with her palm. "Now remember honey, it's an investment. You know what you say about buying cheap things," she reminded him.

At her warning, Sean caught the tag dangling from the exquisite piece and gasped. "You're damn right this is an investment. Alexa, I can buy you three rings for this price!" he exclaimed at the $7500 sales price. "I know I said buying cheap things is tacky, but babe I know plenty of women who'd be ecstatic with a $2000 rock."

"But I like this one, sweetie," she whined, saddling up beside him and nuzzling her face into his neck. "You can get whatever you want and I won't complain about the price."

With a grunt, Sean searched and settled for a $500 diamond band for himself. The two made their purchases on their respective credit cards and Alexa exited the store walking on air.

The next place Alexa headed for was the bridal shop where she found the Vera Wang gown that she'd been eyeing in a designer bridal maga-zine. The dress cost as much as her ring, but she rationalized purchasing it because she had a sizable savings and deserved to have the fairytale wedding she always dreamed about.

In addition to purchasing the right dress, they reserved the hall, ordered the flowers and cake, selected the menu and paid for the honeymoon package in full. Despite all of her efforts to do things *right*, Alexa's world came to a screeching halt two days before the wedding. She was enjoying a day of pampering at her favorite spa salon when she received a call on her cell phone from Sean. It was apparent by his slurred speech that he was intoxicated. A creepy feeling came over her. Her fears became real when he confessed that he couldn't go through with the wedding. He stated that he didn't want to ruin either of their lives by getting married.

Alexa was sure it was simply a case of pre-wedding jitters and after hanging up from him, she quickly called his best friend Glenn, who was also the best man, to talk some sense in him. Glenn located Sean at a gentlemen's lounge, nursing a bottle of Hennessy, gazing up at the topless dancer gyrating before his face. According to Glenn, Sean told him that while he loved Alexa, he was not "in love" with her and because of that, he didn't want to ruin things by going into a marriage doomed from the start.

Alexa dropped the phone when Glenn repeated Sean's exact words later that evening. Not only was she devastated, but humiliated as well. The worst part was that she didn't even get a chance to talk to him herself because hours following his confession, he left town "to get his priorities in check" as he put it, leaving her with the responsibility of explaining to family and friends that the wedding was off.

Her wedding day was spent in bed crying while a variety of emotions surged through her like volts of electricity, changing as rapidly as the wind. She was affected physically as well, dropping more than 20 pounds in a two-week time frame. She also ended up cutting her hair short because the stress caused much damage to her otherwise healthy mane. Although she appeared to be strong on the outside, she was hurting inside. Eventually, she sought counseling because a sheath of depression had draped over her and wouldn't diminish after a few months.

Just when it seemed as if she had sunk to an all time low, a light turned on and poured in, bringing new life. It happened while she was sitting at home, watching television. She was flipping through the channels when she came across a brother with a raspy voice talking to an audience of women on the Christian network.

The man's tone was so commanding, yet gentle, that Alexa's hand froze on the remote. As he began to read off ailments holding women in bondage, tears rolled down her cheeks as she could identify with many of the labels. Had she really been so out of touch? Some of his examples hit home and made her sob. His soothing voice reminded her of a concerned father, gently reprimanding his daughter with love. The words of his message pierced her heart like an arrow and the hurts and pains from her past were washed away along with her tears.

His words provoked Alexa out of her slump and out to the nearest bookstore to find his latest book. Alexa was so hungry to get beyond her stage that she read the entire book in one night and began practicing the principles immediately. The results did not appear overnight. It took six months before she could get up in the morning and face her day without worrying about what others were saying or thinking about her.

From that point on, she made a conscious effort to concentrate on herself. Not only was she putting more stock into herself mentally and physically, but most importantly spiritually. She began going back to church and decided to take the pastor's advice to step back and allow God to have his way in her life. She came to accept that if it was meant for her to marry, then the right man would come along. If it was not God's will for her, then she would accept it and be at peace. Although she was able to rebuild her confidence, occasionally she had lapses.

Her reminiscing was interrupted by a light knock on the window. She turned to look into the smiling face of a well-dressed, older gentleman.

"Are you okay?" he shouted against the howl of the wintry winds whipping around him as he tried to keep his leather cap on and his heavy leather trench coat closed.

Alexa rolled down the window. "Yes, thank you. I. I was," she searched her mind for a lie to tell when she spied her cell phone resting on the seat beside her. She reached for it and held it up. "I was just making a call."

He gave her the thumbs-up signal. "It's good to see you young folks taking precautions."

She exhaled when he walked away and waited until he pulled off before edging her own car back onto the road.

To take her mind off her troubles, she turned on the CD player. The smooth alto voice of Toni Braxton flowed from the speakers. In the song, Toni was reprimanding her boyfriend for not being a man enough in their relationship to tell her that things were over. The song struck a painful chord in Alexa and she found herself blinking back tears.

However, she refused to slip back into that depressive state, so she quickly changed the CD. This time, the music made her head nod rhythmically to the beat and slowly her spirits began to lift.

She promised herself she was not going to wallow in self-pity again. Whenever the urge to sink came over her, she was going to force herself to think positive thoughts and redirect her energy onto something else. She also concluded that she needed to apologize to Teressa for her distant behavior and be the supportive friend that she was supposed to be.

In the meantime, she was going to do something special for herself like spend an afternoon at the day spa. She was sure that in order to keep her spirits high, she would have to dig deep into herself. "A nice pampered weekend is probably all I need," she said to herself as she exited the expressway.

*   *   *

After her split with Sean, Alexa found a place to live. *When one door closes, God opens another.* A colleague was moving out of state and needed to sell her house immediately. Because of their relationship, she accepted Alexa's offer. The purchase was quick and two weeks after completing the necessary paperwork, Alexa moved into her new home. Although she didn't have much to start with, she managed to slowly fill each room with her personal style.

Her house, a three-bedroom brick traditional, was located on a quiet suburban block in Aurora. Since living there, she could count on one hand the number of times she had seen, let alone talked to her neighbors within a month's time. However, she didn't mind that because she liked to keep to herself anyway.

After gathering the mail from the box, she went inside. The small stack looked more promising than it actually was. There was nothing to get excited about bills, a couple pieces of "dear resident" mail, and the weekly supermarket circular. The room immediately warmed up when Alexa flipped the switch just inside the kitchen door thanks to the rich gold and amber art glass Tiffany fixture hanging above. With a sigh, she placed the envelopes on the kitchen table, and headed for the answering machine on the breakfast bar to check for messages.

The flashing light on the machine indicated that there were four messages waiting. She pressed the button to rewind the messages before easing out of her pumps. While the first message began to play, she sauntered over to the stainless steel refrigerator to retrieve a large bottle of grapefruit juice. A part of her new commitment to good health included drinking at least two glasses of juice every day. She had read somewhere that grapefruit was a great antioxidant and aided in burning fat. When she first started her regimen, her face screwed up from the bitter taste. However, over a short period of time she had acquired a taste for it.

Easing into a chair at the dinette table, she sighed with relief at the opportunity to rest her feet. The first message was from her hair salon calling to remind her of an upcoming appointment. The second was from her mother who wanted to know why she hadn't called in a while. The third message was a hang up, while the last caller was her best friend Maya. At the sound of her friend's radio announcer sounding voice, annunciating each word with such precision, Alexa scurried over to the machine. She caught the tail end portion of the message, "...wonderful news. Return my call as soon as possible."

Alexa wondered what the urgency was about. Ideas began to fly in her head. She knew she couldn't be pregnant again As far as she knew after their third daughter was born, Maya, and her husband Bryant, had accepted the fact that they would not be trying a fourth time for a son. Glancing at her watch, she picked up the telephone, hoping to catch Maya before she left the television station for the day.

The telephone rang twice before Maya answered in her usual professional tone. "Channel 12, this is Maya Renault."

Sometimes it still surprised Alexa that her best friend was a high profile news anchor for Channel 12 in Detroit. Because of her television status, Maya was regarded as a local celebrity and treated as such. People of various ages and ethnic backgrounds recognized her as she graced their television set each morning and was known to be active in worthy causes in the community. Whenever she hung out with Maya during her visits to Detroit, Alexa was amazed by the red-carpet treatment her friend frequently received.

"What's up Mrs. R?" Alexa greeted, happy to hear her friend's voice.

"Alexa?"

"No, Hillary Rodham Clinton," Alexa sarcastically replied.

"Hey Hill, how are things going with Billy boy these days?" Maya teased, once she recognized Alexa's voice.

"Apparently not as good as things are going on there. I got your message. What's up?" she asked stretching her legs out on the adjacent chair.

"I'm getting married!" Maya blurted.

"But Maya, you're already married," Alexa reminded her.

"No, Bryant and I have decided to renew our vows on New Year's Eve. After nine years of marriage we are finally going to have a real wedding," she sighed dreamily.

Alexa refused to let Maya's news rekindle her own insecurities that had risen from Teressa's announcement earlier that day. It seemed like everyone was being claimed by someone. Even Maya's husband was asking for her hand—again!

"That's great Maya!"

"I knew you'd be happy," Maya exclaimed. "So when can you come?"

"Maya, I know you don't think I can come? New Year's Eve is just four days away."

"And?" her friend replied matter-of-factly.

"You know how busy I am. Don't you think I need more notice?"

"Maybe *any* person would need notice, but you are my best friend. I know regardless of how much notice I give you, you'll be there. Bryant and I are counting on you. Plus, I want you to stand for me."

Tears swelled in Alexa's eyes. Maya and Bryant were two very special people whose lives she shared in years back. The three of them had been through a lot, giving each other mental, and when possible, financial support. Alexa could recall many times when she didn't go to bed hungry because Maya and Bryant called her right on time to go out for pizza. In addition to hanging out and partying together, they at one time shared the same townhouse. Now the two of them wanted to reaffirm their love before God, friends and family and wanted her to stand again in their circle of love. She was touched by the request for her presence.

A tear slid down her cheek and before Alexa knew it, she was crying for a second time that day. "You know I would be honored," she replied with a sniffle.

"Are you crying Alexa Kirkwood?" Maya asked softly.

"I'm so happy for you both," she admitted as she reached for a tissue. She blew her nose. *At least somebody is happy.*

A slight sense of panic hit Alexa as she realized her role in the wedding. As the made of honor and best friend to the bride, she had to be there for Maya in a big way and she wasn't about to let her friends down.

Immediately she began to run down her list of things to do in preparation for her trip. "I'm going to have to call my travel agent to see if I can get a cheap flight and I'll probably have to beg De Angela to see if she can squeeze me in for an earlier hair appointment, probably get my nails done too."

"Alexa, Alexa, just get here. We'll deal with those things later," Maya assured her.

Alexa wiped away the warm tears settling on the rim of her eyes and exhaled softly. *Here I go again.*

*   *   *

Upon entering her office, the first thing one would notice was the breathtaking view of downtown Denver at dawn from her window. Having a corner office with a wide view was one of the many perks she enjoyed at Marks-St. Claire. Without turning on her lights, she sat her things on her desk and walked over to the ceiling to floor windows behind her desk. She leaned against the panel and stared in awe at the waking city below.

Despite the fact that she had been in the City of Denver for several years, she still was captivated by her beauty. Hints of sunlight breaking through the mountains in the East left her speechless. Her eyes traveled down to the slow moving vehicles below. The various shapes vehicles merging in and out of traffic, pressing towards their destinations reminded her of her own life—erratic, busy, yet focused and unchanging.

Her thoughts drifted onto the night before and the episode in the car. She realized later that her emotional breakdown had nothing to do with neither Teressa's good news, nor the last minute break up by Sean. They came from a remote place in her mind that posed the inevitable question of what if? What if she had remained in Michigan with Darius? Would they have married? Would nine years have guaranteed wedded bliss with a child or two? Or would the itch have settled in, resulting in divorce? Would he have continued to pursue his master's degree? Or would he have settled for a job to take care of his family as he pledged? Would they have lived comfortably? Would she have aspired to be anything more than Darius' wife? All of the questions remained unanswered and swirled like a tornado through her head.

With a sigh, she turned from the window and her eyes came to rest on the wall displaying her awards and achievements. She smiled as she privately recalled each awards banquet, down to the gown that she had worn that evening and the well known attendees in the publishing industry. The affairs were always grand and were held in different cities across the country. The formality of it all put her in the mind of the Academy Awards given the attention surrounding it. She was proud of her success and wouldn't trade anything to take back those experiences.

Unlike some of her friends, she did not have reason to complain about the corporate culture. Her company paid well. They believed in personal development and growth as well as promoting from within. They offered their executives excellent benefits and took great strides in maintaining a creative, stress-free work environment. She had a vision for where she wanted to go in the company, and she felt she had the backing to execute those dreams at the appropriate time.

Easing down in the black, leather chair, Alexa reclined in thought. She had made the right decision. Not very many women, especially the African American ones, could say that they got where they were today in so little time without entertaining the boss after hours. She thanked

God that she never had to compromise her self respect to get where she was. Her promotions were either based on her merit or hard work, nothing more nothing less. A feeling of celebration came over her. Turning to her CD player on the credenza, she pulled out her favorite Jill Scott CD. She forwarded to one of her favorite songs and began bobbing her head to the jazzy beat, finding the energy she needed to begin tackling those items in her inbox.

*   *   *

There was something magical about taking early morning flights that captured Alexa's attention. The way the sun made an entrance against the dawn, transforming the skies from a purplish pink to a yellowish orange was like magic. Then to be so high above the floor of clouds, witnessing the rays stretching out across the endless heavens was like a warm invitation calming her sometimes, restless spirit.

She needed to feel a sense of calmness as she was a ball of anxiety, trembling like a frightened cat. From the moment she received Maya's call, the butterflies had not stopped fluttering around in her stomach. She couldn't eat anything because the thought made her nauseous. The anticipation of confronting her past made her lightheaded. A past filled with unresolved issues; one that involved Darius Riverside.

Upon hearing of Darius' participation in the wedding, Alexa's immediate reaction was to change her plans, but she knew she couldn't do that. Especially since she promised Maya that she would be there for her. Although nine years had passed, she was surprised that hearing Darius' name still caused her heart to race. Their relationship was so close that sometimes all they had to do was look at each other and seemingly feel what the other was thinking. It was amazing to Alexa how they were so in tuned with one another. Although they weren't together for very long, Alexa had always felt like their paths were destined to cross sooner or later. She always had a sixth sense about him.

Most important than the physical attraction, was their friendship. Because of this, Alexa often wondered if she made a mistake by walking away.

She could vividly remember the precise time that they met. Her recollections were so fresh in her mind that she could actually bring the colors and smells to life from the intimate etchings in her mind.

It was spring time in Ann Arbor and for the first time it looked as if Mother Nature was going to make good on her promise for an early summer. The snow had all melted and Alexa could see little sprigs of green budding from the tree's bare branches. Students were out in droves seated sporadically throughout campus catching rays or killing time between classes to people watch or just skip all together. Alexa drove her little Ford Escort through campus on her way to her new apartment to drop off some personal items.

"Finally," she yelled out loud. "Freedom!"

Her father had finally agreed to allow her to move into an apartment off campus. She was a senior at the university and after committing herself diligently to her studies he had taken notice and granted her wish to move out of the cramped dorm room into a roomy townhouse with her best friend Maya.

A smile spread across her mouth when the apartment sign at the entrance came into view. A sense of accomplishment came over her. Yes, she has managed to pull an "A" average since attending the university, but moving out on her own was a much greater feat in her eyes.

Dressed in a hooded sweatshirt and matching sweats with the school logo emblazoned on the front, Alexa hopped out of the car and raised the hatchback. She lifted the box of books with a grunt. She recalled advising Maya not to over pack the box, but to no avail, her friend had ignored her wishes. Alexa held the box close to her and rushed to the door with help from the weight of the box. She was grateful that they lived on the ground level. Sweat began to bead on her forehead as she struggled to open the door. She continued fumbling with the knob when suddenly the door swung open. She would have fallen inside if it were not for the strong arms catching her around the waist.

Alexa immediately let out a scream and dropped the box, escaping the unfamiliar arms. In haste, she quickly grabbed the first item at hand to defend herself. She knew that she looked funny standing there with the telephone hand set held high above her head with the base dangling to the floor.

With a frown on her face, she looked up into the most incredible pair of eyes she had ever seen. "Who are you!" she demanded. Her heart was pounding a mile a minute not only from the fact that she was face-to-face with a man she didn't know, but also because despite everything, she couldn't help but notice how handsome he was.

"Here, let me help you," he quickly offered, lifting the box with ease to his broad shoulder. "Where would you like this?"

"First things first, who in the hell are you!" she demanded again, not wanting to look into those dark eyes again for fear of her anger dissipating. She quickly averted her eyes to his chest but had trouble in that area as well upon seeing the tiny hairs peeking through the open collar of his shirt he wore beneath a black leather jacket. Her eyes rose back to his face and she forced a frown.

The stranger had deliciously dark features. A smooth pecan brown complexion, thick coal black hair styled in a low cut curly top fade. Equally black silky brows hovered above intense midnight eyes which gazed upon her through long lashes.

Alexa's lips parted slowly just when Bryant burst into the room with Maya riding on his back.

"Hey guys!" Maya greeted cheerfully.

"Good, you two have met already." Bryant added, looking from one to the other.

"Actually we haven't," Alexa replied her eyes still locked with the stranger.

"My bad," Bryant said with a laugh. He bent down so that Maya could hop off of his back. *"Alexa this is my cousin Darius. D this is Maya's best girl, Al."*

"The name is Alexa," she quickly corrected Bryant.

"Pleased to meet you," Darius replied, extending a large but well manicured hand. *"And I do apologize for scaring you."*

Alexa hesitated before taking his hand. When she did, something happened. Some sort of transference of energy. The connection caused them both to freeze and their eyes to meet in silence. Alexa quickly released his hand and stepped back, holding it close to her breast. She turned away and pretended to be busy doing other things. She grabbed the telephone and replaced the receiver on the base.

"Darius is helping us move. Isn't that nice of him?" Maya asked with a glowing expression. It was clear to Alexa that Maya was quite fond of Darius.

Alexa could not hear Maya's words for she was watching Darius. She tried not to gawk at the sight of him slipping out of his jacket to reveal a complete view of his expansive upper body. She had admired many men for their physical statures, but none kept her tongue tied like this one.

"It's no problem," Darius assured them. *"Bryant asked me to help when I finished registering for my classes. It was the least that I could do with all he's done for me."*

"I didn't know you were going to school here Darius!" Maya said with surprise.

Alexa pretended like she wasn't the least bit interested and began to fumble around inside one of the boxes all the while listening to their conversation.

"Yes. It was sort of a last minute decision. I'm enrolled in the MBA program. Everything has been smooth thus far with the exception of finding a place to stay."

"Why don't you stay here with us?" Maya blurted out.

Alexa whipped around with a shocked look on her face and Darius' brows shot up in astonishment. His eyes immediately turned to Alexa.

"*I can't impose,*" *he quickly interjected.*

"*Why not? I am,*" *Bryant added proudly. He quickly explained how he had waited too late to sign up for a dorm room.* "*Besides we could all stand to save some money. With us splitting the rent four ways, we could save about—Bryant paused as he calculated the savings in his head.* "*About $200 a month a piece.*"

"*Yeah, we have 2 bedrooms and an extra room off of the kitchen. Kind of like a sun room. If you want, you can have that room,*" *Maya offered.*

"*I don't want to put anyone out.*" *He turned to Alexa more obviously now.*

All eyes turned on Alexa who squirmed nervously. The last thing she needed was for her father to find out that she was living with a man and all hell would break loose. Yet, she had to take into consideration that he was Bryant's cousin.

"*I guess its okay with me.*" *After much contemplation, she reluctantly relented.* "*But I do think it is wise for us to set some ground rules first.*"

Every one agreed to her suggestion. Alexa would keep the master bedroom while Bryant and Maya would share the second room. The women would share the master bath while Darius and Bryant would occupy the other. Everyone would chip in for groceries and split the utility bills four ways, with the exception of the telephone.

After spelling out the particulars, Darius moved his things in that same evening. Later as she lay in her bed, Alexa prayed that she wasn't making a mistake in agreeing to allow him to stay.

Over the years, she often wondered what became of Darius. She never dared asking Maya because she knew her friend too well. Her nose for news would start sniffing around for hidden agendas or repressed feelings. Besides, she did not want Maya to start preaching to her about having let a good man go. Darius definitely possessed the qualities that would earn him that title, and Alexa accepted the consequences for not appreciating him early on.

She was sure Darius loathed her to the point that any thoughts of reconciliation, let alone a friendship, was out of the question. With that in mind, her sole purpose of attending the wedding was to support her friends, not run around fretting over an encounter with Darius. When it was all over, she would leave the following day and not look back.

*   *   *

The Detroit airport was more crowded than Alexa had anticipated, making her wish she had worn something other than the casual sweat suit. She guessed that the crowd of travelers was probably returning from spending Christmas with family in time to kick off the New Year in the Motor City. It didn't take her long to spot Maya standing to the side, trying to keep a low profile in a brimmed hat, leather walking coat and a pair of jeans, chatting away on her cell phone.

With a mischievous grin, Alexa scurried out of Maya's view, hiding behind a pole. She peeked at her friend, like a lioness stalking her prey, while at the same time trying not to draw too much attention.

Maya was so deep in her conversation that she did not notice Alexa slip past. Alexa smiled and then, quick as a wink, zipped back in for the kill, pouncing on her unsuspecting friend with a big hug. Maya immediately let out a frightened shriek and pulled away causing all eyes to fall on the two women.

"Alexa!" she shouted, relieved to see it was her friend and not some crazed fiend. She pulled Alexa to her for a hug.

Soon the two were crying and hugging like long lost sisters. Passersby watched the two with curious expressions. A few could be heard murmuring if that was indeed Maya Renault in disguise.

Minutes later, the two eased back from their embrace, smiling at one another.

"You are looking good girl!" Maya affirmed as she walked around Alexa looking her up and down.

"Girl, you're the one," Alexa responded, smoothing down her hair.

Maya reached up and fluffed Alexa's shoulder length mane. "You really let it grow out didn't you?"

"Yeah, I got tired of using those irons everyday," she sighed. "I was glad when those layers finally grew out. With it being this length, I can pull it back into a ponytail when I get lazy."

Despite her attempts at looking casual, Maya looked like she was ready to step out on some runway in her casual attire. "Always looking good Mrs. R," she commented.

Maya groaned. "I just hope that not too many folks recognize me looking like some vagabond out here."

"Yeah right," Alexa scoffed as she draped her arm over Maya's shoulders. "You hardly look like some vagabond and ya dang sure ain't getting paid like one."

Maya laughed. "Don't be deceived girl friend. I have bills like everyone else. Plus, I have three children."

"Speaking of which, where are my sweeties?" Alexa interrupted, looking around as they headed towards the baggage claim area. She had been fortunate to be named godmother to all three of Bryant and Maya's daughters and wouldn't trade the honor for the world. The girls were the closest thing she had to motherhood which satisfied that maternal instinct that popped up at least twice a year.

"Home, with Bryant," Maya replied. "But they are all excited to see their Auntie Alexa."

Alexa smiled as she pictured the three girls: six-year-old Monaye, the inquisitive one was very bright for her age and acted very much like the big sister she was to her two younger siblings: four-year-old Brielle and two-year old Sasha. Brielle was mild mannered and nurturing with a very sweet disposition, while Sasha was independent, outgoing, free-spirit who loved to explore. All three were little darlings whom Alexa cherished as if they were her own.

Upon retrieving Alexa's luggage, the women walked the short distance outside to Maya's Cadillac Escalade and before long they were headed to the Renault's home in Southfield. It was Alexa's first time seeing Maya's new home and her jaw dropped in awe at the sight of the gigantic, three-story, brick structure standing grand on the large lot surrounded by tall, stately pine trees out back. Tall, oak doors guarded the entry-way and were nestled between two tall columns that reached up to the second floor. A large window above the door frame revealed a decorative chandelier as well as the banister of the winding stair case. Attached to the house was a three-car garage.

"It's beautiful!" Alexa gasped as they pulled up the long circular drive. She was both impressed and proud of her friends' success.

Maya smiled as she reached up to press the button on the garage door opener hanging from the visor. "Girl, God has been good to us."

"Amen," Alexa agreed as Maya eased the truck in beside a late model, midnight blue Jaguar. On the other side of the Jag was some type of small, sporty vehicle beneath a tarp. She guessed it was probably something that belonged to Bryant.

Bryant and the girls must have heard them arrive because before they could get out of the truck the foursome shot out of the connecting door to the house.

"Auntie!" the little girls shrieked happily. In a few seconds, Alexa was covered in tiny little arms. She gave each of them a kiss on the head and a hug before reaching up to give Bryant a tight squeeze.

"What's up, big brother?"

"You," he replied, giving her a tight hug.

Before she could reply, the ruckus from the girls swarming around them stole her attention and she gave Bryant an apologetic look.

"It's okay," he assured her, knowing how excited the girls were to see her. "We can talk later."

Alexa smiled and refocused her attention on the girls. "My goodness, you girls have grown so," she said, her loving gaze gracing each one of them. The last time she saw them, Sasha was only 10 months old and barely walking. "Guess what? I have presents for all of you."

"But Auntie, we already got a present from you," Monaye announced, hanging onto Alexa's coat sleeve. The small party moved from the chilly garage into the cozy family room where yellow and orange flames danced in the fireplace.

"Those were Christmas presents sweetie," Alexa explained, with a loving smile. "I have something else for you."

"Now you know they don't need anything more," Maya protested. All Alexa had to do was go up to their playroom and see what Maya was talking about. They had toys to last them a lifetime.

Alexa ignored Maya's comment by assuring the girls that they would get their presents after dinner.

As promised, following dinner, Alexa distributed the one of a kind, handmade rag dolls created in each of their likeness. The girls loved them. Later after they were bathed and ready for bed, they also enjoyed Alexa's animated bedtime story about three African Princesses going to a royal ball.

When she had kissed them all goodnight, she joined her friends in the family room where Bryant had just poured three glasses of Zinfandel. Maya carried in a tray of sliced cheese, crackers, and fresh fruit and placed it on the table before them.

"You looking good Alex," Bryant complimented as he stabbed a toothpick into a cheese cube.

"I told her so, but you know how she is," Maya added with a smile.

"Me? You both look great and I am definitely feeling the crib." Alexa replied, kicking out of her sneakers. She took a seat on one of the plushy sofas, curling her feet beneath her.

The family room was cozy yet embodied a lived in quality. A marbled hearth was the focal point where a pair of white slipper chairs accompanied two charcoal-hued loveseats in a u-shape. The white walls contained interesting pieces like mirrored candle sconces and black and white prints in boxed frames, giving the room a cozy yet elegant quality. Alexa marveled at the black baby grand that dwelled in the alcove of a floor-to-ceiling pane glass windows.

Maya sank down beside Bryant on the opposite facing sofa and reached for a handful of grapes. "Yeah girlfriend, it's been a long time."

Alexa took a sip of her wine. "I know."

"So how is Denver?"

"Same."

"And, your job?"

"Actually, it's going quite well. I got a raise," she proudly announced, holding up her glass for a toast. In her nine years at Mark-St. Claire, Alexa had been promoted three times. The most recent promotion was an upgrade to a corner office along with a staff in addition to a salary increase and heftier bonuses. "You are now looking at Managing Editor of *Mountain High* magazine."

"You go girl!" Maya congratulated, touching her glass to Alexa's.

"Here, here," Bryant joyfully added.

"Another toast is in order," Maya continued. "Bryant is going into business for himself."

"Congratulations!" Alexa asked with surprise. She knew that Bryant worked in computers, but had no idea he was interested in venturing out into a business of his own.

"I can't take all of the credit. D is taking the plunge with me. Since we are both handling some really good contracts, we figure we could merge forces, eliminate the middle man and bring in the bucks directly."

He continued to discuss the plan, but his words fell on deaf ears. Alexa knew she heard him right when he said D. That was the nickname everyone called Darius except her. Her nickname for him had always been Darry. So, he was thinking about going into business with Darius.

Rather than comment about Darius, she continued conversing as if she hadn't heard him drop Darius' name at all. After getting up to speed on their lives, Alexa yawned, succumbing to jet lag and announced that she was ready to hit the sack. Maya showed her to the spacious in-law suite located over the three car garage that was accessible off of the kitchen.

Mirroring the rest of the grand home, the room was decorated with impeccable taste. The four-poster rice bed was elegantly decorated in sophisticated, camel-colored faux suede bedding. Paprika, butter and coffee colored pillows of the same material were neatly stacked against the headboard. Beyond a pair of shutter doors was the bathroom with separate garden tub and shower, which was also decorated in the same colors as the bedroom.

"May, this is gorgeous!" she said eying the tub longingly. She looked forward to languishing in it amid lavender-scented bath salts.

"Actually I had you in mind when I decorated it." Maya said as she stretched out on the bed. "I'm so glad you could come. I just wish it was you getting married."

The look of disdain on Alexa's face did not equal Maya's glowing expression. "Keep wishing," she smugly retorted as she leaned up against the dresser.

"Come on Alexa, I know you want to get married and have some bay bays?" Maya chided.

Alexa raised her hands in surrender and walked away from her friend. "Maya, I've come to realize that what I want isn't necessarily what I am going to get. If the Lord sees fit for me to have a family, He will bless me in His time. I'm not going to force things anymore."

"Do you think you were forcing things with Sean?" Maya asked, sitting up on the edge of the bed.

Alexa paused before answering. "Back then I probably wouldn't admit it, but today—yes."

"Why?"

"Because I thought I was ready for marriage and a family. You don't understand the pressure that women my age have to endure. You and Bryant have been together since you were 19. If a woman is over twenty-five, and not married, or at least dating someone, people look at her as if something is wrong. Sean was a nice guy and I loved him as a person, but he really wasn't somebody I could see myself spending the rest of my life with."

"And you were willing to marry him knowing that's how you felt?"

"Yes." She admitted, taking a seat beside Maya on the bed. "I guess I was hoping that my feelings would change, but now my outlook is different. When I look at you and Bryant, I see something that I want in a relationship. You two are soul mates. You got each other's back and the love and respect that you have for one another is apparent. Sean and I could barely live together without arguing."

"Do you hate him for what he did?"

Alexa hesitated before responding, pondering the question for a few moment. She was more humiliated than anything. "I did at first, but I got over it when I realized that us breaking up helped me to understand what I really want in a man."

"Which is?"

"I want a man who is not afraid of my success, who is my friend, who has my back, understands my dreams, and encourages me to pursue them. I need somebody who can love me for me."

"Sounds like a pretty special man," Maya wistfully replied.

Alexa nodded. "I know. I also know that you don't come across these types everyday, and this time I won't settle for anything less."

"Well then I pray that you find who you are looking for."

A hint of sadness laced Alexa's giggle. "No, I hope he finds me."

Without comment, Maya leaned over and gave Alexa a tight hug. "I'm glad you came."

"I'm glad I did too," Alexa replied, pulling back. "Now go to sleep blushing bride. We have lots to do in the morning."

CHAPTER 2

The minute Maya and Bryant agreed to renew their vows, one of the first people Maya called was her friend Margaret Cade. Margaret owned an exclusive boutique, where she sold her original creations. Her styles were so popular that her list of clients consisted of several high profile community figures and celebrities.

Alexa's eyes widened when Maya stepped from the dressing room in a champagne hued, strapless silk gown with elbow length satin gloves. The skirt was long and fitted with a twisted knot in the back that gave it a bustle-like appearance.

"Well, what do you think?" Maya asked, noticing Alexa's awed expression in the three-way mirror.

"It looks great on you." The sales clerk commented.

Alexa nodded in agreement, "Maya, that dress is tight."

"It is!?" Maya cried out in horror. "It's a size 6. I hoped that I wouldn't gain any weight."

Alexa and the young sales clerk looked at each other and burst out laughing at Maya's misunderstanding.

"I'm sorry," she apologized through her laughter. "You have got to forgive my sister. She's been out of the loop so long she kind of lost touch." She didn't want to explain that tight was slang for nice.

Maya still wore a look of confusion until Alexa assured her the dress was just fine. The ensemble was complete with an elegant rhinestone tiara and a pair of matching silk mules with a clear heel.

At Last!

The bridesmaid's attire turned out to be silk midnight-blue camisoles with matching floor-length, A-line skirts. Alexa thought they were beautiful and was grateful that Maya didn't pick out just anything for her bridal party.

"You are going to knock Bryant off of his feet!" Alexa announced as they exited the boutique.

"I am so nervous. Can you believe I have the nerve to be anxious?" Maya said as she laid both dresses across the back seat of the truck. She smoothed out the plastic so there were no folds to prevent wrinkling.

"Yes, I can." Alexa replied, turning forward in her seat. However, her comment was for a different reason. The possibly of Alexa coming face-to-face Darius made her anxious too.

"Could your anxiety be Darius related?" Maya asked, eyeing her out of the corner of her eye as if she had been reading her mind.

Alexa's silence answered the question.

"Alexa, I was wondering when you were going to get around to Darius being the best man at the wedding. I hope you are okay with it considering."

"You guys want him in the wedding too. What can I say? It's your wedding," she replied, hoping that her tone and posture gave off an air of indifference.

"Now, now," Maya soothingly replied. "I know that there's animosity on both your parts, but maybe you two need to get it over with by facing your fears and talking it out."

"What is there to talk about Maya? Darius told me all that I needed to know years ago."

Alexa had set aside her pride and reached out to him. Just thinking about that dreaded phone call made her wince. His words stung just as sharply today as they had then.

They had been apart for almost a year. She was settled in her job at Marks—St. Claire's and was living in an apartment of her own.

It was a Saturday evening and Alexa was stretched out on her sofa sipping a wine cooler while flipping through the channels on the television.

Who would have guessed that she would be home on a Saturday evening? She loved to party, but since coming to Denver, she didn't know where to go let alone who to go with. Although she had met some good people in Denver, no one could replace her friends back home.

As a result, she opted for a date with the television. Before settling in, she poured herself a glass of the fruity mixture.

She began flipping through the channels, not finding one thing that caught her attention for more than a few minutes. Suddenly, her eyes came to rest on the telephone. She wished she had someone to call. She entertained the idea of calling Maya, but she had just talked to her the night before. When they talked, Maya asked if there was something wrong. Although she denied it, she knew that if she called Maya at that moment, she would surely suspect something. Besides, she and Bryant were out celebrating Maya's new job as a beat reporter for the local television station. And if she knew her friends as well as she thought, celebrating would mean a highly charged romp in the sack.

With a sigh she picked up the telephone to call her mother, but then thought again and quickly slammed the phone down before she answered. Her mother had been acting quite strange. Alexa thought it was premenopause. Whatever it was, she couldn't deal with her right then. Her brother Justin called one day talking about her going on this crocheting rampage having draped the beds, chairs, table tops and toilets in every color imaginable.

Finally, her thoughts came to rest on Darius. She wondered if he had the same number. There had been many times when she wanted to call him and apologize, especially during those times when she felt lonely. When it seemed like the world was against her and all she wanted to do was press her face against his sturdy chest and cry. But there was no Darius at home waiting with open arms to lick her wounds. Besides the shame of leaving him the way she did still hung over her head like a storm cloud.

Now after a year, she felt she could talk to him. Denver was okay. She had been right about Marks-St. Claire. Already she was promoted to an Editor position. She wanted to let him know that her decision was a good one and that leaving, though not in the manner in which she did, was the right thing to do and maybe, just maybe he would understand and forgive her.

So, she slowly dialed his number. The phone rang several times before the answering machine picked up.

"You've reached Darius." His speech was strong and mature. She smiled at the sound of hearing his voice again. "I'm sorry, I can't take your call—"

The greeting cut off with a screech, and suddenly a male voice cut through the message. "Hello!" Alexa's heart began to thud rapidly. "Hold on while I turn off the machine."

She was a bundle of nerves as her frozen hands trembled while trying to grasp onto the phone.

"Hello!" He repeated. He sounded somewhat cheerful, not somber for which she was glad.

Alexa took a deep breath and lightly whispered, "Hey stranger."

"Who is this?" Darius asked slowly, his voice laced with suspicion.

"It's me Darius, Alexa."

Silence hung between them like an iron curtain.

"What do you want?" he finally huffed after several minutes.

"Hey is that anyway to greet an old friend?" she teased, going for the lighthearted approach. Her heart was beating so rapidly, she wondered if he could hear it as well as the quick nervous breaths she tried to contain.

"Friend?" he threw back harshly. "I'd hardly call you a friend."

"Darius," she sighed. "I know how you must feel-"

"You don't know a damn about how I feel!" he cut in. "Why are you calling me anyway?"

"I just wanted to tell you how I'm doing."

Her heart sank when he began to laugh sarcastically. "Do you honestly think I care?"

"I hoped that we could talk."

"Talk about what?"

Darius' responses were so full of bile that it made her want to hang up in his face. She expected some kind of lashing, but thought he would at least be civil given the feelings they once shared.

"About us," she stammered. "About what happened to us."

Her answer caused Darius to rear back in laughter. She couldn't make anything of it because she wasn't used to him behaving in such a way. She sat there in silence through his amusement, hoping that it meant she was getting somewhere with him. When he finally caught his breath, his response turned iced cold.

"Alexa, I don't care about what happened anymore. In fact, as far as I'm concerned nothing did. And for the record there is no us, never has been and never will be. So, if you are sitting alone in your house flipping through your little, black book in search of an old flame to torture, just bypass the R's. You did it once before and that we both know you are really good at!"

The next thing she heard was ringing in her ear from the slamming of the receiver.

"He was so mean, so ugly," Alexa stated after recalling the story to Maya. She hadn't shared their conversation before now.

"Have you ever thought that his words could have been said out of anger?"

Alexa shrugged. "Whatever the case, it's been said and was buried years ago. I don't want to revisit that chapter in my life and I prefer if you didn't either. Although I may have some misgivings about being here, I will be civil for you and Bryant's sake."

"Alexa," Maya began, but Alexa cut her off with a firm shake of her head. Finally, Maya gave up and the two rode home in silence.

As they approached the house, Maya gasped, but Alexa pretended to hear nothing. She was firm on her stance of not wanting to discuss the issue any further.

Had she known anything about the owner of the black Chevy Suburban parked in the driveway she would have prepared herself, but it didn't provide her with any clue. The secretive smirk Maya flashed should have given way to what was to come, but it too had passed without comment.

Still silent, the two women went inside the house.

"Honey, I'm home!" Maya called from the kitchen.

"We're in here May!" Bryant shouted back from the family room. Maya lead the way and Alexa humbly followed. As soon as she entered the room, her eyes widened. Sitting there surrounded by the girls sat Darius.

*   *   *

Alexa felt like her feet were glued to the hardwood floor. Darius gazed up at her looking every bit as handsome as he did back then and more. Neither of the two said anything as if they both were tongue-tied. Little Sasha, who sat on his lap pulled his bearded face to hers, nuzzling her face against it. The innocent gesture brought back to Alexa's mind memories of herself in the same position.

It was Monaye who broke the awkwardness of the situation when she ran up to Alexa and hugged her waist.

"Auntie," she exclaimed with a bright smile, pulling Alexa's arm. "Say hi to my Uncle Darry."

Alexa allowed the little girl in all of her innocence to make the first move for her. "Hello Darius."

"Alexa," he returned. The cold tone in his voice mirrored the equally cold look in his eyes causing Alexa to turn away with a shudder.

Bryant and Maya exchanged glances.

"So when did you get in Mr. Darius?" Maya asked, breaking the tension. Alexa stood by and watched as Maya pranced over to the man who stood to give Maya a hug.

"Just this afternoon," he replied over her shoulder, his eyes never leaving Alexa's face. She averted her eyes to the floor. However, her attention was restored from Maya's next question.

"Are you going to stay with us?" Maya asked.

Alexa's breath caught from Maya's invitation. It was a suggestion followed by awkward silence. She couldn't bear to stand before him now, how could she withstand four days in the same house?

Her eyes flashed in Darius' direction. He sarcastically laughed in reply. "No thanks. I don't think there's room enough for all of us."

Alexa caught onto the double meaning that was intended and rolled her eyes.

"Nonsense," Maya retorted. "We have plenty room."

"I think it's for the best that I stay at the hotel." Darius continued.

Maya was about to challenge his response when Bryant intervened by slipping his arm around his wife's waist. "If that is what you want D, we understand."

"But..." Maya started in.

"May, if he says he can't stay, we shouldn't press the issue," he quickly interjected in an obviously firm tone.

A wave of warmth permeated Alexa's collar. She knew Darius' reasons for not wanting to stay at the house were because of her being there. As far as she was concerned, she was not about to let him take a potshot at her.

"Yeah, Maya, let the man go," she piped up. "It's apparent that he doesn't feel comfortable with me around and frankly I don't care to be in his company either." With that comment, she did an about face, picked up her shopping bags and marched upstairs to her room.

Once behind the confines of her door, she let out an irritated growl. Seeing Darius had taken her by surprise. A rush of complicated feelings that even she didn't understand had surfaced.

Alexa knew that it was inevitable that their paths would cross, but she didn't think it would be so soon nor did she feel it would be hostile. They didn't even say more than two words, when Darius came with the lame excuse as if she was not even in the room.

She broke her pace to halt before the mirror above the dresser. "If there is one thing he will see is that I am no longer an insecure twenty-two year old," she promised in a huff. She gripped the edge of the dresser with both hands to calm her rapid breathing. Although his comments infuriated her, she was more angered by the fact that she couldn't deny the power of his mere presence.

The years had been good to Darius. His handsome features were matured by a close-cut beard. He looked like he put on some weight, in all of the right places, filling out his tall, athletic build.

Deep inside a little voice scolded her for letting go of the best thing that ever happened to her, but a louder voice told her it was for the better. After all it was her decision to split up. The night of her big decision was as vivid as if it were yesterday.

Alexa had just received the job offer from Marks—St. Claire, a magazine publishing company located in Denver. Darius did not want to see her go which he had expressed several times. The last time the discussion came up, the two were at home preparing dinner together.

"There are plenty of jobs in Detroit, Babe," Darius pointed out as he stirred the red sauce in the pot on the stove. "I know you've applied for some of them. Just give it time. Somebody will reply."

"I can't stay here forever Darius. I need to know what it feels like to have a place of my own. I want to create my own bills and pay them. Marks-St. Claire is offering me a good salary with great benefits and stock options. Tell me, how can I say no to that?"

"With your talents, Babe, I know you can find something just as good here. Why don't you wait it out?" he tried coaxing, but it only made her increasingly frustrated.

"I can't keep depending on you," she sighed. Darius had been paying her bills after her work study job ended following graduation. "I have to make my own way."

"I like taking care of you," he assured her by wrapping her in his embrace and kissing the tip of her nose.

A wave of anxiety gripped her as her mother's voice came to mind. Five years down the line, she didn't want to be saddled down with kids she wasn't ready for. Nor did she want a man to feel like he was keeping her. As her mother said, her education was the ticket to a self-sufficient lifestyle. Marks-St. Claire was offering her that life. She wasn't sure she wanted to chance a relationship with Darius that could be potentially wrong for them both. If they were meant to be then they would come together again, she told herself countless times.

The decision to accept the position hung over her head like a dark cloud. To make matters worse, Darius had hinted around to marriage to sweeten the deal.

As a last attempt to keep her in Detroit, Darius had proposed to her after a night filled with passionate love making. Lying in his protective arms, Alexa was glad that it was dark for it hid her tears. Darius felt the sobs racking throughout her body and had mistaken her tears of sorrow for tears of joy. While Darius slept with a contented smile on his face, Alexa placed his ring on the nightstand and slipped out of his embrace and essentially his life.

It seemed like the taxi driver was an accomplice to her escape that morning as they sped down the expressway. She turned her tear-streaked face from the window to the driver with a questioning look. Was this supposed to happen? There was hardly any traffic about and he was driving like his life depended on getting to their destination.

At Last!

It was when she noticed his slightly bobbing head and heard the reggae beat popping through an old transistor radio perched on the dashboard that she realized he was in his own world. She sank back in her seat and closed her eyes with Darius' face haunting her silent reverie. How could she make him understand that it was the right thing for both of them? She loved him too much to mess up his life, but leaving was something she had to do. She knew that if she didn't leave now, she never would. Her mother's words rang through her mind. "Don't tie yourself down before you've experienced life."

For many years, her mother had preached that sermon to Alexa and her brother. However, the words were especially meant for her to heed to for she didn't want her daughter to make the same mistakes as she did.

Alexa's parents were married the summer following graduation from high school believing that it was the only thing to do because they were in love and were expecting their first child. After 15 years of marriage, the two grew up and eventually grew apart.

Alexa made it a practice to never talk much about her family, so telling Darius how much her mother's words impacted her decision never presented itself. Rather than reveal the dysfunction in her family, Alexa took the low road, journeying to a future she embraced and praying that fate would shine favor on her. However, when her eyes met Darius' upon entering the room, there were no signs of fate being kind as animosity filled the air.

She sat on the edge of the bed, "I don't know why I thought he would behave any other way," she murmured to herself. "But nine years is a long time to hold a grudge."

She was interrupted by a soft knock.

"Come in," she called. She knew it was Maya coming to save the day.

She was right when her friend poked her head in. "Are you okay?"

Alexa nodded, and then laughed half-hearted. "As okay as I can be."

"I'm sorry."

"You didn't do anything, Maya," Alexa replied. She noticed that her friend's way of taking on other people's problems had not diminished over the years.

"I should have left things alone."

"Well, apparently he has some place to stay, so I wouldn't worry about it," Alexa replied. "Besides, you have other things to worry about."

Alexa hoped she sounded convincing because she didn't want Maya to worry about her or Darius.

CHAPTER 3

Early the next morning, Alexa was shaken awake by a very distraught Maya. She knew that something was wrong judging by the anxiety in Maya's tone and the urgency in her actions. Alexa immediately sprang up into a seated position, her eyes wide with wonder and her heart hammering in her chest.

"Wh-what's wrong, Maya?" she asked, clutching the front of her gown in terror.

Maya sank into a nearby chair and covered her eyes with her hands. "It's Bry's mother. She had a diabetic episode last night and they had to rush her to the hospital."

"Oh, my Lord," Alexa moaned. "Is she okay?"

Maya shrugged, "We haven't heard anything as of yet and Bryant and I need to go to the hospital. I don't know if I can handle this right now"

"Is there anything I can do?" Alexa asked.

"Do you mind watching the girls?" Maya asked as she began to remove the scarf from her head, allowing the silky curls to fall in disarray around her face.

"Of course I don't mind!" Alexa replied. "I just pray that Bryant's mom is okay. How is he holding up?"

"To be expected. He's upset because he knew how excited his mother was about the wedding. We believe that in the excitement of it all, she may have forgotten to take her insulin."

Alexa paused. She understood how easy it was to forget important details when your mind is focused on other things. Just the other day, she left her purse at home while on her way to work. Since the wedding announcement, she frequently found herself nervously awaiting her confrontation with Darius that she'd forget the simplest task.

"By the way," Maya began as if reading her mind. She rose from the side of the bed. "Darius is supposed to swing by to work on Bryant's computer in his office. Bryant tried calling him when he found out about his mother, but he couldn't reach him. He must have already left his hotel room."

Alexa's first instinct was to protest, but given the delicate situation her friends were facing, she refrained from doing so. Instead she tried her best to ensure her that everything would be okay.

"Don't worry about a thing, Maya. I've been looking for an opportunity to spend sometime with my goddaughters."

Maya turned around before exiting the room. "Thank you Alex for being here. I'm so grateful you came early, you just don't know."

Had it been any other day, Alexa would have remained in the bed until noon, but godmother duty called. When Maya closed the door, she got out of bed and opened the dresser drawer in search for something to wear.

The first thing that she laid her eyes on was a snug black sweater and a pair of fitted boot-cut jeans. Although casual, the outfit complimented her size 10 figure. However, she had second thoughts when she remembered Darius. She didn't want him to entertain the idea that she was dressing to get his attention. So, she quickly laid the outfit to the side and selected a loose fitting pair of sweats and an oversized long sleeved t-shirt. Ordinarily Alexa wouldn't be caught dead in her sweats; however, they came in handy today. She hoped that choosing the sweat suit over something more visually appealing sent a strong message of indifference to Darius.

Before stepping into the bathroom, she stopped to turn on the CD player. She fingered through the CD's in the holder, before selecting Cassandra Wilson's latest.

Once the composition started to play, she gathered her things and went into the bathroom and turned on the shower. As the water warmed up, she bobbed over to the sink and began brushing her teeth.

Moments later she emerged from her quarters feeling fresh and ready for the day. To her surprise the Renault family was seated at the breakfast table before 8 a.m.

Bryant, who was pouring himself a second cup of coffee, glanced up as she entered. "Thanks Al, for staying with the girls."

"No problem. I just pray that your mom is okay."

Bryant didn't respond and Alexa could see the concern in his eyes. "Are you ready, Maya?"

"Mommy, where are you going?" Brielle asked.

"We told you, boo," Maya answered patiently. "Daddy and I have to see Granny because she is sick."

"Is Granny gonna be okay?" Monaye asked, her little face contorted as if she would cry. She was definitely the emotional one.

Bryant and Maya exchanged worried glances.

"We hope so," Bryant finally answered.

Maya quickly added. "You can do your part by praying for her in the meantime."

"I will," Monaye quickly replied.

"I'll pray too, Mommy," Brielle said, not wanting to be left out.

"I pray Mommy, okay?" Sasha added.

Maya smiled at her precious children with loving eyes. She leaned down and pressed her lips to each of their foreheads. The tender exchange was like a Kodak moment.

"Call me as soon as you hear something," Alexa called out.

"We will," Maya promised, releasing her hold on the girls. Alexa could see the lines of worry furrowing her brow. She walked to the door behind Bryant and Alexa followed.

"Thanks again, girl," Maya said turning back to her friend for a hug before departing.

Alexa squeezed her tightly. "Don't worry. Everything will be okay."

Maya solemnly nodded and left to join Bryant in the warming vehicle.

Alexa watched them from the door way. As they began backing out of the driveway, she closed her eyes and said a quick prayer. When she opened her eyes a black SUV pulled up the drive and stopped along side the truck.

Alexa's stomach fluttered when the window rolled down and she spied Darius poking his head out to talk to Bryant. In a flash, she closed the door and scurried over to the front bay window. She peeped through the drapes to see the two talking. After a few moments, Bryant continued to back the truck down the drive. Alexa waited for Darius to do the same, but was surprised when he pulled in and parked.

She exhaled, her breath creating a fog on the window. *Why is he staying?* She asked herself. It would be awkward having him around without Maya and Bryant around to be buffers between them to alleviate possible tension. Darius had a way of stealing her control, which really unnerved her.

She watched him fiddling around inside the truck for a few minutes before opening the door and stepping out. So as not to be seen, Alexa hurried off to the kitchen where the girls had just finished eating their breakfast. The three of them had wandered into the adjoining great room where they were watching cartoons.

In an attempt to look busy, Alexa began to clear the table when the door opened.

"Good morning." He greeted in a voice as smooth as a caress.

Alexa looked up right into his smoldering eyes. *How could he look so sexy at this hour of the morning?* She wondered digging his style. The reversed leather Kangol cap on his head and the belted, black leather jacket look good on him.

"Good morning," she responded, turning her back to him to place the dishes she was holding inside the dishwasher.

"Uncle Darry!" Monaye and Brielle screamed in unison. They scrambled up from the places on the floor and charged him like miniature linebackers on a quarterback.

"Hey little bits!" he returned scooping them both up in his arms. "How are my girls?"

"Guess what?" Monaye asked, completely ignoring his question. "Our Granny is sick."

"I know," he sadly replied. "Your Dad just told me."

"Mommy said we should pray so she can get better."

"That's a good idea." Darius replied.

"Okay, let's pray," Monaye suggested as she had seen her mother do on countless occasions. She motioned for Darius to place her back on the floor, which he obliged.

Alexa, who had heard everything as she watched from her side of the room, found her goddaughter's approach touching.

Just as they did at the dinner table, Monaye locked Darius' hand in one of hers and Brielle's in the other.

Darius glanced up at Alexa with pleading eyes as if begging for a way out. Alexa, in turn, pretended as if she hadn't noticed believing that she was exempt from the circle. However, that was not the case as Monaye had called her over to join them.

"Are you sure?" Alexa asked, stunned by the child's astuteness.

Monaye nodded, "Mommy said that if more than two people pray in Jesus' name, God will answer our prayers."

This time it was Alexa who looked to Darius for a way out. But just as she had treated him moments before, he returned the favor by ignoring her pleas. To stress his point, he released Monaye's hand and extended his hand therefore creating a space for her.

Seeing no other way of getting out of it, Alexa joined them. The point at which she entered required her to hold Darius' hand. It was the first time they had touched in nine years. His hand was more massive than she remembered, yet amazingly soft.

For a few seconds they stood there looking at one another to see who would take the initiative. Alexa thought Darius would and vice versa. Again, they were surprised when Monaye stepped forward with a sweet, short prayer for her grandmother. When she was done, Brielle followed suit. Alexa was impressed and made a mental note to praise her friends for the great job they had done in developing their children's spirituality.

Upon the completion of Brielle's contribution, Alexa prayed for complete healing and energy for the upcoming celebration. When she was done, all eyes fell on Darius. Alexa didn't know if it was his nerves or the warm jacket he wore that produced the beads of sweat on his brow, but he surprised Alexa with a short yet eloquent prayer.

When they were done, Alexa instructed the girls to play in the family room while she finished cleaning up the kitchen. Darius slipped out of his coat and tossed it on the ottoman before getting down on his knees to initiate play with the girls.

Alexa moved back and forth from the table to the dishwasher, occasionally stealing glances at the foursome roughhousing in the next room. The girls screamed with delight each time Darius held one of them high above his head and pretend to drop them only to cradle them against his solid chest. At one point, she paused to watch them tumbling into a pile on the floor in fits of laughter.

As Alexa observed their play, memories of their playful days back in college came to mind. Darius loved to wrestle with her. He claimed that the tough image she tried to portray energized him and he liked showing her who the "champ" really was. Any signs of boldness or bravery challenged Darius and he would lift her high above his head before tossing her on the sofa. If she talked back, he would pin her down beneath his weight until she admitted that he was "the king."

She recalled one occasion when they were spread out on the living room floor after watching WWF.

Darius was on top of Alexa and had one of her arms and one of her legs pinned down. "You give?" he panted, searching her face for signs of surrender.

"No!" Alexa screamed, squirming to set herself free.

He responded by raining kisses over her face and neck. As he worked his way down and inside her button down shirt, she screamed out that she gave up. Upon hearing that, Darius' grip loosened and his kisses soften. Minutes later, they would be wrapped in each other's arms.

With Darius nearby, in the other room, Alexa grew uneasy as thoughts of them being intimate entered her mind. She always believed that what they shared was unique. Making love to Darius was like exquisite art, beautiful music, comforting scents, and freedom of expression all rolled into one. It bothered her to know that Darius would always possess a part of her that she could never, ever share with anyone else.

"Whatever you're thinking about must be good." A voice said from behind, causing her to jump with surprise. Alexa turned around to find Darius leaning against the door frame with his arms crossed before his chest.

"Excuse me?" she asked her face warm with embarrassment.

"I would like to be in your head right now," he replied.

Heat radiated from her collar. *Little did he know that he was already in her head.* "I was just thinking about something," she uttered.

"You were smiling so wide, I thought you won the lottery," he continued.

"If that was the case believe me I would be doing more than just smiling," she retorted, turning back to the cupboard to retrieve the box of dishwasher detergent. Pouring some into the dispenser, she set the timer and turned it on. All the while, Alexa knew Darius was watching her and knowing this made her uncomfortable.

From where Darius stood, he had a good view of her backside and he couldn't help but smile with appreciation. Her efforts to thwart his attention had failed as he found her as appealing in the nondescript clothing as he would in a sassy red dress. He was curious to know what had her paralyzed in thought just moments ago. Whatever it was, she turned down the glow like a halogen lamp. He mistook her quiet muse as an invitation for company and thought it would be a good time to ask her out to dinner as friends. However, the idea quickly escaped him when she closed up like a clam.

"Well, I played long enough," he announced. "I guess I better get to work."

"Good idea," Alexa quickly agreed. Then as to not sound too harsh, she added, "I have to get the girls dressed anyway."

At the mention of their well being, the girls groaned in protest.

"Come on girls, you know you have to get ready for the day," Alexa ushered them towards the stairs.

Darius watched as they trudged past with sad expressions. He waited until they disappeared upstairs before heading for Bryant's office.

The work that needed to be done to Bryant's computer took longer than Darius anticipated. It was after 4:00 when he emerged from the office tired and famished.

His stomach growled as he made his way from the back of the house into the main living quarters. The house was as quiet as an empty church. Thinking Alexa left with the children, he headed towards the kitchen in search of something to devour. As he rounded the corner leading into the kitchen he came to a screeching halt, surprised to find her seated at the table; his mouth agape with awe.

Alexa appeared to be deep in thought as she gazed out of the window, grasping onto a mug of hot tea. Darius almost didn't want to disturb her.

She looked so peaceful and radiant, with the natural light warming her nut-brown complexion. He fought the urge to approach her and stroke her ebony tresses, but he knew he could not do that. The act would have been too intimate and much too forward considering the circumstances.

"Alex," he said her name softly. So softly, that he thought only he could hear, but she had.

She turned around, her honey brown eyes aglow.

"The house is so quiet. I thought you all were gone."

"The girls are taking their nap." She whispered as if speaking aloud would wake them way upstairs.

The mention of the girls brought a smile to his lips. "Those girls are something else, especially that Monaye. She is Maya all over again."

Alexa smiled and nodded in agreement. Her response encouraged him to enter the kitchen.

"Are you hungry?" she pointed over to the stove. "I just made some potato soup."

His brow lifted. Potato soup was his favorite. "I am starving!" he alerted and went over to the kitchen cabinet to grab a bowl.

"Have you heard from Maya and Bryant?" he asked, taking a seat.

Alexa nodded. "They are on their way home. Ms. Lily is stable and will be fine in time for the wedding."

Darius exhaled in relief. "That's good news." He knew how close his cousin was to his mother as he had the same type of relationship with his own mother.

Alexa gazed down at the mug between her clasped hands.

Darius felt her slipping away and tried to drum up something to say in order to retain the pace of the conversation.

"Since you're back, are you going to take some time to reacquaint yourself to the city? Maybe see some old friends?" He hoped to keep her talking in an effort to bring forth ease and hopefully fade away the tension.

"I didn't plan on it," she replied. "As you know, we moved here when I was 10 years old and my folks left the area while I was away in college. The only tie I really have here now is Bry and Maya."

"Well, let me know if you change your mind. I could go for a night out on the town. It seems as if every time I come here its all about business."

Alexa shook her head. "I don't think that would be a good idea."

"And why not?" He spooned up some of the soup and blew on it to cool it off before eating. When he put the contents in his mouth, his eyes close with pleasure. Alexa had made it just the way he liked it with chunks of potato, leeks and chives.

"Because, we are not exactly friends," she retorted, recalling his words from that telephone call she made.

"That is precisely the reason why we should do it."

"What would that prove?"

"That we are two mature adults who can set aside our differences and at least be civil towards one another," he offered.

"While that would be idea, we both know that too much has been said for me to pretend like things are okay."

"If my memory serves me correctly, I can recall that the exchange of words may not have been said at all if certain actions by a certain party were not made."

Alexa's eyes widened at his words before narrowing into angry slits. She couldn't believe that he had the gall to go there. "And you say set aside our differences. How can we if you make comments like that?"

"Well, it's the truth Alex," he charged. "Your actions led to my words, plain and simple. I just call it as I see it." He pushed aside the half-eaten bowl of soup, totally losing his appetite. The muscles in his jaws tightened in anger. He wasn't prepared for this and was upset at himself for allowing her to witness his agitation.

"Who are you to sit up here and condemn me!" she exclaimed. His accusation may have been true, but she was not in the mood to hear it.

"The truth hurts doesn't it?"

Alexa was not prepared for a confrontation, nor did she desire one. Her response was silence.

Darius couldn't take it anymore and announced that he was leaving.

"That's probably for the best," she hastily agreed.

He rose from his chair and marched into the next room in search of his coat and hat.

Alexa went straight to the closet where she hung it shortly after he deposited it in the family room. She removed it from the hanger and handed it over.

"You know, you still should take me up on my offer," he said in a thick voice.

"Whatever," she couldn't believe that he still wanted to go out after just picking a fight.

"What's wrong?" he asked, leaning in closer. "Are you afraid that your feelings for me haven't disappeared after all?"

Her eyes widened, and her mouth parted in disbelief. "I can't believe how full of yourself you are."

"And so are you," he returned. "The years may have come between us but you are the same Alexa."

"What's that supposed to mean?"

He stepped closer to her. "You know exactly what it means. I know you Alexa especially when it comes to me—you are easy. You were easy then and you're easy…"

"Stop while your ahead!" she warned her eyes ablaze with fury. "I don't know who you think you are coming in here trying to put me down. I could say a lot about that situation, but I won't because I don't want to stoop to your level of game playing. I'm not into playing games. If that is what you're all about these days Darius, then you can leave me alone."

With a smug look on his face, Darius shook his head and departed without another word.

*   *   *

Alexa was fuming when she later repeated her altercation with Darius to Maya over dinner that evening. The two had the house alone. The girls were spending the remaining part of the week with Maya's mother while Bryant went to spend time with his own mother.

"I don't know who he thinks he is trying to make me look like some bad person," Alexa huffed as she took a sip of her wine.

"That doesn't sound like Darius," Maya replied.

Alexa threw her a surprised look. *No she was not sticking up for him.*

"Well it was him. He is such an ass. I swear I don't know what I saw in him to begin with!"

Maya knew, but she refrained from replying.

"He called me easy, Maya. Can you believe that?"

Maya grunted in response.

"So you're playing silent now," Alexa voiced, noticing Maya's silence. "Normally you would be on this story like a cat on a mouse!"

"I've just learned to keep my peace at certain times," Maya replied, clamping her teeth down on a piece of spicy garlic chicken.

"Yeah, right," Alexa scoffed. "I don't care, I am not going to play his childish game. I'm just going to avoid him until I leave."

She knew what she was proposing would be hard. Just thinking about him made her stomach feel all fluttery inside. Over the last few days, her emotions were as unreliable as a weatherman—stormy one minute, sunny the next.

"Then you'll ruin things." Maya whined.

"No I won't. I just won't deal with Darius."

"There will be instances where the four of us will have to come together like when we take pictures. I don't want you having an attitude and ruin my wedding day." Maya huffed as she dropped her fork on her plate and slumped back against her seat, pouting like a child.

Alexa rolled her eyes at Maya's display, frustrated that her friend did not understand her dilemma. "I'm not trying to ruin your wedding Maya. I'm just pissed off at Darius' for his comment. He was wrong for what he said."

"What you *did* was wrong too," Maya shot back. She immediately covered her mouth as if regretting her comment.

Alexa was equally surprised by her outburst. "What do you mean by that crack?"

"I think his actions were as justified as yours."

"So you think I'm easy too?"

"No, no," Maya interjected waving her hands. "I'm not saying that. What I am saying is that you hurt him. Regardless of how long ago that occurred, Darius was hurt. He's probably still hurting. People don't realize how first loves leave lasting impressions on a person."

"I loved him too, Maya. You sound like I reacted totally without emotion and that was not the case."

"I was hurt, too."

"But, you were the one who left. The man asked you to marry him. You slept with him, packed up your things and left. How would you have felt if the tables were turned?"

"But I told you how necessary it was for me to establish my career before getting involved in a serious relationship."

"I believe that was your mother's suggestion," Maya corrected her.

Alexa's frown softened. "That's not fair, Maya."

"And you think it's fair to Darius?" Maya asked. "I understand what your mother had gone through, Alexa, but that was *her* experience. She had no right telling you not to fall in love until a certain age. Love comes when it's ready. We can't conjure it up when we think the time is right. Darius loved you. It tore him up when you left. I should know because I was there.

"I'm not saying that you were wrong for not wanting to get serious at a young age, but I think you could have gone about things differently. Bryant and I have been through the fire and the flood and we have managed to stand strong. He's been supportive of my career, and I support him wanting his own business. If you truly love someone, it's about give and take. Maybe your father didn't know much about that, so don't use that as an excuse with me because I know things can work out especially if it was meant to be."

With that she slid back from the table and placed her soiled dish in the sink.

*   *   *

Darius was reminded of Alexa's cognac-colored eyes as he sipped Grand Marnier from the snifter. Regardless of the number of times he replayed the scene in his mind, he couldn't understand why he had behaved the way he did. All he knew was that seeing Alexa again made him realize how much he had missed her.

She looked the same except more mature. Her eyes still possessed that tranquil, yet smoldering gaze laced with wonder and mystique.

The whole scene, which was blown out of proportion, occurred so fast that the next thing he knew he was leaving. As he climbed up behind the wheel of his truck, he resolved that the years had failed to diminish his feelings for her, and the Alexa he knew possessed the same feelings for him as well.

His love for her was enough to make him happy. When Alexa announced that she was offered a job in Denver, he was sure she'd turn it down especially if he asked her to marry him. When he told his parents of his plans, his mother had asked him to take his time, and his father had left it alone all together. But Darius was in love, and he wanted to share that with the world.

When he had awakened that morning to an empty bedside, panic hit. Jumping from the bed, he prayed that Alexa was in the shower or maybe preparing their breakfast, but the house was quiet as ever and absent of her presence. In bewilderment, he sank down on the sofa and wondered what could possibly cause her to leave him. The only thing he could think of was his proposal. But, in his mind, he thought that would be the one thing that would draw her nearer, not push her away.

Suddenly, nothing mattered anymore. Not school, not his job, nothing. He probed everyone, Maya, Bryant, even her school counselor about her whereabouts, but no one knew anything. He even went as far as to contact the company Marks-St. Claire, but the receptionist told him in a nasally voice that it was against company policy to reveal personnel information. Empty handed and heart broken, he returned to Cleveland.

It was a slow process, but Darius managed to accept what had happened and after a year stopped devising ways to get Alexa back into his life. He eventually completed his graduate program and accepted a computer analyst position with a reputable software development company. After he deemed himself ready, he began dating again. The women were not hard to come by, and his nights were not often spent alone. Even so, no woman came close to capturing his heart, body and soul like Alexa.

Darius laughed to himself as he raised the snifter to his lips once more when the bartender approached and placed another glass before him.

"Compliments of the cutie in the red, potna," the bartender announced, nodding towards the door. Darius glanced over his shoulder to the woman sitting all alone. She smiled and raised her glass exposing her cleavage spilling from the black lace camisole. His eyes bucked at her feminine endowment, and she giggled as if she knew he was checking her out.

"Some women need to be arrested for making a man want to sin," the bartender muttered before walking away.

Darius held up the glass with an unsteady hand and nodded a gesture of thanks. She apparently thought that was a cue for her to come over and she did not hesitate to sashay to his side.

With each step, more leg was exposed in the butt-hugging short skirt. She was throwing so many of her feminine assets around that he could barely concentrate on her face.

"You looked like you could use another." She announced upon approach.

"Don't mind if I do," he replied. If somebody wanted to provide him with the means to distract him from his thoughts then so be it.

"My name's Cherise," she held out her hand as she took a seat on the available bar stool.

"Darius," he said, shaking her hand.

"What brings you here, Mr. Darius?"

He wasn't sure if he liked the way she sultrily sang his name or the suggestive glances she threw his way.

"Just needed a place to think," he replied.

"Hmm, you're thinking on an awfully expensive drink," she cooed, referring to the sip of cognac remaining in his glass. She motioned for the bartender to send over another.

"Only the best for me," He replied with a light chuckle.

"Is that so?"

He nodded. "What about you?"

She giggled, more like purred. "I like the best too baby, believe me. A couple drinks always relax me." She raked her long, blood-red nails through her mane and shook it wildly until it fell across her face and down her breast. "I love to let my hair down, and kick my heels up. You know how much fun it is having your heels up don't you?"

Darius nodded until he realized what she was hinting around to. "Oh, well, I watch football to relax. Yeah buddy. There's nothing like a good football game, throwing that pig skin around." If he wasn't so occupied with thinking about Alexa, he would have flirted back, but all he could see were those sexy eyes flashing before his eyes.

"Skin, huh? I like the sound of that." Cherise laughed. Her hand slid under the table and rested on his knee.

Darius pulled back. He had too many drinks. This woman wanted to be taken advantage of tonight and he was in the mood to take advantage of someone. But Cherise wasn't who he was after. The only one he could think about was Alexa.

Cherise rambled on with innuendoes, but Darius did not hear as his thoughts were on Alexa. He felt bad for their earlier encounter and suddenly felt the urge to make things right again. He pulled his wallet from his jacket pocket and removed a twenty-dollar bill.

"Hey baby, where ya going?" Cherise asked, snagging onto his jacket and pulling him back.

"I gotta go," he replied, placing the bill on the bar. He stood. "Thank you for the drink, Ms. Cherise. I apologize for having to dip out on you, but I have business to attend to."

"Would you like me to join you?" she asked with a look of desperation in her eyes. Curiosity made him wonder about the contents beneath the skimpy clothes, but the idea of enduring Cherise's company did not appeal to him. "Thanks, but no thanks." Before she could utter another word he departed.

*　　　　　*　　　　　*

Darius sat outside Bryant and Maya's home peering up to the window where Alexa slept. He wasn't sure if she was home, but his drunken state had lowered his inhibitions causing him to act first and think later. He was aware of his actions and justified them by his curiosity. Had he been sober and in his right mind, he was sure he would be somewhere else rather than lurking outside of his friends' home.

He opened the door of his truck and staggered across the street and up the drive. Digging into his pockets, he retrieved a handful of change, along with his keys and some tic-tacs. He took a quarter from the small pile of change and threw it at the window. It hit the stucco frame just beneath the window. He cursed lightly as he caught the glint of the coin spiraling into the brush below.

Digging into his pocket once more, he pulled out a nickel and with his best aim hit the window right on target. He waited for a few minutes but got no response. Searching once more, he tossed up another coin, which made its mark again. He decided that if Alexa didn't answer this time he would call it quits. When no light came on, he resolved that he was not meant to be there and turned to leave when he heard someone whisper his name in the darkness.

"Darry?"

He turned around to find Alexa standing at a side door dressed in an emerald green, satin robe. "Alexa," he sighed. *Man was she a sight for sore eyes.*

Darius' immediate reaction was to take her in his arms, but he didn't want to repeat their earlier encounter by crossing the line.

"Can I come in?"

Alexa paused for a moment then beckoned him inside. "What are you doing out at this time of night?"

"I came to see you," he replied, stumbling past her.

"Are you drunk?" she asked, catching a whiff of alcohol as he passed by. She turned on the light above the stove.

His eyes widened at the sight of her standing there in the thin wrapper, her feminine curves bringing tempting images to mind.

"I had a little to drink," he replied as he flopped down on one of the kitchen barstools.

She crossed her arms before her chest. "Darius, why are you drinking and driving? And more importantly why are you here at this hour?"

He exhaled loudly, "Because I want to apologize to you. I don't know why I said what I said. No, I know why I said it, but I shouldn't have, and I'm sorry."

His attempt at an apology was a little loud and jumbled, so rather than have him waking the whole house and risk having to explain his being there, she ushered him up the stairs to her room for privacy.

The first thing Alexa did when she closed the bedroom door was excuse herself to go to the bathroom. She did not want to give Darius any ideas by lounging around in her robe. She pulled out a pair of boxer shorts and a t-shirt and slipped them on.

As she exited the bathroom, she immediately spotted Darius' coat and shoes on the floor beside the bed. He, on the other hand, was stretched out on her bed with his hands behind his head staring up at the ceiling. The hem of his fitted T-shirt was raised just enough to expose the downy hairs on his packed abs. She recalled the treasure hidden just beyond the band of his jeans.

Darius raised up catching her by surprise, "Alexa."

She took a seat on the bulky chair away from the bed. "Yes."

"I'm really sorry about today," he started again. Alexa knew it was his induced state that caused him to continuously apologize because the Darius she knew was more reserved with his feelings.

"You were wrong for calling me easy. You, more than anybody, know that there is nothing easy about me."

"I know," he replied sitting up.

Alexa's heart began to beat fast. "Then why did you say something so stupid?"

He paused, "Because I wanted to hurt you. I wanted to see you hurt like I was. I've forgiven you, but I know I can't forget it. You hurt me when you walked out on us."

"What?" She exclaimed unsure if she was prepared for what was to come. "When you left me like you did," he repeated. He proceeded to go on with a faraway look in his eyes. "Young brother was in love. I would have done anything you asked me to, but you were totally oblivious to my feelings."

Alexa searched for words to say to ease his pain, but she couldn't come up with an excuse that would be fitting.

"You were my world girl," he whispered. "How could you end things like you did?"

The topic of conversation was too much and Alexa did not feel like discussing the past. The way she handled the situation was wrong and she realized it, but she wasn't prepared to discuss it. Not at the moment, anyhow. The last thing she wanted to talk about was what she did wrong because that had been haunting her from day one.

"Look Darius, it is apparent that you are intoxicated," she announced, standing. "You are in no condition to discuss serious subject matter."

Darius shook his head. His movement so exaggerated that he looked as if he might give himself whiplash. "I may be a little faded, but I'm not incoherent."

She shrugged. "Okay, how about I don't want to talk about it."

Darius looked at her strangely. "Alexa. Don't you think I deserve to know?"

Rather than respond, she turned away from him, focusing her attention on the dresser before her. The next few days would be hard on both of them. For Alexa, trying to maintain a civil posture would be easy under other circumstances, but if every time she peered over her shoulder to find Darius watching her every move, she would likely falter.

Darius groaned and fell back on the bed.

The sound escaping from his throat caught her attention and she turned to find him stretched out on her bed. "What's wrong?"

He moaned holding his hands to his head. "My head is killing me. Can you get me an aspirin and some water?"

"Sure," she quickly replied heading to the bathroom. She located a bottle of Tylenol in the medicine cabinet. She turned on the faucet and filled a Dixie cup with water. When she returned to the bedroom, she found Darius fast asleep. Rather than wake him, she placed the cup and pain reliever on the night stand.

Although she wanted to leave the room, she couldn't help from remaining in her place watching him sleep. Even in slumber, Darius was a fine piece of art. His sculpted arms and washboard stomach revealed that fitness was one of his priorities. The rise and fall of his chest with each breath, followed by the familiar growl like snore added to his powerfulness. The slight furrow of his brow caused her to wonder what he was thinking.

It was funny how she couldn't recall him frowning in his sleep in their younger days. She remembered how much she used to love watching him sleep. He seemed so masculine. His snoring always made her feel secure. The memory caused a sinking feeling to settle in her stomach.

Shaking away the longing like rain off of an umbrella, Alexa made herself walk away. She returned, moments later, only to lay a quilt on top of him before snuggling under one herself on the chair.

As soon as she propped her head against the cushioned padding, she fell fast asleep.

*   *   *

In the middle of the night, Darius awakened to find Alexa curled up on the chair in what looked like an uncomfortable position. He glanced at the alarm clock. It was a few minutes after 2:00 in the morning. He decided he could sleep the alcohol off for another two hours and be gone before the other inhabitants woke up.

Watching Alexa snoring peacefully made Darius determined not to sleep alone. He slipped out of bed and gently picked her up from the chair and carried her over to the bed where he laid her down. After covering her with the comforter, he lay down beside her, on top of the covers, pulling her into his arms. His heart beat like an African drum. He imagined, actually dreamt about this moment many times. Having Alexa in his arms again felt so right. Like it was where she belonged.

CHAPTER 4

Just as smoothly as he had come in the night, Darius was gone the next morning. Through blinking eyes, Alexa wondered how she got into the bed. A secretive smile curved the corners of her mouth when she concluded that it was Darius' doing.

That smile faded when she rolled onto her side and gazed out of the window, realizing the complications she was creating by allowing him to place her in difficult situations. Letting Darius inside the house and into her room could have been a mistake. While she was supposed to be there for Maya, most of her quiet time was spent reflecting on her feelings and past with him.

With a heavy sigh, she closed her eyes once again and allowed herself to escape into the past filled with passionate memories that touched her every essence.

Despite her initial reservations, Alexa and Darius hit it off. If there was one thing that she recalled about her relationship with him in comparison to other guys she dated, was the fact that their personalities were a perfect complement. While Darius was talkative, Alexa was more of a listener. He taught her how to express herself more and she showed him how to listen well. Any tension that was apparent in the beginning had quickly dissolved as they fell into a comfortable place. Everything about their relationship was special, including their first time. Darius was her first lover. And oh what a lover he had been, Alexa thought with a smile.

Because she was a virgin, Darius felt it was important that they discuss how she wanted their first time together to be like beforehand.

Alexa took the necessary precautions to prevent pregnancy while Darius concentrated on fulfilling her wishes by making the evening special. When that special night had arrived, Darius fronted some money to Bryant for him and Maya to stay the night at a hotel. Once the apartment was vacated and while Alexa was away, he began to create an evening that his woman would never forget.

Alexa remembered being nervous the whole day. However, when she crossed the threshold of her bedroom, her anxiety dissipated when she saw the care Darius had put into making her first time special.

There were candles all over the room, giving it a warm, inviting glow. Darius had searched through his music collection and made a compilation cassette of the best love songs of the time by great artists of love like the Isley Brothers, Force MD's, Ready for the World and Luther Vandross. The bed was redressed in white linens and was scattered with rose petals. On the bedside was a small plate containing strawberries, pineapples and chocolate dip along with a bottle of chilled champagne and two glasses.

In the dimness she called out his name.

"Yes, babe," he responded softly.

She turned to the sound of his voice and blushed at the sight of him standing in the doorway, shirtless, wearing nothing more than a pair of jeans. He reached his hand out for her to come to him and she responded, her heart pounding in her chest like a bass drum. As she slowly moved towards him, she couldn't help but get caught up in the ambiance that he had created. Once she reached him, Darius pulled her into his embrace. With his hands on her hips, he began swaying her into a slow dance.

He whispered sweet endearments into her ear as he held her tightly. She relaxed and rested her cheek against his smooth sturdy chest with a sigh, feeling like she could stay in his arms like that all night long.

They danced to several love ballads before Darius took her by the hand, and led her over to the bed where he began to feed her some of the chocolate covered fruit.

At Last!

As she savored the sweet treat, Darius reached for the bottle of champagne and poured some into a wineglass. Holding the glass to her mouth, he tilted it for her consumption, deliberately allowing some of it to leak out of the corner of her mouth and trail down her chin to her neck and finally into her blouse. With a mischievous grin, he cleaned up the liquid with his warm tongue.

No words were exchanged as Darius proceeded to remove each piece of her clothing in slow motion until she was standing naked before him. He stepped back to gaze upon her with love-filled eyes. Alexa blushed under his scrutiny and immediately glanced away her hands covering her femininity.

However, Darius wouldn't have it and looked into her eyes as he took her hands in his.

"I don't want there to be any secrets between us Alex," he whispered as he stood before her. His lips tracked feathery kisses down her neck and shoulders while his hands caressed her soft skin. It didn't take Alexa long to forget about her nudity and in moments her inhibitions gave way to the warm need stirring in her abdomen.

Darius was gentle. He loved her slow and sweet. It was everything Alexa wanted her first time to be like. When it was over, she cried because she knew she was in love. Darius whispered sweet promises as he kissed the tears away. The next morning, instead of eating they had each other for breakfast in her bed several times before falling asleep curled up to one another as if connected for life.

When they exited the bedroom later that evening, Bryant and Maya were grinning like Cheshire cats. However, Alexa's smile was only for him because she knew her life had changed forever. The whole year, the two were inseparable until that fateful night when Alexa stepped out of his life.

Although she tried Alexa could not shake Darius' memory, which burned like a torch in her heart. She believed that her disregard for their relationship came back to haunt her when Sean called off the wedding, reaffirming her belief in the saying "what goes around comes around."

Since then, she accepted the responsibility of what had occurred and chalked it up as a learning experience.

Yet here they were, nine years later and she felt helpless around him again. The ever-present chemistry between them hovered above as a reminder of how good they were together.

There was also the ever present fact that the situation had driven a wedge between them. In time, she had learned to gain control of her emotions and move on. Yet she could not help but be reminded that she may have lost the one true love of her life.

Right now she had no place in her life or her heart for distractions. For the remainder of her stay, Alexa vowed to concentrate on her role in the wedding and not on Darius or their history. Once the festivities ended, she would catch the first flight back to Denver.

*   *   *

The orange sphere swirled around the rim a few times before sinking into the net. Darius jogged up to retrieve it, bounced it three times, looked to his left then to his right before pivoting sharply back to his left only to drive down the middle of the court for a lay up.

He was up most of the night thinking about her. It felt so good holding her in his arms again and took everything he had within him to get up and leave. He left her curled up, hugging the pillow. Later in his own bed, he tossed and turned. He tried watching television, but there wasn't anything on that held his interest, so he decided to get up and workout to clear his mind.

After shooting hoops for another half-hour, he went up to the locker room to get ready for the day. He was glad Bryant was able to obtain a temporary pass to a 24-hour gym for him during his visit. Working out was a great tension reliever for him.

At Last!

Sweat poured down his face as he peeled off the saturated T-shirt and shorts before stepping into a steamy shower. When the hot water hit his tired muscles and streamed down his body, thoughts of Alexa entered his mind. Darius had come to understand that seeing her again was like never having lost sight of her at all. They were three months into their new relationship and every day was like their first time meeting. He recalled in his mind the exact moment that he knew he was in love.

He had been studying for a test when Alexa returned from her campus job.

The minute he laid his eyes on her, he knew that there would be no studying taking place.

Her image stayed with him long after she left his presence for the kitchen. All he saw on the pages of his textbook were her smooth, shapely brown legs, soft feminine curves beneath her tank top and short denim skirt and those smiling brown eyes. He stole a glance at her pulling books out of her backpack and was mesmerized. Damn, she's beautiful, he murmured to himself.

"Let's go to the park," he suggested a few moments after her arrival.

There was no denying the attraction between them. Alex, as he liked to call her, was the first woman who captured all of his senses. He knew that it would be a matter of time before their playful wrestling and the late night company they kept while watching old movies would eventually lead to something more.

For right now he was content with being in her company. Not only did she have the temperament that complemented his own, but she was a beautiful person both inside and out and lot of fun. Darius also enjoyed her sense of humor that came across as naiveté. This made him feel so relaxed in her presence and he appreciated that he could be himself.

"The park?" she asked, stepping from the kitchen. She smoothed her bangs, a habit of hers that he found to be so cute.

Darius nodded emphatically as he stood up encircling her waist in his arms. "I need to take a break from the studying. C'mon," he urged.

Alexa relented with a smile. "Okay, let me change."

"No!" Darius blurted. "Don't change. You are fine just the way you are." He meant that in more ways than one and judging by the grin Alexa threw his way, he was sure she caught on to the double meaning.

They drove to their favorite park and walked the bicycle trail until they came upon a bench facing one of Michigan's many lakes. Several people had their boats out on the lake, some sailing, others fishing. The one which caught Alexa's eye was bright yellow. The gentle breeze made the colorful matching sails flap lazily.

Alexa sighed and leaned back on the bench up against Darius' chest. "That's pretty," she cooed.

Darius turned to her, his heart fluttering like the winded sail before them. She was so close to him. He could smell the sweet cherry fragrance of her hair oil. She looked so stunning even with her hair pulled back into a silky ponytail. No, she did not possess model-like features like Maya, but she had a more wholesome splendor which attracted him more; an untouched beauty that he had to claim as his own.

He then proceeded to do what his heart had been telling him the moment he caught her in his arms the day they met in the apartment. Without warning, with his hand on her cheek Darius gently turned Alexa's face to his own and lowered his head meeting her lips with his own. His rapid breathing began to calm when she opened her mouth to receive him like she had been waiting all along for the moment to happen.

When Darius finally pulled away they sat there for a few seconds smiling at one another. Then with no words exchanged as none were needed. Darius just entwined his fingers with hers and they continued to watch the wind rippling across the waters.

He shook his head as if to erase the vision from his mind onto current matters and emerged from the shower refreshed.

As he proceeded to get dressed, Darius ran through his itinerary for the day. He planned to pick up his tuxedo as well as a gift for the "oldly-weds" before heading to the church for rehearsal.

As he passed the front desk, Patricia, the desk receptionist called out goodbye. She had made it known, at check in that her "friendliness" reached beyond the front desk. Although she was attractive, he was not interested. It seemed to be the pattern in his life lately. Some sisters had no shame at all in approaching brothers these days for 'no strings attached' sex and he had turned down many.

However there were a few he considered.

There were certain qualities in the women he liked which allowed them to last longer than others. He could count those few women on one hand. Valerie Fontaine was one of them. Valerie was a beautiful, weight trainer and part-time, swimsuit model who could cook her butt off. Her culinary skills involved all sorts of exotic vegetarian dishes. She was an upbeat person with a positive outlook on life, happy with herself and mentally and spiritually balanced. However, Darius noticed that her appointment book was filled with more social & business activities than free time. After a while, he grew tired of being penciled in at odd hours in order for them to spend time with one another so they eventually parted.

Then there was Lanai Edwards. Lanai was a successful attorney, gorgeous, very professional, and very committed, but because she had placed her personal life second to her career in the past, she was dead set on achieving her goals for making wedding plans a year into the relationship. When Darius couldn't agree to her terms, the relationship quickly dissolved.

Then there was Tori Stackhouse, a down-to-earth, single mom who attracted Darius with her easygoing personality. He liked how she put her son's needs before everything and how she didn't expect much out of him. She had a good heart and was attractive as well. However, he couldn't help but be reminded of Alexa in her presence. Once, when they were making love, he whispered Alexa's name into her ear. That was enough for Tori to not take things any further. She wasn't about to play second fiddle to any woman, and Darius couldn't agree more.

The past six months were spent trying to find what made him happy in life. Upon reaching his thirty-third birthday, he had come to the conclusion that he may never experience the love, trust and honor that a good woman could bring to his life. In the meantime, he decided he wasn't going to sit around and dwell on what he didn't have. He had a lot to be thankful for. For one, he was in good health as was his family. Secondly, he had a decent job and held a position as an active administrator of a predominantly black, inner-city high school for boys in which he found many rewards. He was lucky to sit on many high profile boards throughout the city and was involved in several professional and service organizations where he met some good people.

Just when he thought he had reached the level he wanted to, he got the call from Bryant urging him to fly to Detroit to stand as best man in his wedding. Darius was all for it until he learned that standing opposite of him was his old love interest Alexa Kirkwood. His stomach practically fell to the floor, but for the sake of his cousin, he agreed to be there with his game face on. However, from the moment they came face to face, he turned weak in the knees like a schoolboy and his reservations were tossed out the window.

Although his heart ached for her, he knew he couldn't sacrifice his soul again. As he parked his truck outside of his hotel room, he knew that he had to do whatever was necessary to get through the weekend, regardless of the circumstances.

CHAPTER 5

Alexa sprung for a new outfit for the rehearsal dinner. She wore a black velvet dress with long sleeves and long skirt. The most attractive feature of the dress was the back, which temptingly dipped to the small of her back. She completed the outfit with a pair of black pumps with rhinestone straps. She twisted her hair up in the back, bringing attention to her dramatic eye makeup.

Alexa stepped from her room in time to see Maya sashaying down the hall, looking equally nice in a silver-gray cocktail dress with spaghetti straps and slim-fitting skirt, silver sandals and a matching sheer wrap.

"You go girl with your bad self!"

"No," Maya replied with a shake of her head. "You are the one."

"Does it look okay?" Alexa asked smoothing her palms on the sides of her skirt. Her question was for more reasons than one.

"It looks real nice." Maya replied and spun around to show off her attire. "What about me?"

It was apparent that Maya had an eye for fashion. Everything she owned, including her casual, wear looked great on her size six figure. She always managed to find really nice articles of clothing in out-of-the-way boutiques and tonight was no exception.

"Bryant better watch out. He may want the honeymoon tonight!"

Maya smiled and draped the wrap over her shoulders in a dramatic fashion. "Remember, you always have to keep them on their toes." Maya dropped her advice with a mischievous giggle. They stepped into the hall bathroom and headed straight for the mirror. They both fingered their hair into position and simultaneously stopped what they were doing to step back and admire their reflections.

Maya reached over and placed her hand on Alexa's shoulder. "Hey, I want to apologize for my comments the other day," she began.

"Oh, forget it," Alexa replied with a wave of her hand. She was hurt by Maya's comment, but she had to admit that she had gone somewhat overboard with her tirade.

"No, it is none of my business. I talked to Bryant about it and he gave me a new perspective. I'm sorry for trying to act as if something was there between you two. What you and Darius had is over and it's time that I stop hoping for some sort of reconciliation because it is apparent that both of you have buried the past and I promise that I will too."

Alexa's eyebrow rose from Maya's comment, but she avoided responding. That wasn't what she gathered from Darius' conversation the other day. However, he must have told Bryant otherwise since they last saw one another. And, although she wasn't expecting anything from him, it hurt to hear it.

"I promise not to get into your business like that anymore," Maya continued as she began applying some mascara to her eyelashes.

"Thanks girl. I just want to be here for you without any distractions," she sighed deeply. "And like you said, the past is in the past. I don't want to stir up old memories. Let's just focus on the New Year."

Maya turned to Alexa and stretched out her arms as a peace offering. "Friends?"

Alexa nodded with a smile, "Always."

The two leaned in and exchanged hugs.

*　　　　　*　　　　　*

The rehearsal went very well. After running through the entire ceremony a second time, Bryant and Maya were satisfied that things would fly without a hitch. While at the church, Alexa kept her attention focused on serving Maya. She didn't want to even be left alone in Darius' presence. It was hard not to engage in the bantering with the men along with the other women. The men were trying their best to agitate the women who received them good naturedly.

Alexa stayed to the side, playing with the girls. On occasion, she'd glance over at the group to find Darius' eyes on her. When this happed, she would quickly turn away not acknowledging him.

So it was with a sigh of relief that Maya had the foresight to not seat her near Darius at the rehearsal dinner. It would have definitely been a task if she had to avoid him in close proximity. As they took their seats, she immediately struck up a conversation with the young man seated beside her named Chris.

Chris was a student at the nearby college majoring in pre law. He was a fraternity brother to both Bryant and Darius. So, most of his conversation was about the fraternity and Alexa tried to appear interested by asking questions.

Again when she broke eye contact with Chris to take a break from his ramblings, she'd find Darius watching. Instead of looking away like he had all day after being caught staring, he continued to challenge her by keeping his eyes set. After awhile, Alexa got tired of being intimidated by his looking and accepted the challenge, but when she looked into those dark eyes, she quivered.

Finally, when she couldn't stand it any longer, Alexa excused herself. She was glad that there was no one else in the restroom as she entered. Standing before the mirror, she reached into her purse and retrieved a tube of lipstick. When she held her hand before her face to apply the color, she frowned at the sight of her hand trembling. She couldn't believe Darius was acting up like he was. Why couldn't he just leave her alone? It was bad enough that both of them had to be within each other's presence. He didn't have to make it worse with his silly games.

With a sigh, she rolled down the tube and tossed it into her purse. She didn't feel like going back into the dining room. What she wanted to do was get tomorrow over with and be on the first flight back to Denver.

She wasn't going to get caught up in Darius' control games which were sure to continue throughout the course of the evening. Rather than go back and endure his intense stares and smirks, Alexa detoured to the coat room. The attendant handed over her coat with a gold toothed smile and had the nerve to ask for her telephone number. She rolled her eyes in response and abruptly turned away.

The night air was chilly and instantly bit her face causing her to shiver despite the warm coverings she wore. Thank goodness there was a cab driver waiting out front reading a newspaper. Alexa rapped on the passenger window with her knuckle. The East Indian man peered at her over the rim of his glasses and lowered the window a couple of inches.

"Are you on duty?" She asked. She shifted her weight from side to side to keep her blood circulating.

"Depends, where to?" he asked.

Alexa swore that if there had been another cab waiting, she would have told him to kiss her butt and move on. She hated when cab drivers, especially the foreign ones, acted like all black passengers were potential thieves or prostitutes.

"Southfield," she gritted through her teeth.

"In that case, I'm open for business." He said with a smile as if trying to make up for his ignorance.

Alexa opened the door, slipped inside and quickly rambled off the address.

"Wow, are you an entertainer or something?" he asked, obviously familiar with the neighborhood where her friends lived.

"Yes, something like that," she wryly replied. Then so that he wouldn't ask any further questions, she turned her head and gazed out of the window. It was like deja vu, she thought to herself, driving away in the night, escaping the same man who haunted her thoughts in the present.

As the cab exited onto the expressway, Alexa contrived a story in her head that she was sick and didn't want to interrupt Maya during dinner just to tell her so. The plan was to get back to the house and relax a moment before packing. Then following the wedding, she was out of there.

*   *   *

Darius tried to concentrate on what Bryant was saying about their business venture, but his thoughts were on Alexa. From where he sat, it appeared as if the young Will Smith look-a-like was talking her ear off. He almost wanted to rush over and free her from the boring conversation that she endured, but he didn't. Alexa hadn't given him much thought all evening. What attention she did give him was short lived and then she ended up easing out of the room.

Darius was so caught up in Alexa's whereabouts that he didn't hear Bryant's question.

"Damn man, what's with you?" Bryant asked, rapping his knuckles on the table in an attempt to get his attention.

Darius turned to Bryant with a sheepish grin like a child who had just been caught with his hand in the cookie jar. "Whassup?"

"I don't know you tell me? I've been trying to talk to you about the business and you've been spacing me off."

Darius eased back in his chair and tossed his napkin on the table. "Now you know this isn't the time or the place to be discussing business," he reprimanded his cousin. "You're supposed to be talking about wedding bells and stuff."

Bryant laughed and his eyes traveled over to where Maya sat chatting away with her mother and aunts. "I already got the bride in more ways than one. All of this was May's idea. She said she always wished she had that big wedding. I told her it didn't make a difference to me, because I love her as much now as I did then. But you know women always trying to come up with ways to spend some money."

Darius laughed. "Don't give me that crap man. I know you are just as down as Maya." Darius sat up in his seat and held a fork to his ear like a telephone imitating Bryant's call. "Hey brother you got to come to Detroit for New Years. Maya and I are renewing our vows!"

Bryant burst out laughing and playfully punched Darius.

"Mind your manners boys!" Maya called from her place at the end of the long table.

Darius watched as the two exchanged loving glances. A blind man could see that the connection between the two of them was tight and he envied that closeness. Lately, this feeling seemed to invade his thoughts more often than not in the last year. His eyes traveled from Maya and across the room where he last saw Alexa seated. All that remained was an empty chair and a lipstick stained wine glass. He quickly scanned the room for her, but did not see her anywhere.

Wondering where she was, Darius stood up. "I'll back right back."

Then, as if on a secret mission, he breezed through the party room and into the dining area of the restaurant. He glanced about the room once more just in time to see her slipping out the front door.

His dinner bill was the last thing on his mind and he hoped Bryant would forgive him for leaving without paying. He didn't know why he chose to follow her, but he did, right back to Bryant and Maya's house. He parked a little ways down the street and observed the cab turn up the circular drive. She got out and leaned over to give the driver his money. He rolled his eyes when the driver took off without even waiting to make sure she was safely in the house. Minutes later, he noticed the light in the guest suite turn on.

Darius continued to sit in the truck, staring at her window when the light went out. He glanced at his watch. It was a little after eight. Surely, she wasn't in bed, he thought. Rather than sit there and be mistaken for a peeping Tom in the high-brow neighborhood, he started to leave when he noticed the light filtering through the trees, in the solarium located on the side of the house. Curiosity got the best of him and he decided he had better check out what was going on.

*   *   *

Alexa eased down into the Jacuzzi's hot foaming water and immediately began to feel the tension leave her body. The tub was located in the solarium off of the master bedroom and was also accessible through a pair of French doors off of the family room. It was well hidden from outside view by lush foliage and trees. The room was a wise investment, as far as she was concerned. The dim lighting and jazz music pumping through the built in intercom system further enhanced the ambiance and Alexa was grateful for the opportunity to relax.

She took a deep sigh as she stretched her neck from side to side before reaching for the bottle of Dom Perignon and wineglass. She poured some of the liquid into the fluted glass and brought it to her lips. Her taste buds seem to shout for joy as the sweet elixir trickled down her throat. She credited Maya for her good sense of taste as she was the one who insisted on the builders adding a wine cellar just off of the family room for the purpose of entertaining, which she loved to do. Alexa closed her eyes and leaned back against the cushion, getting lost in the music, frothing water, and wine.

Immediately, Darius' dark eyes and sexy smile trespassed in her mind. A slow smile formed on her lips as she visualized him walking towards her with outstretched arms.

"Looks mighty tempting," a male voice cut through her mental milieu.

Alexa's eyes immediately popped open and she gasped. Leaning there in the doorway with his arms crossed before his expansive chest was Darius. He looked enticing as ever in a charcoal-gray ribbed turtleneck sweater and black trousers. It was as if she conjured him up.

"Darius," she gasped. "How, what are you doing here?"

"I saw a light," he replied and stepped into the plant filled room. He had to admit that one would have to look hard to see light through the Amazon forest that Maya and Bryant created. They playfully referred to it as "The Jungle."

"I wasn't sure if there were prowlers on the premises."

Alexa averted her eyes as she treaded her arms through the water. "Well, as you can see all is well so you can go before they miss you at the party."

Rather than be derailed by her comment, Darius ventured closer. "How do you know if I want to go back to the party?"

"Why would you want to be here?" she returned, trying to remain cool although she couldn't look him in the eyes.

"Maybe to see you," he bluntly replied.

Alexa was taken aback by his response, but pretended she wasn't affected. Shrugging her shoulders, she picked up her glass and casually took another sip. "I guess."

Then, in an attempt to block him out, she closed her eyes and began to concentrate on the soothing music when she heard a dull thud. Her eyes sprang open to find Darius standing there with nothing on but his trousers. "What are you doing?" she nervously demanded.

He grinned wickedly. "I thought maybe I could join you?"

"What made you think that?" she retorted, her expression and tone clearly showed her irritation. "I can't believe you're half naked already!"

"Baby, you ain't seen naked," he teasingly replied as he slowly undid his belt buckle.

"Look Darius, if you want the tub to yourself, I'll be glad to go." She was about to stand up when she realized her compromising position. Had the room not afforded her the privacy, Alexa probably would not have entertained the idea of getting inside in just her panties, but with everyone gone, she thought she had nothing to worry about.

Darius noticed her hesitation. His eyes traveled down her face to her neck and onto her bare shoulders. *She couldn't be.* The delicious thought had his mind racing. A playful smile spread across his face and he swept his arm to the side. "Be my guest."

Alexa rolled her eyes and edged to the furthest side of the tub, crossing her arms before her bare bosom. "I guess it couldn't hurt if you got in, but don't get too comfortable because I need to go to bed."

"What's the rush?" he asked, slipping the black trousers down his strong, muscular thighs to expose a sexy pair of black boxer briefs. Alexa's eyes took in the contour of his manhood clearly remembering there was no myth about his well-endowed package. She flushed with embarrassment upon raising her gaze meeting his eyes.

Darius smiled as his eyes locked into hers and he stepped down into the foaming water like a lion stalking his prey. Just as he neared her, he submerged himself into the water, disappearing for several seconds before shooting up like a chocolate Poseidon, dripping wet and looking very enticing.

Wiping the water from his face, he eased close to Alexa. So close, that she could hear his ragged breaths. She fidgeted nervously. Just as Darius was determined to test her will, Alexa resolved to be unmoved. Yet she could not deny that his familiar masculine form, sexy dark eyes, and full lush lips had her blood flowing in all of the sensitive parts of her body.

Darius stood tall before her, their bodies were mere inches away. Alexa knew that resisting him would be a challenge. Thoughts of succumbing to his advances entered her mind. Not only did he still have an affect on her despite how hard she fought, there was still a touch of curiosity.

She licked her lips nervously just as Darius raised his hand towards her. She expected him to pull her close, but was surprised when instead; he reached for the wineglass behind her head.

Raising the glass to his lips, Darius emptied the contents in one swallow. "Mm, that's pretty good. May and Bryant sure have some good taste." He took the bottle and glass and treaded through the water towards the other side of the tub.

The whole scene was humiliating. Warmth brought about by embarrassment flushed Alexa's cheeks "You jerk!" she shouted, slapping the water so that it splashed across his sturdy back.

Darius spun around, his eyes boring into hers. "What's that for?"

"You know why!" she retorted. Her quivering voice matched her untapped physical yearnings. "Stop playing games with me Darius."

"Games? Who's playing games?" he asked with mock innocence. He set the wine bottle and glass on the edge of the Jacuzzi.

"You know exactly what I am referring to, so don't even try pretending you don't," she replied, rolling her eyes.

"No, I don't. Tell me."

Alexa cut her eyes at him again and crossed her hands over her bosom. Now would be the perfect time to exit, but she was too proud to humiliate herself again by storming off. "Forget it. Just leave me alone. Please."

He softened at her requests. He was purposely toying with her emotions, but he couldn't help himself. His desire for her was strong and he hoped that she felt the same.

He slid over to her side once more. "I can't Alexa," he admitted. "You see, being around you is intoxicating. Every time I look at you I have an incredible urge to say or do something that I know I would not in ordinary circumstances."

"Try containing your self," she said sarcastically.

He shrugged, "I guess I can't help myself. Like right now I want to do this." He pulled her into his arms and possessed her mouth with a warm urgent kiss. Her lips parted with ease as he tasted her sweetness.

Alexa immediately pushed her hands against him to free herself, but Darius held her tightly against his strong chest. Mixed feelings of exhilaration and fear swirled inside her like a tornado as her will unfolded before her eyes, resulting in her melting against him in defeat.

Darius smoothed his palm up the back of her delicate neck, raking his fingers in the silky tangles of her hair. He tipped her head to the side and ran kisses from her mouth to her jaw line down to the hallows of her neck.

"No, Darius," she groaned as his tongue made tiny swirls on her neck. She was falling fast and he knew it. "You know…"

Her words cut off as he gently suckled the tender spot, making her writhe out of control. Her neck was the spot he knew he had to attend to first and she would be his again, if only for one night.

Darius pulled her tightly against him so that she could feel the full length of his masculinity, hard with need. He pulled back temporarily, halting their growing desire to gaze upon her as if she was the most beautiful woman he had ever seen. She blushed from his open adoration.

Shifting his stance, Darius lifted her higher in his arms, placing her chest directly before his eyes. He always thought her breasts were beautiful, but now they were fuller and more womanly, making him want to nurse them like a newborn infant. He closed his mouth over one and began to suckle.

Alexa's body and mind battled between her sensuality and sensibility. The reasons why she should not release control were compiled on a list and contained very good points. However, her heart and her body reassured her that everything was okay because this was someone whom she loved deeply even though he did not know it.

Darius gently lowered her back onto her feet yet continued to cover her with kisses as if making up for all of the lost years. When he could go no further without sinking into the water, he scooped her up in his arms and carried her through the French doors into the master bedroom where an inviting fire burned in the white marble fireplace. The fire equaled the fires burning within them.

With her in his arms, Darius got down on one knee and was about to lower Alexa on a large plush pillow on the floor before the fireplace when Alexa immediately went stiff in his arms. Pulling back, Darius searched her face with questioning eyes.

"I'm sorry, I can't Darry," she murmured with downcast eyes. "There's too much behind us to go out like this."

Although Darius wanted her badly, he released her from his hold. His desire for her was great, but not enough for her to compromise her integrity.

Alexa, too, understood the repercussions of an intimate encounter with a person you love without a commitment. It could be as dangerous as playing with fire. She couldn't continue on with him then go about her life again as if nothing happened. She wouldn't do that to herself or to him again.

"Darry," she whispered his name. She wanted to touch his back which was towards her, but knew that touching him again may weaken her resolve and she could not, would not go back on her word.

Darius slowly turned around. "I understand Alex," he murmured. "You are right. We have a lot of things to deal with from the past before we can even think about sharing ourselves in this way again." With that he went to retrieve his clothing from beside the hot tub.

Alexa's hands shook nervously as she slipped into her robe. She couldn't believe that she had let things get as far as they did. She glanced at her reflection in the dresser mirror and guilt swept over her. She wasn't sure she could even look Darius in the face.

"Oh, what he must think of me," she groaned disappointedly, covering her eyes with embarrassment. She came to Detroit wanting Darius to see nothing more than the exterior of the confident, accomplished woman that she had become. Not the lonely and frustrated woman inside.

Only after a few moments, when she thought he was fully dressed, did she dare to reenter the family room. The room was dark, with the exception of the blinking lights on the Christmas tree. Alexa found him leaning over the back of a high back chair. He turned around upon her approach.

"About tonight," he began, but she stopped him with a wave of her hand.

"Let's just forget about it, okay?"

"No, I have to say this," he interrupted her. "I have to admit, I can't leave you alone. Every time I see you, there is nothing more I want to do than to make love to you even if you won't admit it I know you feel the same. However, I know we have a past that we haven't even dealt with."

Alexa was at a loss for words. She never would have expected him to say anything, let alone reveal the depths of her heart

"I also know that neither of us are ready to address our past just yet and having sex, no matter how bad we want to, won't do anything but damage things further. So, for both of our sakes, I'm going to stay away from you. Don't think I'm being rude or anything, but I need to do this for both of us."

Before she could even respond, Darius opened the door and strolled out into the cool night.

His direct words coupled by the heaviness in Alexa's heart made her want to cry. Darius had stirred up so many emotions inside, leaving her more confused and out of control than ever.

She missed the sense of security that her routine life had provided for her. However, she knew that going home wouldn't be the same. Things would be different because she wouldn't be returning the way she had left. Darius made sure of that. She resolved that the tender part of her heart would probably always ache for him, yet the sensible half knew leaving without any strings attached was for the best. Turning off the porch light, she turned and went upstairs without even a backwards glance.

CHAPTER 6

"What is wrong with you?" Maya asked. She was seated at the vanity in the bridal dressing room before Alexa who was helping her to adjust the tiara on her elaborate hair style.

It was the big day and the bridal party was running around like busy little bees, helping Maya in every way each one could. Alexa, on the other hand, didn't show the typical wedding jitters like everyone else but a unique silence of her own. If Maya could bet on it, she knew her friend's behavior had something to do with Darius. She noticed this yesterday at the rehearsal dinner. Shortly after Alexa left, Darius disappeared as well. Maya repeated her question and watched for Alexa's reaction in the mirror before them.

"Nothing," Alexa replied without raising her eyes. "Now hold still."

"Yeah, right!" Maya hissed as she whirled around to face Alexa. She seized her arm, pulling her close. "Did you and Darius get into another fight?"

Alexa glanced up into Maya's eyes at the mention of Darius' name as their previous night's encounter came to mind. She shook her head, wanting to erase all memory of that evening. "No, I kept my promise on that."

"Then what's wrong?" Maya pressed on. "You're not acting like yourself."

Alexa shrugged, trying to come up with a good story to ease Maya's suspicions.

"Honestly, I just have some things on my mind," she replied nonchalantly. Maya was way too perceptive to deceive at times and her best defense was to appear indifferent during one of her inquisitions.

"Like what?" Maya probed, her eyebrows raised with curiosity.

Alexa rolled her eyes. "Maya, you are getting married in exactly," she glanced at her watch "one hour. Stop harassing me about my problems. I am fine really."

Maya sighed, unsatisfied with her response, but decided not to press the issue because she had her own matters to contend with. For this Alexa was grateful as she did not want Maya's mother, Aunts, and others in the room all in her business. Although she would have liked the opportunity to talk to her friend, now was not the appropriate time.

Alexa realized that adjusting the headpiece didn't require mind effort, leaving her thoughts to drift. Last night was sleepless. Just thinking about what could have happened between her and Darius made her nervous. Although he was gone by morning, her uneasiness increased. The anxiety she felt was so apparent that she decided to skip out on the prenuptial brunch. She needed to clear her mind of Darius and get her emotions under control.

She hated that she wasn't there for Maya considering that she promised to be by her side until she walked up the aisle. But she was afraid of seeing Darius and having to look in his face after he so clearly read her innermost feelings.

Alexa had always believed that they had some kind of "mind thing" going. Their connection allowed them to read each others emotions and thoughts because they were so in tune with each other's body language and facial expressions. The components of their shared chemistry was so complex yet intriguing that it actually drew them closer, which only heightened their desire to be in each other's presence even if neither of them would admit to it.

At Last!

Once the headpiece was secured, Alexa stepped away to allow the makeup artist, Angie, to do her thing. Standing there made Alexa hungry. Since there was no food around to be thought of, she decided a cool drink would have to suffice. On her way in, she recalled passing a Coke machine and thought a Sprite would be good.

"Maya, I'm going to get a drink," she announced, digging through her small purse for some loose change. "Do you want anything?"

"No thanks," she replied. "But please hurry back."

Alexa promised she would as she left the room. To her relief she didn't have far to walk as she found a closer machine around another corner. She purchased a Sprite and popped the can right there and took a long swig. She exhaled with satisfaction as the clear liquid burned the back of her throat like harsh liquor. Rather than go back into the swarming dressing room, she decided to stay out in the hall.

Her nerves were so rattled that one would think it was her wedding day. The proof was in her sweaty palms and weak knees. In exactly, 10 minutes she would be walking down the aisle and all eyes would be on her. Under ordinary circumstances, she probably wouldn't think twice about it, but knowing that Darius was out there unnerved her.

She pressed her hand against her fluttering abdomen in an attempt to calm herself when Bobbi, the coordinator, decked out in an elegant tuxedo jacket with a long matching skirt, breezed past.

"Time to get ready!" she announced. She stopped at the dressing room door and poked her head inside informing the others inside as well. Alexa could hear a shriek from inside and within minutes, the bridesmaids exited the room followed by Maya's aunts.

Only Alexa and Maya's mother remained. However, they did not stay there for long as Bobbi poked her head in a second time to inform them to line up in the main hall.

"I'll see you in the sanctuary baby," Mrs. Jameson announced as she placed a kiss on Maya's forehead.

Alexa knew that she was up next, so she quickly got her hug in and whispered, "Keep smiling, it's your day."

Monaye and Brielle, who were spinning around the room making their frilly white and gold dresses swirl around their little knees, stopped long enough to give their mother a kiss before leaving with Alexa.

Sasha had grown tired and fell fast asleep. She found refuge in the loving arms of her great auntie.

Alexa assembled the other two in the foyer of the church with their gold baskets filled with ivory rose petals before handing them over to one of the ushers who promised to make sure they went down the aisle on time.

While she waited for her cue, Alexa poked her head inside the door and her eyes widened in awe. The room was dark with the only light illuminating from the ornate candelabras positioned on stage.

White tooling was attached to each aisle pew and flowed up to the stage where it entwined gracefully up the base of two tall white columns, which held two huge baskets of black roses.

The church was full, which was not unusual as the couple had lots of family and friends. According to Maya, their guest list consisted of several well known local celebrities and political figures that she had befriended over the years.

In the reserved seating sat author and Maya's namesake Maya Angelou. Also in attendance were gospel greats CeCe and BeBe Winans, comedian Steve Harvey and his wife, as well as the R & B singer Anita Baker. There were even some professional sports figures that Alexa recalled seeing on television but whose names she could not recall.

Bobbi jetted out of no where, wearing a headset that she used to direct commands to her assistants located in other parts of the building.

"Moms, you're up next," she announced, stepping aside for the elegantly dressed women to get into place. Both mothers stepped into place and began to fuss playfully over the handsome usher designated to walk them down the aisle. He blushed with embarrassment from their comments about his debonair good looks.

When the large oak doors opened, the mothers each entwined an arm with the usher. Everyone beamed with joy at the sight of the attractive trio strolling down the aisle. Bryant's mother looked healthy as ever. Everyone was grateful that her setback had not prevented her from enjoying her son's day. Alexa smiled broadly as they strolled down the aisle waving and smiling like a pair of beauty queens. When they arrived at their seat, the women surprised the usher by simultaneously placing kisses on his cheeks, making the crowd burst out in laughter.

With shaking knees, Alexa took her place next in line. She didn't know why she was so nervous because if anybody knew how to walk down the aisle as a bridesmaid, she did. She had been in so many weddings that her closet was full of frilly dresses she had been meaning to donate to the Goodwill.

When she spotted Bobbi's assistant raising her hand from the front, she knew it was her cue to begin her walk down the aisle. With a fixed smile on her face, Alexa proceeded forward to the beat of the music.

Camera flashes filled the room from every direction. Determined to keep her cool, Alexa looked straight ahead and smiled, focusing on nothing but the spot where she was to stand.

Once she made it to her spot, she glanced in Darius' direction. Fortunately for her, he was busy whispering something to Bryant and didn't see her looking at him. Even in her short glimpse, Alexa could tell how handsome Darius looked.

The Armani tuxedo with crisp, white collarless shirt looked like it was tailor made for him. She could also tell that he had cut his hair and trimmed his beard, making him look all the more tempting.

Alexa's thoughts were disrupted when Bobbi's assistant stepped forward and grabbed on the cord of the lacy white runner. She pulled it all the way back to the door and securely fastened it down.

At that moment, the doors opened again and in stepped Monaye and Brielle looking like miniature angels. Again bulbs flashed and "oohs" and "aahs" could be heard throughout the sanctuary as the little girls delicately tossed white rose petals on the ground, announcing their mother's entrance. Once they reached the front, Alexa beckoned for them to join her side. Monaye did as she had practiced at the rehearsal, but Brielle was another story. At first sight of her Daddy, little Brielle dropped her basket and ran giggling into Bryant's arms. Again, the guests united in laughter as Bryant scooped her up and carried her over to Alexa, managing to coax her into remaining there with a kiss.

The tender exchange between father and daughter was touching. Alexa glanced over at Darius to find him looking at her in return. Rather than look away as she expected him to, he continued to stare as if he was trying to send a message. Alexa was relieved when the beginning bars of *"I'm Lost Without You"* by BeBe and CeCe diverted his attention. Collective gasps could be heard throughout the sanctuary when both BeBe and CeCe, dressed in shimmering black attire, rose from their seats and took their places up front before the microphones.

Alexa was surprised that her traditional friend had not chosen the wedding march. However, she quickly understood once the two began to sing the lyrics to their hit contemporary gospel song.

The pastor stretched out his hands signaling that it was time for everyone to stand for the bride's entrance. All attention was now focused on the opening doors where Maya stood with her oldest brother Kenneth.

Although she had seen Maya in her dress beforehand, Alexa inhaled along with the others as if it was her first time. She looked at Bryant who stood there admiring his wife with adoring eyes. Maya boldly blew him a kiss which he returned.

The music faded when the pair reached the altar but not before BeBe and CeCe gave a stellar performance. The guests cheered as they made their way back to their seats. Pastor Mitchell waited until it quieted before asking, "Who gives this woman to this man?"

"I do," Kenneth proudly replied. He turned to face Maya and took both of her hands in his. "No one deserves this special day more than you. I love you sis. The only thing that I regret is that Papa couldn't be here for your big day because I know he'd love Bryant as much as we all do." With tears glistening in his eyes, he placed a kiss on her forehead.

His loving words and tender gesture brought forth tears to Maya's eyes. Alexa was grateful that she had the foresight to tuck some tissue beneath her nosegay and she immediately stepped forward to hand one to Maya.

Pastor Mitchell announced that Maya and Bryant had composed their own vows and stepped back to allow them to share their heartfelt words. While everyone thought Maya would be the one to break down from the sentimentality of it all, they were surprised when it turned out to be Bryant. Upon Maya completing her vows, Bryant took her hands into his. He cleared his throat and looked back at Darius who gave him a quick nod of encouragement, which he returned, getting a laugh out of the crowd.

Bryant clasped his hands and paused, closing his eyes in an effort to get serious.

When he gathered his bearings, he reached out and took Maya's hands in his own.

"I thank God for blessing me with this woman who is the sweetest most loving person I know. I love and admire everything about you Maya Dionne Renault. I want to spend many more years with you as you have been a blessing in my life. From the moment we first met, I knew the Lord had blessed me with an angel. With that I say, thank you for being my best friend, thank you for being my best girl and thank you for being the best woman to be called mother of our three beautiful daughters. I want you to know-" Bryant paused in mid-sentence when his chin started to quiver. Suddenly he broke down in quiet sobs of joy after realizing the magnitude of how the woman before him had affected his life. Maya immediately threw her arms around him and there wasn't a dry eye in the house.

Alexa dabbed her eyes with a tissue and looked over at Darius in time to see him wiping his hand across his face. She thought to herself how lucky Maya was to have Bryant in her life. Here was a man who stood before God, family and friends to profess his complete love for his woman. Through the tears in her own eyes, Alexa knew at that very moment that she wanted the same thing.

*   *   *

The reception was held in the luxurious ballroom of the Ritz Carlton Hotel.

The elegant setting at the church was carried out in the hotel ballroom as well. The room was divided into two parts. One side of the room was reserved for the sit down dinner while the other half was for the wedding party table. The band and dance floor were located in between. Next to the wedding table was an ornate wishing well, where Maya and Bryant asked for donations. Rather than receive gifts, the two thought it would be a good idea to accept donations for the local Boys and Girls Club.

As Darius entered the ballroom, he nodded in approval. The Renaults had gone way out. Not only was the reception hall tastefully decorated and the gift idea honorable, a gloved wait staff was on hand to serve chilled flutes of champagne and delectable hors d'oeuvres.

Darius didn't get a good chance to look around when one of the waitresses approached carrying a silver tray with the bubbly liquid.

"Thank you," he said picking up the glass by the stem.

"My pleasure," she cooed giving him a look that said *I want to eat you up*. Darius smiled in return but his mind was not focused on anyone or anything except Alexa. He hadn't seen her since the reception line at the church. He hoped that she wasn't holding the night before against him because she had no reason to. However, he couldn't help but notice how she was avoiding him.

The ceremony was deep, so deep, that it had him thinking. To love someone so completely and so deeply and have her love you in return with the same intensity had to be an amazing feeling. Bryant's tears left him speechless. He commended his friend for displaying his heart like that. His take on the ceremony had him thinking how much he missed that feeling and how much he desired to have it back in his life.

After breaking through the crowd of people milling about, Darius spotted the rest of the wedding party seated at their reserved tables. His attention immediately zeroed in on Alexa. Like a schoolboy, his heart began to beat fast and joy grew from the mere sight of her. He longed to be by her side and within minutes, before he could even think about what he was going to say, he found himself approaching the table.

Alexa must have felt him near because she looked up just as he approached and smiled shyly.

"Hey lady," he greeted as he took a seat beside her.

"Hi," she softly replied. He noticed how she acted as if she could not look him in the eye.

Could his confession from the other night, coupled with the emotional wedding ceremony, have had the same affect on her as well? He wondered. He took his place beside her and turned to say something when he was interrupted.

"Can I please have everyone's attention," the leader of the band called out. Everyone turned around respectively.

"I want to welcome you all to the wedding reception of the year!"

The guests cheered in response.

"I would first like to say that it is an honor to be able to provide the entertainment for my good friends, Bryant and Maya Renault. I would like to take a moment to say that I pray that God blesses your marriage for years to come. You are the most genuine, loving and special couple that I know. You do so much for others in the community through generous donations and you're both so giving of your time. I wish you all the best. We hope to get the opportunity to perform at your silver and gold anniversary affair."

Everyone cheered and clapped again.

"This is the part of the reception where we ask the couple to come to the center so that we can honor you in song for your first dance."

The smiling pair rose from their seats with hands clasped and gallantly approached the dance floor.

Bryant immediately pulled Maya into his arms and all eyes were on them as the lead singer serenaded them with LTD's "Love Ballad." The couple swayed to the beat, as they softly exchanged words of love and occasionally shared tender kisses totally oblivious to those around them.

Alexa felt a tug at her heart once more as she deemed her friends the most romantic couple in the world. The rehearsal dinner, ceremony and now this was starting to get to her. She didn't know how much more of it she could take.

So it was to her surprise when Darius interrupted her thoughts by sliding his finger seductively down her bare arm.

"Hey, woman."

Alexa jumped then shivered as his touch ignited a current of electricity which ran all the way to her abdomen. She gazed up at him through fluttering lashes.

"Hey, yourself."

"Some wedding, huh?"

She took a deep breath and nodded. "It was something else, that's for sure."

"About last night," he started.

"Shh," Alexa cut him off gently placing her fingers to his lips. "Let's not talk about that right now. Today is their day." She nodded towards the dance floor.

The two glanced over just as Bryant spun Maya away from him and twirled her back into his embrace. The movement caused the spectators to cheer. When the song ended, the band began to play an upbeat tune.

"Okay let's get the party started in here!" the lead singer said, waving his hands above his head. The crowd began swaying to the beat and waving their hands in the air in response as they made their way out onto the dance floor.

Alexa bobbed her head to the beat. She didn't get out much in Denver. Clubs just weren't her thing anymore. However, the music had her pumped and she felt like dancing.

She glanced at Darius out of the corner of her eye. Back in the day, he was two left feet. She wondered if his skills had improved any.

Darius felt Alexa's eyes on him and he turned to find her grinning mischievously. "Yes?"

Alexa leaned over and breathed into his ear, causing him to shiver down to his core. "There's something I wouldn't mind doing."

"And what would that be?" he asked, trying to keep his cool although he was yearning to allow his imagination to take over. All it would take is a sweep of his arm, he thought glancing at the contents on the dinner table. Her eyes traveled over to the dance floor.

"Dancing," she innocently replied, hunching her shoulders rhythmically to the music's beat.

Darius rolled his eyes with a smile. Instead of commenting, he took her by the hand and led her out onto the floor.

Alexa noticed that Darius had honed up on his dance skills judging by his moves. They exchanged knowing smiles in acknowledgement of this fact. Alexa's eyes traveled around the room to keep from having to stare at Darius, but she could feel his eyes on her, penetrating her clothes, down to her skin. She was relieved when the music switched from the smooth groove to a thrust-like reggae beat and was ready to call it quits.

However, Darius would not allow her to leave the dance floor. He grabbed onto her hands and pulled her close to him, rocking their bodies from side to side. Alexa gulped when Darius accidentally brushed up against her. Or was it an accident? She glanced up at him only to find that he was dancing another dance in a world of his own with his eyes closed.

Alexa took a couple steps backwards, but Darius gently placed his hands on her hips and pulled her back into his possession. In a slick motion without missing a beat, he turned her around so that her back was to him, causing her eyes to widen when she felt Darius' gyrating hips against her backside. When his hands encircled her waist and he rested his chin on her shoulder, she knew that it would be hard conducting herself with a cool head.

Closing her eyes, Alexa allowed her senses to be her guide. It wasn't long before she too had lost herself in "their" dance. Turning so that she was face-to-face with him, Alexa stepped up close and wrapped her arms around his neck. Darius' eyes locked with hers as they moved their hips to the arousing beat. Just as they were getting into their groove, the music slowed. She could feel the heat burning her skin, not only from the crowded dance floor, but also from her aroused state. She didn't know if she should vacate the dance floor or not.

Darius answered that question by reclaiming her hand and leading her deeper into the crowd. With no words spoken he pulled her tenderly into his arms and rested his chin on top of her head. With others surrounding them, Alexa felt secure in Darius' arms so she allowed herself to relax again. Nuzzling against his neck she prayed that she could remain in his protective captivity as long as she could so that she could savor the sweetness of his tender touch. As they dragged slowly from side to side, Darius began to sing along with Will Downing about going crazy when he looked into his lover's eyes.

Alexa did not know if he was singing for her benefit or not. So she closed her eyes and pretended that he was revealing the intimate impressions from his heart for her alone like he did back in the day when they were in love. She so badly yearned to experience that exhilaration again, the freedom of innocent love. Although he had only confessed to wanting her physically, she decided if tonight was the night, then she was going to take what she could get just to be with him, even if it meant never seeing him again. The song ended sooner than either of them cared for it to as they were caught up in the solace of each other's arms.

The band announced that in five more minutes the New Year would be upon them. He might as well said "last call for alcohol" because the crowd scattered about the room just as fast to find their significant others or someone to ring the New Year in. Darius took Alexa's hand and managed to secure them both a glass of champagne from the server whom he ran into earlier. When she saw him hand one of the glasses to Alexa, she sucked her teeth, rolled her eyes and marched away in a huff.

"What's her problem?" Alexa asked as she watched the woman retreat.

Darius didn't answer but continued to lead her by the hand through the throng of people. He wanted to find a place for them to be alone.

He brought her hand to his mouth and kissed it tenderly before proceeding to lead her about the room. The simple gesture evoked memories of how passionate Darius could be. Alexa recalled a statement Darius made in their youth about holding her hand. According to Darius, Alexa's hand was a perfect fit to his own which is why he enjoyed holding it so much.

Darius spotted a vacant table against the wall and led Alexa through the thick crowd to claim it. Just as they were about to sit down, two women in short, body-hugging dresses approached and announced that the table was taken.

"But brother we can make a concession for you!" The honey-blond one boldly declared. Her eyes rolled down the length of Darius' body like he was a piece of meat.

Alexa pretended she did not hear the comment and slid her arm around Darius' waist. "No, thank you. We need some privacy," she suggested linking her arms through his. Alexa did not care what was said in her wake. Tonight Darius was in her company and she wasn't going to let anyone spoil their evening.

Practically every seat, with the exception of the wedding party table, was taken. Therefore, Darius had to settle for a spot against the wall. He leaned against it and positioned Alexa in front of him wrapping his arms around her waist and the two waited for the countdown to begin

"We got one minute left people!" The DJ announced.

When the time was upon them, the countdown began.

"Ten, nine, eight," the crowd began in unison. "seven, six, five, four, three, two, one—HAPPY NEW YEAR!"

Confetti and balloons fell from the ceiling and horns and whistles went off in celebration. Surrounding couples embraced one another and glasses clanked as the previous year went out with a bang, making room for the new. The band began to play a jazzy rendition of Auld Lang Syne and the crowd sang along through hugs and kisses.

Oblivious to it all was Darius and Alexa who were wrapped in each other's arms, locked in a deep kiss in the back of the ballroom. Suddenly, an old adage of her grandmother's came to mind. *"The man you kiss at the stroke of the New Year is destined to be the man you'll wake up to for the rest of your life."*

Darius noticed her body tense in his arms and he eased back, searching her face for a problem. "Is there something wrong?" he asked through ragged breaths. The last thing he wanted to do was break their kiss, but he also wanted to be aware of her feelings. His eyes traveled down to her sexy kiss-swollen lips and his body hardened.

Alexa shook her head. "Nothing," she murmured, pulling his face back towards hers for a kiss "Nothing at all."

CHAPTER 7

"So what do we do now?" said Darius as he placed an endearing kiss against Alexa's forehead.

The words caused Alexa's head to spin as all sorts of thoughts came to mind. She may not be sure of what the future held for them, but she was certainly sure that she never felt as secure as she now did in Darius' strong arms. For the moment, there was no other place on the earth where she wanted to be.

Burying her face into the musk scented hollow of his neck, she inhaled deeply and closed her eyes, "Whatever you want to do."

Darius tipped her head with his forefinger and gazed lovingly into eyes. His head lowered until their mouths met and through tender caresses, he proceeded to communicate exactly how far he wanted things to go. Pulling back, he brought one of her hands to his mouth. He placed a gentle kiss on the smooth back of her hand before opening it. His tongue then whirled down the peak of her thumb and into the valley at the palm of her hand where he tenderly suckled.

Alexa shivered from his touch in addition to the fiery connection burning between them. With no further ado, Darius draped his arm protectively around her shoulders and led her through the crowd of merrymakers and out of the building. As they exited the building all Alexa was conscious of was the feel of his heart beating thunderously where her cheek rested against him.

$$\ast \qquad \ast \qquad \ast$$

At Last!

Darius' temporary accommodations were very nice, Alexa noticed as she entered the room behind him. The grand suite was elegant, yet provided a comfortable homelike atmosphere. There was a sitting area complete with a plush sofa and matching chair. A large entertainment unit, which housed a 36-inch color television and state-of-the-art home stereo system. The focal point of the room, however, was the beautiful marble fireplace. Alexa thought how romantic it would be to sit in his arms before a roaring fire, while placing the cares of yesterday behind them.

There was also a kitchenette complete with stove, microwave oven, refrigerator and breakfast bar for those desiring a longer stay. The sleeping quarters were located in the loft which overlooked the seating area. It consisted of a king size bed and a large bathroom with garden tub and separate shower.

It was apparent that the housekeeping crew had come in Darius' absence because of the cozy fire burning in the fireplace and the small basket containing a mixture of expensive chocolates left on the counter top.

Darius tossed his keys on the breakfast bar and proceeded to slip out of his suit jacket. Alexa watched him recalling every inch of his body with admiration. Again their eyes locked. As he removed his dress shirt, Alexa eyes roamed over the contours of his well sculpted torso and arms. She had been mesmerized by his defined masculine build then, but was even more captivated by his more manly form now.

Darius stepped away momentarily to turn on the stereo. He scanned through a few stations when the saxophone from a slow jazz piece caught his attention. Turning around he opened his arms, inviting her to step into his waiting embrace.

She melted against his chest, relishing in being close to him once again.

When the song came to an end, Alexa continued to hold him tight. She knew that they were about to engage in an activity that if it were any other individual, she would think twice about. However, with Darius, there were no second thoughts. She was his to begin with and now he was here to claim her. He had captured her heart nine years ago and there was no doubt that her feelings had not changed. Even if he didn't feel the same, she wanted to know his loving again although it could mean giving up a part of her self.

Darius noticed her hesitation and pulled back searching her face. "Are you sure you want to do this Alexa?" he whispered. He wanted to make sure that she wanted him as badly as he wanted her.

She responded with a gentle push, making him edge backwards until the back of his legs came in contact with the sofa. He fell back with Alexa falling down on his lap. He murmured her name as he held her close into his arms while raining gentle kisses over her face and neck. In turn, Alexa smoothed her hands over his head and down his shoulders and up again to his face as if reacquainting her memory with the actual feel of his body.

Her touch was delicate like a feather and he began stroking her face, shoulders and breast in return. Alexa proceeded to kiss him all over, finding those spots that had lain dormant since her last touch.

When he could no longer holdout from having his way with her, Darius scooped her up into his arms, stood and carried her away to his hideaway in the loft above.

His hands were practically shaking as he unzipped the back of her dress and slid it down her shoulders. He gasped when he saw what was beneath. The shell-colored French cut panties along with the laced top thigh highs were both sexy and virginal sending his senses into an upward spiral. It didn't take long for them to dispose of their clothing before they were kissing, caressing, touching and tasting one another. Finally, when neither of them could stand it any longer, Darius lifted her onto his lap and gently eased himself into her warm feminine core; the only place that he dared to call home.

Alexa let out a soft moan as he entered her body and she wrapped her arms around his neck wanting to hold onto the feel and memory of the moment forever. Darius lifted his head back and reached up to cup her face in his palms when he proceeded to kiss her long and deep. Not withholding themselves any longer from the total physical expression, Darius captured her hips in his strong hands and began moving his body beneath her. It didn't take long for their lovemaking rhythm to come back to both of them.

Pleasure radiated throughout Alexa's body like an electric current awakening places that only Darius knew. Their bodies moved to a rhythm that only the two of them could understand. Through satiated eyes, Darius looked at Alexa and admitted to himself what he always knew: *Alexa Kirkwood was his woman. She always had been and always would be.* In turn, Alexa's eyes fell on him and she knew that Darius never stopped being her man for a moment. If neither of them recognized this before, they definitely did at that moment.

Alexa exploded first murmuring unintelligible words against Darius' strong shoulder as her body went through its different levels of release. The warmth flowing from her body caused Darius to follow suit.

When it was over, Alexa held onto him tightly, not wanting to let go just in case it was all just a dream leaving them lying alone in their separate beds. In addition, she didn't want him to see the tears rolling down her cheeks for she knew that if she looked into his eyes at that moment, there would be no letting him go.

*   *   *

In the wee hours of the morning, the two consummated their love again and again. Each time their connection was more intense and more passionate than the last. No words were spoken, just the satisfied moans of long lost lovers reunited into one.

They only took a break when hunger pangs hit and they escaped to the kitchen in search of something to eat. However, Darius couldn't think about food when he saw Alexa standing at the counter opening a can of nuts. He stepped up behind her and kissed her on the neck, fanning the flames all over again.

After their last encounter, the two laid side by side on the kitchen floor catching their breaths. Darius rolled his head towards Alexa with a sedated smile on his face. Alexa's eyes were closed and she lay there peacefully like she was sleeping. Darius reached over and tweaked her nipple to see if she was awake.

She turned with a smile. "Yes?"

"Let's get married." He said.

"Yeah right," Alexa sniffed in reply and closed her eyes.

"Serious babe, let's make this official. What I feel for you, I know you feel for me. We both know that what we have been doing over the past 10 hours was not insignificant. The look in your eyes when we made love was the same as when we used to be together. I don't know about you, but I know I haven't stopped smiling since you walked through that door. In fact, I can't stop." To prove his point he gave her a toothy grin.

Alexa rolled over, propping her head with her arm. "You're serious, aren't you?"

"I am." He replied. "I don't want to let you go again Alex. I think we were good together. Despite what occurred between us, I still love you, and I know you love me too."

A moan escaped her throat and she covered her eyes with her hands. "Darius don't you see how complicated things are. We have issues. You even said we haven't even addressed them."

"All couples have issues." He interrupted.

"But we are not even a couple," she reminded him.

"Yet we can be." he interjected, caressing her hair lovingly. "All you have to do is say yes."

Alexa stared into his eyes and she knew he was more serious than he ever.

"But we live in separate cities."

This time, Darius cut her off with a firm kiss. "Minor details darling that can be handled very easily."

Alexa would have thought she was dreaming if it were not for the cool linoleum sticking to her damp back. How could a few days bring her face-to-face with her first love and a marriage proposal to boot? Everything was happening so fast. She couldn't jump at the chance for the fear of being seen as flighty. Yet, she didn't want to pass up the opportunity to marry the only man she ever really loved.

"Sweetie, I must admit, the 23-year-old Alexa in me is screaming yes, but the 32-year-old, sensible Alexa is telling me to be rational. I'm not turning you down, but this is a big step. If you don't mind, I need some time to think before I can give you an answer."

After a pregnant pause, he finally conceded with a nod. "I can respect that. But please don't leave me waiting."

CHAPTER 8

Fresh fallen snow greeted Alexa on Saturday morning. However, the cold winds and gray skies could not put a damper on her mood because the sun was shining in her world. With a smile, she snuggled beneath the down-filled comforter thinking of Darius. His spontaneous proposal left her teetering between feelings of exhilaration and apprehension. The whole weekend was like a dream with her fairytale wishes coming true and she wasn't prepared for that to happen.

Due to their late night, the two had overslept on the day Alexa was to leave. She ended up having only an hour and a half to get back to the house, collect her belongings and jet to the airport to make her flight. Darius suggested that she catch a flight the next day, so that she wouldn't be so rushed, but Alexa declined because she knew how much work waited for her at the office.

A warm sensation flowed throughout her body as she pictured him lying beside her in the bed. She hugged the pillow tight, wishing instead that it were Darius. Closing her eyes, she imagined his virile body moving in sync with her own. Her body tingled as she remembered the pressure of his lips exploring areas that made her cry out in joy because they hadn't been caressed in such a loving way for some time. She could almost feel the kiss he planted on her forehead before she entered the jet way to board her plane. It was both tender yet somewhat desperate as if he was afraid to let her out of his sight again. The ringing of the telephone interrupted her daydreaming and she growled in disappointment as she picked up the receiver.

"Hello."

"So how was the wedding?"

Alexa recognized Beverly Kirkwood's nasally voice anywhere. The warmth she felt about her weekend quickly dissipated.

"Hello, Mother."

"Are you sleeping?"

With a yawn, she stretched and sat up, crossing her legs beneath her in one movement. "I just got up. How are you?"

"I'm fine. So how was the wedding?"

"It was beautiful," she said and began to give details surrounding the event leaving Darius and marriage proposal out of the story. "Maya told me to send you her love."

"That's nice. I always did like Maya. She's such a good girl," Beverly replied fondly. Then like turning off a light, she switched to another topic of conversation.

"I'm thinking about making a trip to Denver. What's your schedule looking like this month?"

Alexa rolled her eyes and sank back beneath the covers. She couldn't take her mother on the telephone sometimes let alone in person. Since her parents' divorce, her mother changed into a person she hardly recognized. The first change was the tinting of her hair and then she dropped 20 pounds and began to dress like she was twenty years younger. Although Alexa admitted that she did look good and seemed happier than ever, she couldn't help but worry about her new lifestyle. All of the new men calling her and traveling to far off places at a moments notice made Alexa worry. It was like the tables were turned and she was the mother now.

"I thought you were going to go out to California to visit Justin. Didn't you want to meet his new girlfriend?"

"You sound like you don't want me to come," Beverly said with a hint of hurt in her voice. Alexa immediately felt bad for trying to pass her off on her brother.

"No mother it isn't that. It's just that the beginning of the year is always my busiest time. I'd hate for you to come out and I wouldn't have time to show you around. You know how you like to shop and tour the city."

The older woman snorted in response as if she didn't believe her daughter's story.

She sighed in defeat. "Let me check my schedule to see what it looks like for February. Is that okay?"

"I guess it will have to be."

The two talked for a few minutes longer with Beverly revealing what was going on in her single life. The stories made Alexa ill. There were some positions Alexa did not even want to imagine her mother being in.

"I hope you are using condoms mom. Old folks get diseases too." She preached after her mother gave the details about her latest sexual adventure.

"Do I have idiot written on my forehead?" Beverly snapped. "I know these old men carry diseases too. For your information, I do use protection."

Alexa sighed with relief. The first time she learned of her mother's sexual prowess's, she got all bent out of shape. Although her parents had been divorced for some time, she didn't think her mother should be sleeping with other men. To top it all off, her mother proudly boasted of her exploits.

The first time she had sex with another man outside of Alexa's father, Beverly could not conceal it. The only man that her mother had ever known was her father James Kirkwood. But when a new man had introduced Beverly to the joy of sex, she was blown away. Now most of her time was spent among the mature single set dating, partying, and traveling. She was gone so often that Alexa couldn't keep up with her schedule.

At Last!

Sex wasn't a topic discussed in the Kirkwood household. For a long time she thought all her parents did when they closed their bedroom door was write out checks for bills and talk about what they had to do the next day. By the time they ended their call, Alexa prayed that Justin had the time to fit her in his schedule.

*   *   *

"Have you tried to shut down?" Darius asked the caller. It was Saturday morning and he was already working. He realized early on after getting the word out about his computer consultation business, it was going to be successful. Through his company he had made lots of good contacts and consequently had received a lot of good referrals. Within a week of disbursing his business card at a networking social, he had begun to receive calls. However, Saturday's were typically reserved for the nearby college whose campus computing office requested his contracting services for their students.

"I tried everything," the young woman on the line wailed in exasperation. "I just need to have it fixed. I have a term paper due on Monday and I don't want to start over if I don't have to." Her voice gave way to soft sobs.

"Okay, okay calm down," he tried to comfort her. "If you give me a half hour, I'll be up on campus. How does that sound?"

"Thank you, thank you, thank you," she shouted with relief. She proceeded to give Darius directions before releasing the call.

Darius placed the receiver down and opened his planner to place the address inside when he spotted the piece of paper containing Alexa's address and phone number. The memories of their weekend flashed before his eyes, bringing a smile to his face. It was as if what they had had never ended, which was why his proposal came so easily.

Darius didn't know what came over him when he asked Alexa to marry him, but he found that when he was in her presence, he did some pretty unusual things. There seemed to be a sense of urgency in him, for a response to the smallest of things, in order to prevent her from changing her mind.

This time, he opened the door and was determined to go all the way, but if she wasn't ready he was prepared to put everything they had shared behind him once and for all. He could not deny that her desire to keep her scheduled flight had struck a raw nerve with him and did not want to be placed on the priority of her **TO DO** list. At the same time, he was grateful to have spent time with her. Knowing this scared him because it put her in more of a position of control and he didn't want to have that happen again. He hoped that he didn't reveal too much of himself too soon, but rationalized that without doing so he would not have been able to get as far as they had. Either way the situation looked very grim.

Picking up the piece of paper again, he brought it to his nose and sniffed it as if recalling her scent. Yes, Alexa Kirkwood had lassoed his heart again. He couldn't remember the last time that he had felt so alive and energized. The emptiness he once felt had disappeared the minute he held her in his arms. And making love to her as he did—all night long had satisfied his aching hunger. He couldn't remember possessing that level of stamina since his college days. The irony of it all was that this was the same woman who captured his passions in his past; the one who held the key. Those days were so special, he thought. He closed his eyes again and allowed his recollections to guide him back to their days of innocence.

The sun was setting across the horizon. Darius and Alexa were at the park on the hood of the car cuddled beneath a thick old Army blanket watching the twilight set in with an orange kiss.

Darius sighed as he held Alexa tightly to him blocking out the cool winds. He inhaled deeply, taking in the aroma of her floral scented perfume. Alexa, sitting before Darius, turned around and planted a soft kiss on his mouth.

At Last!

⚭

"Mmm, what was that for?" he murmured against her ear, while at the same time thinking that she should stop before he took her right there on the hood of the car. The thought made him squirm with excitement. Since they'd crossed the line of intimacy in their relationship he found her even more irresistible.

"For making me happy," she said smiling sweetly into his eyes.

"Is that all I do?" he asked, probing for more strokes of her gratitude.

The fluttering feeling in his stomach made him feel like jumping twenty feet into the air. He realized what he was experiencing was deeper than infatuation or lust. Alexa possessed all of the qualities he wanted in a woman. She made him happy. He knew these feelings stemmed from the fact that he loved her. Even so, he didn't want to be the first to say so without knowing her feelings for him.

"There's more," she replied, securing his hands in hers. She looked him directly in his eyes causing him to melt. "You make me feel so special. So, so, loved."

"Shoot that's because I do love you girl," he heard himself confess.

Alexa's brown eyes widened with surprise. Darius' heart began to thud rapidly.

"Oh," she sighed. "I love you too, baby." Placing her arms around his neck, she kissed him passionately to show him how much.

Alexa had always had that affect on him. He carefully replaced the paper inside the pocket of his planner, wanting to hang onto it for reasons he could not begin to comprehend.

CHAPTER 9

With lunch in hand, Alexa searched for a quiet table while Teressa entertained the salad bar once again. She was surprised by how busy it was in the cafeteria, considering that it was a pretty nice day out. Spotting a group rising from a table near the window, Alexa hurried over before the coveted spot was nabbed up.

Once seated, she opened her lunch bag and began to remove its contents. She didn't have much of an appetite and had settled for a small salad and some crackers. She was too anxious to eat. Every moment when she was not concentrating on her work, she was thinking about Darius. She thought for sure that she would have heard from him by Sunday, so she stayed home on purpose all day but the telephone never rang once and if it did it ended up being someone she really didn't care to talk to.

Regret tugged at her conscience though she fought to ignore it. The last thing she wanted to do was beat herself up because of her decision to be intimate with him so soon after seeing one another again. Before she began chastising herself, Teressa approached, relieving the thoughts flooding her mind.

"Tell me all about the wedding!" Teressa exclaimed, taking her seat.

"It was nice."

Teressa beckoned enthusiastically with her hand. "Come on, I want details!"

Alexa laughed and proceeded to fill her in on everything: Maya's dress, the church, reception, food, and the celebrity guest list. As with the case with her mother, she elected to omit the part about her illicit rendezvous with Darius.

Like a wide-eyed child, Teressa listened attentively.

"Wow! What I would have gave to have been in your shoes!"

Alexa wanted to laugh at her dramatic friend who sat there with a jaded grin like a star struck groupie.

"It was nice, I must admit. But, every good thing must come to an end, which leaves me back here."

Teressa rolled her eyes and sighed heavily.

"I know what you mean. This wedding planning thing is starting to get on my nerves."

"Why? I thought that would be the fun part."

"Yeah, you and me both," Teressa replied. "Lewis and I are having a hard time deciding on where to hold the ceremony and who to invite. He wants to have a big wedding so that he can have his boys stand with him but, I think I would prefer something small and intimate with family and close friends."

"Can you two compromise?"

Teressa shrugged her narrow shoulders. "I know that I can bend a little. I just don't want him inviting people from way back in his childhood who I don't even know. You know how our people are. We'll invite one person and they will invite their cousin who will invite their friend who'll bring their little sister and her play brother."

Alexa threw her head back with a hearty laugh. There was truth in Teressa's statement. Some black folks had no problem with showing up at affairs where they didn't even know the honorees all for the sake of free food.

"Then when I want to go back for seconds, there won't be anything left except some mints and nuts," Teressa added, basking in her comedic stance.

Alexa wiped away a stray tear from the corner of her eyes as her laughter subsided. "Girl you are a trip."

"This stuff is making me crazy."

"Well, whatever you decide on, I want you to know that I'll be there for you if you need me."

"Are you sure Alexa?" Teressa asked.

Alexa nodded. "Just let me know what I can do to help."

Teressa almost cried, which made Alexa feel glad that she had agreed to make things right with her. Although she hadn't known Teressa for very long, she thought she was a decent person and was glad to be able to consider her a good friend.

Later that afternoon, Alexa felt like pulling her hair out. The stack of papers that needed to be completed by the end of the week was tedious and required concentration. But she couldn't focus as each time the telephone rang she grew anxious thinking it was Darius. More than anything she wanted it to be him, but she knew that wasn't possible as she didn't give him her work number. As far as she knew, she wasn't sure he wanted it at all.

After rereading the same document twice, she decided to take a break. She removed her reading glasses, closed her eyes, and massaged her temples. Darius Riverside's nude image surfaced the moment relaxation set in. Rather than blink him away as she had been doing all day, she decided to submit to her fantasy. Reclining in her executive leather chair, with her eyes closed seemed a little strange at first but when her reflections began to represent their intimate encounters she threw all reservations out the window.

She blushed when she recalled some of the things they had done in the heat of passion. One instance in particular involved a little creativity on the counter top in the kitchenette and some champagne and chocolate from the gift basket. Her mouth parted as she felt a familiar warmth blossom between her thighs. The image of Darius face wincing with pleasure as beads of sweat laced his brow, almost made her feel as if she was lying beneath him, catching the sweat in her mouth. Her lips parted as if she was receiving his juices when the sound of someone clearing his voice interrupted her reverie.

"I'll have two of whatever you are thinking about."

Alexa's eyes sprang open to find Jesse Mackey, a colleague, standing in the doorway.

"Jesse. Come in," she stuttered. She was embarrassed at him catching her in a compromising position.

"Must have been good," Jesse said, stepping inside. He claimed the first available seat and dropped into it.

"What are you talking about?" Alexa asked. She picked up her water glass and took a sip before slipping her glasses back on her nose.

"I'm talking about that look on your face."

"Please Jesse, what's up?" She said with irritation. She was not about to hint around about her personal life with anyone, especially him.

At one time, the two of them had casually dated. Now she only considered him to be a good friend. Before she ever thought that she and Darius' paths would cross again, she had contemplated involving herself with him again for the male companionship. Jesse was a good listener and conversationalist. Alexa learned early on that the two of them could not be more than just friends. However, he was the perfect person to take in a movie or dinner when she didn't want to do so alone.

"I think I have something you want," Jesse announced, leaning back in the chair with his arms folded boldly across his chest.

Alexa's brow rose. "What are you talking about, Jesse?"

Realizing how he must have sounded, Jesse rephrased his question. "What is the one event you have wanted to attend but haven't been able to?"

She could recall a lot of things in the city that she was meaning to partake in but did not have the time to do so.

"I don't know. What?"

He reached into his shirt pocket and held up two tickets. "*Bring in Da Noise, Bring in Da Funk* with Savion Glover?"

"No way!" Alexa exclaimed. "I've wanted to see that for awhile now, but the show was sold out. How did you get tickets?"

"Remember my boy Simuel?" he asked, leaning back with a confidant smile on his face. "His music store is now one of the Ticketmaster outlets. Whenever something good comes to town, he sets aside good seats for me."

Alexa stared at the tickets that Jesse was now fanning his face with. She didn't want him to get any ideas, yet she wanted to attend the show. Advertisements were everywhere about the popular show and according to the media, it got winning reviews. Alexa wanted to see the show when she was in New York, but it was sold out.

If she didn't have the understanding that she had with Jesse, she was sure that she would turn him down.

"When should I expect you?"

Jesse smiled broadly and gave her the particulars. They would be double dating with friends of his. He would pick her up about six and they'd go out for dinner then on to the show. As he exited her office a twinge of guilt came over her. Was it okay for her to make a date with another man especially since she had just returned from being with Darius? After thinking on it for a few minutes, she resolved that Darius was over 1300 miles away and she and Jesse were going only as friends.

She turned her attention to the telephone and stared at it hard as if trying to send a telepathic message for Darius to call her. When she left Michigan, Alexa slipped her address and telephone number in his jacket. She didn't know why she didn't think to take his in return, but was glad that she hadn't. If Darius was sincere about them sharing their lives together as he claimed, then he was going to have to show her.

With each passing day, she grew more agitated by the fact that it wasn't his soothing voice on the other line when the telephone rang. The glimmer of hope of ever being Darius' wife slowly began to fade. Tears of disappointment clouded her eyes and threatened to fall, but she fought them back. Knowingly, she had given herself to him and tried to be prepared to accept whatever consequences came along with that decision.

She turned back to her articles to get her mind off of the situation, but couldn't see the words for the tears. Why did she have to give into her desires? Had she resisted his charm and advances, life would have resumed the next day and she would have made it back to Denver with her heart unscathed.

Reaching for a tissue, Alexa allowed what seemed like the umpteenth series of tears to come and go. After the last tear had fallen, and her eyes were swollen and red, she wiped her face and reached into her purse for her compact to freshen up. As she peered into the tiny mirror, she couldn't help but grimace. Hadn't this exact scene occurred once before? It was like deja vu. It was getting to be quite embarrassing not keeping the emotions in check.

With a deep sigh, she picked up her pen and reached again for the stack of papers. The words appeared like dots on the pages before her. She had to get beyond this she scolded herself. Eventually, the pain would subside and life would proceed as if nothing ever happened just like with Sean.

*   *   *

It was already 4:30 and Alexa wasn't close to being ready. She noticed the time as she emerged from the shower. With water dripping from her naked body, she scurried into the bedroom and slid open the closet door. She quickly began to push aside one outfit after another hastily searching for the perfect look for the evening. Suddenly, she came upon the little black dress she wore at the rehearsal dinner, and thoughts of the night she and Darius had shared came back to mind. The memory caused a sinking feeling to come over her.

Thoughts of negativity threatened to surface and she struggled to hold them back. Her greatest fear in reuniting with Darius was that it would end on the wrong note. In addition, she was forced to speculate that Darius was giving her a dose of her own medicine. Although she didn't want to jump to any conclusions, she blasted herself for failing to stick to her convictions.

Frowning, she swept aside the evening dress, casting their affair to the back of her mind simultaneously. In doing so, her hand came to rest on her favorite dress. A dark plum colored chiffon dress that dipped off the shoulders and skimmed her slender waist line and hips like a second skin with a flirty flare at the knees. The dress complemented her womanly curves and shapely legs. Before putting on the dress, she smoothed on her favorite scented lotion, 5th *Avenue*, as well as dabbed the matching fragrance behind her ears and on her wrists. Alexa slipped into the dress and spun around in the mirror, smiling proudly at the perfect fit.

She selected a pair of strappy sandals of the same color to complete the ensemble. Satisfied with what she saw, Alexa stepped into the bathroom where she began to flat iron her hair into her signature sleek pageboy. It took her only 10 minutes to do her whole head before combing it out so that it lay gracefully on her shoulders. Just as she was about to apply her makeup, the doorbell rang.

She glanced at her watch. It was only 5:15. Suddenly a feeling of regret came over her. In her experience, when a man came over more than a half an hour before the set time, it meant an attempt to make a "pre-dinner booty call." She rolled her eyes in disgust. If Jesse was coming over early for that, then he could forget the whole evening.

With a disappointed frown, Alexa marched to the front door, undid the lock, turned the deadbolt and flung open the door only to gasp at what she saw.

Standing there filling the door way with his broad shoulders and looking fine as ever was Darius with a half-cocked smile on his face. "Hey lady."

"Darius, what are you doing in Denver?" she asked with surprise while silently thanking the Lord for sending him to her front door.

"Isn't Denver big enough for the both of us?"

"Of course," she replied, stepping aside to allow him to enter. He seemed a bit distant. She could sense it the minute she opened the door.

She stood there waiting for some sign that he was happy to see her like a hug or better yet a kiss, but when Darius stepped past her it confirmed that something was wrong.

"Hmm, nice," he complimented as he walked into the living room, surveying her choice in decor.

Alexa eased up nervously behind him. "Thank you."

He stopped at the living room and nodded, "Very nice. I'm impressed."

When he reached the attached family room, Darius spun around quickly totally catching Alexa off guard. His eyes traveled down the full length of her attire causing her to squirm from his scrutiny. "Looks like you have a special evening planned. Are you expecting someone?"

"I did have plans," she hesitated to reply. "But, now that you're here, I can cancel them."

"No, no." he interjected with a wave of his hand. "Don't interrupt your life on my account."

"It's not a problem Darius, really."

"Go on with your date." He said walking towards the door. "I'll just get me a hotel room and take in the city a little later."

"Darius!" Alexa frantically called out his name. Everything was happening so fast, she didn't know what else to do besides grab him by the arm. "What's going on?"

He whirled around to look at her, his usually bright eyes laced with anger. "Try asking yourself that question Alexa?"

"What do you mean by that?" she asked totally confused.

Darius closed the door and placed his hands on the wall behind her, boxing her inside his arms. His face was so close to hers that she could smell a hint of mint on his breath. "How in the hell can you walk out on us again after that weekend? You got on that plane like you didn't have a care in the world except getting back to your damn job!"

Everything was falling to pieces, which wasn't how she had imagined their reunion to be.

Darius snorted. "Alexa, we made love. We were together all night. Didn't you feel anything? Or have you grown that cold? The way you rushed back here made me feel like what we had was nothing but a booty call—pure and simple!"

"No baby, that's not true!" she disagreed. "Don't say that. It was more, much more."

"You have to explain it better to me then because I can't see it any other way?"

Darius wanted more than anything to give her the benefit of the doubt. He wanted the excuses to come flooding forth, something that would erase the ill feelings that he felt.

"Baby, I've been thinking about that night since I got on that plane." She leaned her back against the door, her gaze dropping to the floor. "I know I hurt you in the past. When you asked me to marry you, I didn't want to give you an answer because I felt like we needed to clear up our past before moving into even a friendship."

Darius groaned, expelling the built up irritation. He slid his hands down to Alexa's sides, capturing her hands in his before leaning in closely. He pressed his nose against her hair, and inhaled her scent with a sigh. "You're right. If there is to be a second time for us, we have to do things right."

She continued. "Don't get me wrong, I was ecstatic from your proposal, I just thought it was too soon."

"So what do we do?" Darius asked, his eyes falling onto the lushness of her moist lips.

Alexa shrugged. "I guess we can take things one day at a time."

Darius chuckled deep down in his throat as he eased against her, molding his body against hers. "Or one week at a time. You know its going to be hard since I'm way over in Ohio."

Alexa nodded with her face against his cologne scented chest. It felt so good to be in his arms again. "I think if we both want it, we can work it out."

"You know what I want?" he asked, tracing her jaw line with his finger.

With a naughty grin, she encircled her arms around his solid mid section. "Could it be this?" she asked, raising her head up capturing his luscious bottom lip gently between her teeth. Darius chuckled as Alexa took charge, parting his lips with her tongue and exploring the recesses of his mouth with fervor. Their tongues proceeded to engage in a playful game of tag when Darius slowed the pace to a gentle joust. His mouth moved away from hers to place tender kisses along her jawbone and down to her neck. A soft moan escaped Alexa's throat as Darius' kisses manipulated her weak spot, making her body writhe in response.

Their mouths made love with Darius moving his tongue in and out between her lips in a slow, gentle motion. Alexa in turn tightened her soft lips around his tongue. With their mouths locked, Darius backed into the family room skillfully avoiding a fall over the furniture until they reached the sofa where they tumbled down into a heap. Darius took his time removing Alexa's dress. As he inched the delicate fabric down her body, he planted a luscious kiss on the exposed skin.

It wasn't long before Alexa lay before him on the sofa totally naked and ready for his taking. Darius eased back and gazed upon her with adoring eyes. His appetite for her was unmeasurable. His desire for her exceeded mere infatuation but a longing that burned like hot embers.

Whatever he was trying to say, she received the message clearly and reciprocated by removing his clothing. Soon they were both completely naked. A caress here and kiss there as both remembered and relished in the touch and taste from their last encounter. Finally, when neither could stand it any longer, Darius quickly protected himself before entering the warm, moist place between her thighs with a content groan. Alexa raised her hips to receive him fully. At first, their actions started out slow as they took their time, savoring one another but things soon escalated into unrestrained, heated passion as if their lives depended upon it. In their case, it did.

As if they had not already been connected, their bodies exploded in unison. When their faculties restored moments later, Alexa tapped Darius' shoulder. "Hey big man, let me up."

Darius raised his head with a mischievous grin. "It's going to cost you." He gently brushed away the stray hairs from her face, causing her to blush under his inspection.

"C'mon baby, I have to use it." She whined.

"Oh do you now?" he teased. "First tell me, who's the champ?"

Before Alexa could respond, the chiming of the doorbell interrupted their bantering.

"Is that your date?" Darius whispered. He had no intentions of releasing her from his hold so that she could go off on some date with some other man, especially not after what they just shared.

Alexa nodded. She wished they were in the throws of passion then they would be too busy to think about answering the door.

"Then be quiet and maybe he'll go away," he suggested.

Alexa giggled. "I can't do that. Let me up so I can tell him that I have to cancel our date."

"That's right," Darius replied, finally rolling off of her. "Tell him your man is in town and he better get on up the road, or else."

Alexa laughed at Darius' jealous remark and struggled to stand. Making love to Darius left her with a sense of being drunk. If she didn't have to get up that minute, she probably would have dozed off. She searched around for something to cover herself. The nearest article of clothing was Darius' shirt.

"You can go upstairs while I get rid of him," she informed him.

"Are you kidding," he replied, scrambling from the floor. "I want to see the competition."

Alexa smirked from his response and slipped his shirt over her mussed hair. Darius' eyes glowed. Even with her kiss-swollen lips and tousled hair, he thought she was the most beautiful woman he'd ever seen.

The doorbell rang again and Alexa tiptoed to the door. She pressed her finger against her lips urging Darius to not make a sound. Although she caught a glimpse of her disorderly reflection in the mirror, she did not bother to adjust herself hoping it would add believability to the story she was fabricating in her head.

Jesse stood at the door holding a small bouquet of flowers. When the door opened, his smile drained from his face from the sight of her. "Alexa, what happened?"

Alexa faked a sniffle. "I know. I got up feeling terrible this morning. I thought I'd get better by tonight but I feel horrible. Please, don't be mad."

Darius tiptoed behind the door and peaked through the glass at Jesse. From what he could see, he was hardly Alexa's type. The man standing there looked way too conservative in his wire framed glasses, steel gray suit and camel coat.

Even so, Darius couldn't contain the resentment rearing up in him just thinking of her being with another man. He had to end the scene fast. A naughty thought came to mind. Before he knew it, he was easing his hand up the back of her shirt. When his hand reached the round, mound of soft flesh, he caressed it softly before giving it a nice squeeze.

Alexa jumped with a gasp.

"Are you okay?" Jesse asked in alarm, taking her response as sickness.

"Oh, uh, no," she stammered then placed her hand on her stomach. "I think I'm going to be sick. I'm sorry, Jesse. I'll pay you for the ticket."

"No, no problem. I'll just call you later," he promised. He quickly handed over the bouquet. "I just hope you get better."

"Thanks," she replied, taking them from his hand and shutting the door.

Upon locking the door, she turned to find Darius smiling like he was up to something. Although she wanted to be mad at him for almost blowing their cover, she couldn't be. Alexa's eyes could not hide the love she had for Darius, making him feel like royalty before her.

Before she could protest, he hurried over and swept her up in his arms. "Where's your bedroom?" he murmured into her ear. "I want to do this right."

Alexa pointed up the stairs. Like a valiant knight honoring his queen, Darius carried her upstairs. He entered her bedroom at the end of the hall and carried her over to the queen sized bed before gently lowering her onto the throne. This time when they made love they took things nice and slow, savoring each other, as if nothing but time was on their side.

*　　　　　*　　　　　*

Alexa moaned as Darius trailed his fingers delicately down her spine. "You like that?"

Alexa nodded through her erotic drunken stupor. She was totally and completely satisfied. They had made love countless times leaving her exhausted from the intensity of it all, but she didn't regret a minute of it.

"Are you hungry?"

She rolled onto her side entwining her legs with his, enjoying the feel of his muscular, hairy limbs against her own. "Not really, are you?"

Darius nodded. "You know making love makes me hungry."

She giggled upon remembering that fact. As she drifted off to sleep, Darius went into the kitchen in search of food. Because she hadn't been shopping, the only thing he could find was fixings for a peanut butter and jelly sandwich. He decided that it could hold him until they went for some real food.

He practically inhaled the sandwich and glass of milk. He couldn't believe that he was there in Denver, but he was. Alexa was sleeping in the bed in the next room. Just to make sure he wasn't dreaming, he quickly returned to the room. Sure enough there she lay on her back snoring lightly. Darius reached over and began to massage her neck. His hand ventured further down to her breast where he ran his finger tips over one of her nipples.

Her eyes immediately popped open. "I thought you meant that you were hungry for food."

Darius laughed. "I did, but I just wanted to make sure you hadn't fallen asleep."

"I heard you," she assured him. She sat up beside him and glanced at the clock. It was 9:00 in the evening. "I guess we can get something to go. What do you feel like?"

"Chinese sounds good." Darius announced as he untangled the bunched covers from her body. He began searching the room for his clothes. Before going off to the other parts of the house, he glanced over his shoulder and smiled at what he saw—Alexa lying peacefully in bed.

He couldn't deny that he wanted this scene to replay itself over and over in their bed in their home as husband and wife.

Their clothes were everywhere. In their haste to disrobe, articles were thrown haphazardly about the room. He found Alexa's panties dangling from a plant and his boxers were on the coffee table. After slipping into his jeans, he trotted back upstairs to get his shirt only to meet Alexa on the way down dressed in a pair of loose fitting jeans and wearing his shirt, which hung almost to the knees.

"Don't you think my shirt is a little too big for you?" he asked with a laugh.

She shrugged. "I don't care." She lifted the collars and took a deep whiff. "I'm going to keep it, because it smells like you."

Her response touched him and he fought the urge to pull her down into his arms again. There would be plenty of time for that so he settled for a kiss this time.

"Hey," she warned, batting him away. "We better get out of here or else you'll never get anything to eat."

They ate their dinner on the floor before a roaring fire sharing shrimp lo mein, chicken egg fu yung, white wine, and conversation.

"So what is there to do in Denver?" Darius asked as he fished through the pile of noodles for a piece of shrimp. He picked up a couple with his chopsticks and popped them in his mouth.

"Nothing really if you're referring to the club scene," Alexa replied, between bites. "I don't go out much."

He nodded, satisfied with her answer. At least that meant he didn't have to worry about her being approached inappropriately by men with one-track minds. However, he knew that her beauty and sweet demeanor could attract a man in almost any circumstance.

He took a deep breath before asking the next question. "What is it that you do at Marks-St. Claire?" He asked while trying to keep the sarcasm out of his voice. As far as he was concerned, they were the enemy. After all, it was their job offer that took Alexa away from him in the beginning. The thought of competing with the organization didn't rest easy with him, but he had to find out what the intrigue was all about.

"I'm managing editor of a lifestyles magazine called *Mountain High*."

"Managing editor, huh? So what does your work consist of?"

"Marks—St. Claire is the parent company of several magazines. I basically manage the senior editors of the different departments featured in the magazine by making sure that each article or feature story correlates with the monthly theme." She paused long enough to take a sip of her wine. "Then there are other administrative type duties, but I don't want to bore you with those details."

"So do you like it?"

Alexa nodded. "I enjoy what I do. The company has been really good to me. It's rare to find women, let alone African-American women in the business. It makes me proud to be representing."

"I see," he replied with a pause.

"What about you?" she asked turning the table. "What do you do in Ohio?"

"You know Bryant and I are joining forces?"

"Yes I heard that," she said with a nod. "So you're moving back to Detroit?"

Darius shrugged his broad shoulders. "We haven't decided. We've been toying around with the idea of me heading up a satellite office in Ohio. I'm just so involved with a lot of community projects, worthy projects that will be hard to walk away from."

"What kind of projects?" Alexa asked, setting her half-eaten container to the side. She took a sip of wine before rearing back on one of the pillows giving him her full attention.

"Well, I am on the board of directors at Frederick Douglas Academy, which is a private elementary and high school for African-American boys. I'm also coordinator of a related program that encourages fathers to be men and either reclaim their families and position in the home or at least be an active presence in their children's lives."

Alexa's eyebrows rose with surprise, clearly impressed by his endeavors. "How admirable," she said. "How did you get involved in such projects?"

"After attending the first Million Man March, me and some buddies decided that we weren't going to return home with the same attitude we had when we left. The school concept was always in the works for Reggie, this friend of mine who is an ex-cop turned educator. He belongs to this huge AME church that wanted to get two schools started—one for all boys the other for girls. The need for the all-boys school presided over the girl's school. All Reggie had to do was get several members of the congregation who were teachers and put people in place. I came in initially as a computer instructor, but felt compelled to do more. When Reggie suggested that I sit on the board, I jumped at the chance."

"That's very commendable of you Darius," Alexa praised. She thought she was doing something by coordinating the annual food drive at her church. Yet, here was a man who was really extending himself to his community.

"That's because I love kids," he wistfully replied. "Kids sometimes get the short end of the stick with their parents having to work to make ends meet or not having positive role models in the home at all. I like to fill the gap anyway I can."

He sat his empty container to the side and reached out for her. Alexa crawled over to him from her spot and planted herself between his outstretched legs.

Darius felt the crotch of his pants stiffen as her denim-covered behind snuggled against him. Slipping his arms around her waist, he kissed the back of her neck. *Man I can sit here like this with her forever,* he thought to himself. He sucked at her neck gently, then more fervently. He could tell that she was succumbing to his touch, judging by the soft whimpers escaping her throat. His hands traveled down her abdomen and played at the button on the front of her jeans.

"Hey!" she warned, batting his hand away. "I'm not giving in to you that quickly."

"And why not?" he breathed into her ear as he hugged her tightly against him.

"Because if I do, most of your trip is going to be spent in bed."

"Would that so bad?" he replied with a laugh.

Alexa reared forward and peered at him over her shoulder. "Yes, because I want to spend some time with you outside of my home. I want to show you the city and I want to take our time and do this right."

"Okay, okay," Darius conceded releasing her from his hold.

Alexa quickly scampered from her place on the floor and picked up the weekly entertainment paper from the coffee table. He watched with glowing eyes as she proceeded to run a list of activities by him. He was glad that his anger had caused him to hop the first plane to Denver, glad that they were able to reconcile and most definitely glad that he was able to be in her presence. Maybe Alexa didn't know this, but he would run to the corners of the earth for her.

CHAPTER 10

The weekend drifted by slowly. Each minute was well spent as Darius and Alexa languished in each other's company. When they weren't cuddled up in bed watching television or lying in each other's arms listening to jazz music, they exchanged introspective thoughts as they sat in a hot bubble bath. As Darius smoothed scented suds across Alexa's moist skin, he dared to visit their past. Their laughter echoed off of the bathroom walls when he recalled the day they first met. In turn, they quietly snuggled when they reflected on the first time they made love. Later that afternoon, restlessness set in and the pair decided to get out.

Alexa gave Darius the standard guided tour of Denver that she usually gave family, friends and sometimes clients when they came down for a visit. As they drove through the downtown area, she pointed out common attractions such as the gold-domed Capitol building, City Park, Museum of Natural History, United States Mint and the Black American West Museum as well as other well known sites. There was also the Cathedral of the Immaculate Conception and the old D& F Tower. Alexa always enjoyed history, especially Denver history. To her, the history behind each landmark was as interesting as the actual structures themselves.

The place she saved for last was her favorite. The historic Lo Do, a mile long strip of old warehouses converted into artsy coffee houses, quaint bookstores, funky fashionable boutiques, unique restaurants, wine bars and pubs. Like two lovesick teenagers, they strolled hand in hand giggling and occasionally stealing kisses, totally oblivious to those around them.

They ducked in and out of the doorways of different shops admiring the eclectic wares.

Just as they exited a watch shop, a hat boutique caught Darius' eye. "Sweetness, let's check out the hats" he suggested, nudging his head in the direction of a classy looking haberdashery.

"Sure," Alexa warmly replied, loving the affectionate name he had just called her.

They entered the store to find a young, serious looking brother sporting a skullcap who was reading a book behind the register. He glanced up as they approached. "Can I help you folks?"

"Yeah brother, I like your stuff," Darius announced, picking up a black hat with a wide brim. It reminded Alexa of those hats worn by many hip hop artists. Darius placed it on his head and took in his reflection in the nearby mirror.

"Looks good on you, bro," the young man complimented.

Alexa nodded. She had always liked seeing men in hats. The hat added to Darius' sexy edge. Darius turned her way and struck a Mack daddy pose with a grim expression and his arms crossed before his broad chest.

"What you think?"

"You look delicious," she replied and playfully licked her lips in a slow tantalizing way to prove her point.

"Why don't you get one?" Darius suggested handing the hat to the brother for purchase.

Alexa shook her head. "I don't think I look good in hats."

"Come on," Darius egged. "I bet you look fine. You just have to find the right one." His eyes roamed over the wide array of wool, felt, knit, velvet, straw, fur, and leather head garments before settling on a deep plum colored velvet hat with a fold up brim. The hat matched perfectly with the plum velvet jeans and matching vest she wore.

Darius placed the hat on her head and turned up the brim. "See you look good, girl."

"Let me look," Alexa peered into the mirror and actually liked what she saw.

"It does look pretty nice, but I probably won't wear it."

"You will because I'm buying it," he informed her as he smacked her on the rear.

Alexa wanted to protest, but she knew what he said was true.

After making their purchase, they exited the shop and continued on their way when Alexa spotted two familiar faces. Vernita Bradshaw and Genevieve McElroy were two older women who were deemed Mothers at the church that Alexa attended. Since her trip to Detroit, she hadn't been to church and she was sure that the two had noticed.

Darius felt her tense under his grasp and he turned to find out what was going on.

"Just play it cool," she whispered through the smile on her face. "These two women coming our way belong to my church."

"Hi baby!" The heavier Mother Bradshaw greeted.

"Mother Bradshaw and Mother McElroy," Alexa greeted each woman with a hug.

Besides being dedicated parishioners, the two women made it their business to remind everyone, especially the younger, members of their commitment to the Lord. Alexa respected their position although she sometimes found their methods to be intrusive. She glanced over at Darius who stood smiling. She loved him with all of her heart. She hoped that the women, no matter how much she loved them, would abstain from comment about them being together.

"How are you?" Alexa asked stepping back holding Mother Bradshaw's hands in her own.

"Blessed child, and you?" The woman asked, peering over Alexa's shoulder at Darius.

"I'm fine," she replied. She turned and held out her arm for Darius. "I would like you both to meet a friend of mine. Mother Vernita Bradshaw, Mother Genevieve McElroy, this is Darius Riverside."

"How are you?" Mother McElroy greeted with a warm smile and firm handshake.

"Do you go to church young man?" Mother Bradshaw quizzed.

"When I can ma'am," Darius quickly replied.

"When you can?" Mother McElroy repeated.

"Why don't you bring him to church with you tomorrow child?" Mother Bradshaw suggested.

Alexa was distracted by their inquisition. She prayed that Darius wouldn't be turned off by their many questions.

"Alexa?" Mother Bradshaw repeated her name.

"Yes ma'am?"

"I said are you bringing your friend to service tomorrow?"

Alexa quickly searched Darius' face for a way out. "Well, I'm not sure. Uh, aren't you leaving tomorrow?"

"Right after church," Darius smoothly replied as he took her hand in his.

The two older women who appeared to be holding their breath in anticipation for an answered sighed with relief in unison.

"Then I guess we will see you tomorrow," Alexa replied.

"It was nice meeting you," Darius said, shaking both of their hands.

Alexa laughed as they departed.

"What's so funny?" Darius asked, recapturing her hand in his.

"You," Alexa replied. "The Mothers are going to have a field day tomorrow."

*   *   *

That evening, the two had a quiet, romantic dinner at a mountain top restaurant with a gorgeous view of the city lights glimmering below. The faint glow from the flickering candle in the centerpiece provided a cozy atmosphere as the two sat talking and holding hands between bites of blackened salmon and shrimp scampi. Their meal ended with Darius feeding them both a decadent chocolate soufflé mousse. He scooped up a spoonful of the tasty treat and fed Alexa the first bite.

She squirmed with delight as the velvety, sweet chocolate melted on her tongue. "Mm, delicious," she hummed smacking her lips.

Darius continued to alternate feedings between the two of them when he reached the bottom of the bowl.

Alexa watched as Darius scooped up the last bit of dessert and held it to her lips. "No thanks."

"Are you sure?" he asked, twirling the spoon temptingly before her eyes. "This is your favorite."

Alexa smiled. "I'm sure."

"Okay, don't say I didn't offer." He warned as he raised the utensil to his mouth. Slowly inserting the spoon into his mouth, he proceeded to remove it in the same manner, pulling it from his full, succulent lips. Exaggerating his expressions, he moved the dessert through his mouth as if it was the best he ever tasted, licking his lips enticingly. His gesture was deliberate as to arouse her and Alexa was ashamed to admit that it was working.

"Mm, that was delicious," he replied. "But baby, your chocolate is the best!"

"Ooh, you are nasty!" she laughed with a playful roll of her eyes.

Darius reached over taking her hands into his. "Yeah, nasty for you," he solemnly replied, kissing her palms. With his skillful tongue, he began licking the delicate tips of her fingers one by one as he gazed deeply into her eyes.

Alexa squirmed in her seat as a light chill ran down her back. "Let's go home." she whispered.

Darius nodded and waved for the server to bring his check.

*   *   *

Soft jazz music played and Alexa snuggled against Darius' shoulder enjoying the relaxing atmosphere in the car. Darius held her against him with a protective arm making her feel secure. Alexa's eyelids fluttered as sleep threatened to come over her.

She tried to stifle a yawn, but Darius was so attentive that he sensed her exhaustion. "You sleepy?" he asked, caressing the back of her neck. His action, along with the soft sounds of Boney James filling the car, relaxed her.

Although she didn't want to admit it, Alexa nodded in response. She didn't want the night to end because that meant one thing, their days together were numbered and Darius would be on a plane tomorrow evening. Alexa had been spoiled by his affection and didn't know if she could stand being apart from him again.

"Go on and go to sleep," he urged in a gentle tone. "I'll wake you when we get home."

Alexa yearned to enjoy their quiet ride around town, listening to the music, but her body had other ideas. Finally, when she couldn't take it any longer, within minutes she was fast asleep.

*   *   *

"Babe, are you ready?" Alexa heard Darius call from the bedroom.

She had been standing before the mirror applying her makeup. She could barely concentrate for thoughts of Darius' impending departure had already begun to consume her. He would be leaving that evening and she wasn't looking forward to saying goodbye. Since putting off his proposal for further scrutiny, Alexa desperately wanted to know what was in store for them. The question haunted her because she realized that her love for Darius was as strong as it had been nine years back. Because of this, she did not want her decision to accept his proposal to be made in haste. It had to be made at the right time after considering many factors.

A knock on the door interrupted her thoughts. When she opened it, she found Darius standing there with a smile on his face. He looked handsome in a light yellow shirt and tailored navy trousers. "You ready?"

She nodded with downcast eyes. "I just need to put on my shoes."

"Are you okay, Boo?" he asked, noticing how she avoided his gaze.

Again, she nodded.

Darius stepped inside the bathroom and enveloped her in his warm embrace. "I know when something is wrong with my baby."

"I'm fine. Really," she replied as she looked up into his eyes. She saw the concern he had for her and she didn't want to bother him with her own insecurities. Rather than confess her fear, she came up with something less threatening. "I'm just nervous about the Mothers of the church. Sometimes they can be so persistent and direct. I just hope you won't let them rub you the wrong way."

Darius chuckled. "My dear, I have a God-fearing, upstanding grandmother and mother. My Pops, brother, and I had to endure them and three nosy, wisecracking sisters. Believe me when I say, I know how to handle the women."

"Yeah, I bet you do," she replied with a hopeful smile.

"I handle you well now, don't I?" he quipped as he kissed her neck.

"Now you need to quit," she warned him. "We are about to go to church!"

Darius chuckled as he released his hold to allow her to continue to get ready.

*   *   *

New Hope Missionary Baptist Church was a tall brick structure that took up two blocks on an established, middle-class, predominantly black neighborhood. The church was a pillar in the immediate community and influenced its neighbors with its strong outreach programs and moving worship services.

Service had already begun when Alexa and Darius entered the sanctuary after the Responsive Reading. They were lucky to find a pew in the back with space for both of them. As Alexa slipped out of her coat, her eyes scanned the room for Teressa and Lewis. She sighed with relief when she spotted the couple sitting closer to the front. She wasn't ready to introduce her friend to Darius just yet and decided that she would try to make a break immediately following services.

The songs were uplifting and the readings were powerful. Pastor Richard Davis was a dynamic teacher and motivator. His sermon really hit home and touched on some points that captured Alexa's attention.

Wiping the sweat from his brow with a towel, Pastor Davis sat his glasses to the side. "I'm telling you brothers and sisters, that there are a lot of temptations out there designed to keep you from hearing God's word."

The congregation responded with "Amen."

"You don't have to go to the movies anymore to be influenced by temptation. It's up in your face on daytime television talk shows and the soap operas. Then there are some of these music videos encouraging youth to partake in illicit sex and violence. And let's not forget the fact that you can learn how to make a bomb on the Internet. What I am saying to you my brothers and sisters is that you need to turn away from these distractions and let the Lord deal with the adversity."

Alexa shifted in her seat as the message struck an interesting chord. She glanced at Darius, who was listening intently, offering an occasional nod. When the service drew to an end and the congregation was called to stand, Alexa slipped into her coat. Darius looked down at her and leaned over, seizing her hand.

"Trying to escape?" he teased.

She smiled. "I just like to beat the crowds."

Darius feigned disappointment. "I wanted to make an impression on the Mothers."

Alexa didn't say anything. The last thing she wanted was for him to not receive his blessing.

"But if you want to go, we can."

"No, I'm sure the Mothers will be looking for us," she replied.

As if speaking them to life, as soon as the Pastor dismissed them, Alexa turned to find Mother Bradshaw, Mother McElroy and three other mothers of the church.

"Hey, baby!" Mother Bradshaw greeted. She leaned over and gave Alexa a hug.

"Hi, Mother Bradshaw."

After releasing Alexa, Mother Bradshaw surprised them both by giving Darius a hug. "Hello, son. Did you enjoy service?"

"Yes Ma'am," Darius replied. "It was very moving. I agree with Pastor about us needing to rebuild a deeper relationship with God. We need to free ourselves from earthly bondage and allow the workings of the Holy Spirit to manifest itself in our lives."

A series of "wells" and "amens" radiated the circle. Alexa felt proud at how Darius was trying to gain their acceptance. She stood to the side watching the Mothers continue their interrogations. After a few minutes, they finally said their good-byes.

"You must come back and visit," the quieter Mother McElroy called as they departed.

At Last!

❦

Darius promised to do so when he was back in town.

Hand in hand, as they exited the church, Darius released the laughter that had been swelling in him. "I told you, women love me!"

Alexa pressed her lips against his cheek and murmured. "More than you'll ever know."

CHAPTER 11

A wave of exhaustion came upon Darius causing him to yawn and stretch his 6'3" frame in response. His muscles flexed before slowly returning to a relaxed state. He had almost fallen asleep at his computer again, thanks to Alexa. The two had been on the telephone until two o'clock in the morning. Since his visit to Denver, their telephone conversations commonly lasted two to three hours every other day.

Despite the fact that they talked so regularly, there always seemed to be something fresh to discuss. And when they weren't talking, they listened to each other breathe. On more than one occasion, one of them had fallen to sleep. Rather than hang up, the other endured the wait until the guilty party woke up.

Although it was taking its toll on his body, Darius wouldn't change things as he was enjoying every moment. If he couldn't have her in his bed next to him, then he could at least have her every other night via the telephone.

Their conversations usually started out discussing their day and almost always, they reminisced about their past.

A yawn broke through again and he stood up to get another cup of coffee when the telephone rang. He snatched it up on the first ring.

"Programming, this is Darius."

"What's up man?" It was his good friend Reggie Thornton.

"Reg, what's up?"

"Got a minute?"

Darius glanced at his coffee cup, and decided that he could wait on his caffeine. "Sure."

"I was calling to let you know that I got the tickets for the Ball. I was wondering when I can get them to you."

"I can run by your office at lunch time today," he said with a yawn.

"Damn man, what you been doing, putting in time?" Reggie exclaimed from Darius' sign of exhaustion.

Darius laughed. "If I am, do you think I'd tell you?" he quipped.

"Yeah, as if I couldn't find out," Reggie scoffed. "You know Tricia would love to give me the details."

"Please this isn't about Tricia," Darius gruffly replied.

In his book, Tricia Herndon was definitely a closed chapter. She worked at Frederick Douglas as a French instructor. Darius was impressed at their first meeting when she approached him with a question in French. Not only was she gifted in a foreign language, she lead an interesting life abroad, which always intrigued him. However, just like all of the others, a month into dating, the interest waned and he broke things off.

Yet, unlike the others, Tricia wasn't about to give up so easily. She frequently sent messages to Darius through Reg. He was thankful that he had his number changed when he moved into his new apartment because now she couldn't call as often as she had before.

"Then who?" Reg asked.

Darius leaned back in his chair and spun around to face the window. "This lady from my past."

"Who? That one babe named Alexa?"

"Damn, man," Darius exclaimed with surprise. "How did you remember her name?"

"Please bruh, you used to talk about her constantly!"

He laughed from Reggie's response. The comment was well deserved because he did talk about Alexa a lot back then.

"So you are talking to her again?"

Darius' silence answered the question.

"Damn, man, what's up with that?" Reggie scolded. "You aren't setting yourself up for more rejection?"

"Rejection?" Darius exclaimed. "Man, what are you talking about?"

"I'm talking about her dumping you. What makes you think she won't do it again?"

"Well, we resolved that."

"Have you?" Reg returned.

Darius' irritation increased. He wasn't about to allow Reggie to talk about Alexa when he didn't even know her.

"Reg, chill out!" he warned. "Alexa and I have worked out our problems. I don't need my friend nagging me about my girl like my mama. In fact, Alexa is coming up for the Ball and I hope you have the decency to pull out that home training."

This time, Reggie was silent before answering, "Whatever you say bro."

Darius smiled. Now all he had to do was ask the same of his family. He wanted to introduce Alexa to the Riversides, but he knew it would be hard for them to put the past where it belonged. His mother was upset, as were his sisters especially Deidra, his younger sister by nine months.

Not only were the two close in age, but they were also best friends. When they were children, people often mistook them for twins. When she heard what happened between him and Alexa, she hurt for her big brother. Deidra immediately let Darius know that she would go as far as track Alexa down so that she could tell her off in person. She also offered to call up some Army friends stationed in Colorado Springs who would be more than willing to ride up to Denver posse-style to scare the crap out of her. Of course Darius talked her out of it, resolving that he would get over the pain one day.

"I'll swing by your office during lunch."

"If I'm not around, I'll leave them with Mrs. Taylor," Reg replied, referring to his secretary.

At Last!

Seconds after Darius hung up, the telephone rang again. Thinking it was Reggie calling again with last minute instructions, he picked it up on the second ring.

"What's up, D?" It was Bryant.

"B, what's up, bro?"

"Nothing, man, I just met with my attorney. We need to get together to go over this paperwork if we want this thing to fly."

Darius flipped through his desktop calendar. "How soon are you talking?"

"Week tops."

Darius groaned, inwardly. Going to Denver had left a lot of work on his desk. Between his job and his home business clients, he had some serious catching up to do. "I guess I can fly up this weekend."

"Cool. So how's it going?" Bryant asked.

"Booming. I picked up two clients today. One of them wants a new setup for the entire office. It will probably involve updating some of the old equipment and—"

"That's not what I mean man," Bryant cut in.

"Then, what are you talking about?"

"Alexa."

Darius paused at the sound of her name. "What about Alexa?"

"Come on, man. I know something was up between the two of you when you were here. Any fool could see that. You don't have to play games with me. Did you two work things out or something?"

"Is it that obvious?"

"Even Ray Charles could see it," Bryant replied with a laugh.

Darius filled Bryant in on the details concerning Alexa with the exception of his marriage proposal. Normally Darius would not withhold important information from his friend, but this time he felt compelled to do so.

"So you two are going to try the commuting thing?"

"For now."

"Does that mean you have a plan?"

"I haven't made any yet, but I'm working on it."

"No kidding?" Bryant exclaimed. "I guess we better consider an office in Denver, huh?"

"Hey, a man's got to do what a man's got to do," Darius found himself smiling. "You know she is my heart. Always has been."

"Well, if I didn't know Al, I would question it all, but I know she is a good woman."

Darius glanced at the playful pictures that he and Alexa had taken at a one-hour photo studio in the Lo Do area. In one, the two of them were posing gangster style with their hats angled over one eye. Another showed Darius crossing his eyes and Alexa making fish lips. In the third one, they were engaged in a deep kiss and the last one showed them staring straight into the camera with serious expressions. He made a point to hang them right where he could see them everyday on the side of his computer. When work became stressful, the pictures would remind him of their time together and the stresses of the day would roll away.

"Yeah, she is something else isn't she?" he fondly replied.

"I'm not trying to get into your business, because I know everybody else will, but as your friend, I am obligated to do so. I know that you love her and she loves you, but do yourselves a favor and take your time. You and Alexa have been apart for a long time. You're not young college students anymore. Both of you have nine years worth of experiences under your belts. Take your time and you'll be all right."

"Like you and Maya?" Darius asked with a hint of humor. "Cuz you know we want to be like y'all!"

"No brother, you can't be like us," Bryant laughingly replied.

At Last!

Darius felt his spirits lift after Bryant's call and abandoned the coffee idea all together.

*   *   *

By lunchtime, Darius was starving. As he maneuvered his Blazer through the downtown lunch hour traffic towards the inner city school where Reggie worked, he decided to take an extra half hour to grab a bite to eat. After all, he could only work so much without eating.

By taking the expressway, the school was only a fifteen-minute drive. As he turned onto the ramp, he turned on the radio. The bass thumped through the Bose speakers and he bobbed his head to an old hip hop beat by the hip hop rapper Notorious B.I.G. Each time he heard a song by the slain, innovative artist, or his equally talented contemporary Tupac Shakur, his heart pained with sadness. Growing up during the rise of rap, Darius had always maintained an affection for the music genre. As far as he was concerned, both artists had unique styles that raised the level of the game. It was sad that both had been gunned down in the prime of their music careers.

He smiled when he recalled Reg giving him a paper written by one of his students to read. The topic was on the influence of rap in the lives of youth. The boy concluded in his essay that he believed that both Biggie and Tupac were probably "kickin' it in God's country collaborating on a new album." Somehow, this image made him feel a little better about losing them.

Soon the school came into view. St. Johns AME church had purchased the brick structure where the school was housed several years back. According to Reg, the building was a former YMCA, but as the city grew, the organization outgrew the facility and moved to a more metropolitan location. Frederick Douglas Academy was a dream that became a reality for the church in 1997. Geared towards young, gifted and black boys the school's aim was to rise up respectable black men who were productive in their personal lives, competitive in the job market and responsible citizens in their community. The school had a math, science and foreign language enrichment program, which was enhanced by a computer and science labs.

Darius parked his truck out front and jogged up to the doorway. Seated right inside the glassed reception area was Tamala Harper, the front office coordinator. Standing beside her was Chester White, the security guard.

"Good morning Mr. Riverside," the two greeted in unison.

"Good morning Ms. Harper, Mr. White. I'm here to see Mr. Thornton."

"Go right ahead," she said, pressing the button to release the security door that lead to the remainder of the building. Security was one of the top concerns for faculty and Board members alike. They wanted to provide an interactive, intense learning environment guarded from the issues pertaining to the streets.

The halls of the school were brightly painted in a warm apricot. As Darius made his way down the hall, he passed several large framed portraits of famous black men such as W.E.B. Dubois, Thurgood Marshall, Martin Luther King Jr., Paul Laurence Dunbar, and Charles Drew, followed by a larger one of Frederick Douglas at the end of the hall. Each portrait came complete with a caption detailing their community contributions.

Reg was pacing in his office and shuffling through papers while talking on the speakerphone when Darius entered. He motioned Darius to have a seat before picking up the receiver.

"As I was saying Albright, I will have to show you these figures. We need some type of compensation, but I have someone waiting for me and I'll have to go over that with you at a later time."

Not only was Reggie a class act professionally, but he had a penchant for fine things. This was apparent to visitors upon approaching his office. The decor consisted of an executive line mahogany desk with a rich, lustrous finish, grouped with a matching credenza and curio cabinet. Black leather Windsor chairs completed the ensemble.

His choice of decoration was minimal, yet tasteful. An oil painting by a local black artist adorned the wall behind his chair along with his highly appraised credentials: Bachelor's from Howard University in Education, Master's in Business Administration and a Ph.D. in Counseling from Ohio State. The curio contained his most prized possessions: a letter from the President of the United States congratulating him on being recognized as teacher of the year along side the actual certificate. On the next shelf was an autographed baseball from Reggie Jackson on a stand, next to it, his fraternity paddle and a picture with a newspaper article detailing the grand opening of Frederick Douglas Academy.

Darius watched as his well-tailored friend straightened the cuffs on his monogrammed shirt. He pretended to pick at some lint then straightened the cuff links. Reggie was such an impeccable person. He was perfect for the principal job at the Academy as he was the perfect example of how a successful man should act and look.

After hanging up, Reg walked over and shook his hand. "What's up D?"

"Looks like you have the best going." Darius replied, his eyes scanning the elaborate office and back to the tailored suit Reggie sported.

Reggie waved him off, the gold bracelet dangling from his wrist. He handed Darius the tickets. "All I can say is sell, sell, sell, because those people think we got money to burn," he replied, referring to the Board.

"Wait a minute, I'm one of those people," Darius defended himself. "What's going on?"

"You know how Albright is," Reggie groaned. "He thinks you can still educate a student on a buck ninety-five like they did back in his day. I keep telling him that this is a private magnet school and that 85 percent of our students are middle to low income. In order to crank out students with competitive test scores, we need to have access to the same tools as their white counterparts."

"Don't worry about him," Darius replied, speaking of the Board's President. "I know how to work Albright."

"I hope so. The students have the CAT test coming up in three months and I want a special study session in place to prepare them."

"I got your back," Darius assured him. "Now what are your plans for lunch?"

Reggie glanced at his watch. "Nothing. I had an appointment with a food distributor who was supposed to call me by 11:00 and it's already 11:30. Why? You want to get something to eat?"

"Yeah, I'm as hungry as a two-headed bear."

Reggie slipped into his Armani suit jacket. "You driving?"

"Sure," Darius replied. "As long as you're paying."

Reggie laughed. "I got your back."

CHAPTER 12

Anybody who knew Beverly Kirkwood knew that she did not appreciate long waits. Alexa spotted her mother immediately as she pulled up outside the airport. Beverly stood out like a sore thumb, with a bright purple silk anorak which contrasted with her freshly tinted, fiery-auburn hair. Despite the chill in the air, she was standing outside smoking a cigarette. The irritated expression clouding her face told Alexa that she was in for a good chewing out.

"Damn," Alexa groaned as she shifted the car in park. She was not in the mood.

Hoping to head off an argument, she fixed a smile on her face before exiting the car.

"Hi, Mama," she greeted as she hurried over to place a kiss on her mother's cheek.

"Don't hi Mama me!" Beverly shouted. "Seems to me I told you my plane arrived at two-thirty, not three."

"It's not even three o'clock, Mama," Alexa replied with a glance of her watch. She pressed a button on the remote and popped the trunk and picked up the two pieces of Louis Vuitton luggage.

"Don't get smart Alexa Denise. I raised you better than that!" Beverly berated.

Alexa rolled her eyes behind the raised trunk. "Ma, please get in the car."

Beverly grumbled to herself as she made herself comfortable in the plush seat.

Alexa continued to piddle around as if looking for something to allow herself the chance to cool off. She was determined to have a good visit with her mother. The last time she visited was right after Sean called off the wedding. Rather than be the consoling shoulder to lean on, she was preachy and critical. Her whole stay did nothing but upset Alexa further. She was relieved when she finally left.

After a few minutes, she joined her in the car. "So, how was your flight?"

"It was okay," Beverly replied. "I met a really nice man."

"Mama," Alexa groaned. "What did I tell you about talking to strangers especially strange men? Besides aren't you supposed to be meeting your boyfriend in Vegas?"

"For your information, Miss Smarty Pants, the man I met was a young man. I was thinking about him for you. His name is Dennis Lawman and he's an investment broker with Merrill Lynch."

Alexa shook her head. "Ma, how many times do I have to tell you that I am okay with being single? I don't need a man on my arm to validate my existence. And if my memory serves me, wasn't it you who said that it was inappropriate for a woman to chase behind a man?"

"Yada, yada, yada," Beverly grunted. "When did you ever start taking my advice?"

"Ma, please can't we just get along for once?" Alexa asked as she turned the car onto the expressway.

Beverly rolled her eyes with a pronounced click of her tongue. They spent the remainder of the ride in silence. The two didn't speak until Alexa pulled into the driveway of her house.

"Oh, this is a nice house," Beverly said in awe.

Alexa smiled. Only her mother could make her fuming mad one minute and happy with joy the next. Beverly's words were touching. She regretted having such ill feelings about her visit to begin with. "Thanks, Mama."

She turned the engine off and popped the trunk while Beverly took it upon herself to go inside, leaving Alexa to retrieve the luggage. After two trips, Alexa had carried in everything. With the last bag in hand, she closed the door behind her. She walked into the family room to find Beverly kicked back on the sofa, flipping through the channels on her 50 inch big screen TV.

"Did you look around?" she asked.

"Yes, I did and I must say that you have a lovely home. I'm so proud of you daughter." Beverly urged with a wave of her hand. "So, what are we getting into tonight?"

"What do you want to do?" Alexa shouted back over her shoulder on her way to the guest bedroom with the luggage.

"First of all, I want to get me something to eat!"

"What do you feel like?"

"What was that restaurant we went to last time I came?"

"Desmond's?" Alexa asked, referring to the Caribbean gourmet restaurant that they ate at almost every night during Beverly's last visit.

"Yes!" Beverly exclaimed. "I talk about that place all the time. I told James about it when I came last time."

Alexa ears perked from her mother's comment. She immediately dropped the bags on the floor and hurried back into the living room. "Mama, are you still talking to Daddy?"

As far as she knew, her parents had been estranged since their divorce was final five years ago. The process was drawn out because her father refused to honor the divorce. As a result, the two had parted more like enemies than anything else.

According to Beverly, their relationship was rocky from the start. Exactly ten months after they were married, Beverly gave birth to Alexa. A year later she had Alexa's brother Justin. James Kirkwood was a hard-working man who prided himself on having a tight reign on his household affairs. Beverly wasn't allowed to work and was issued an allowance along with the children. She wasn't allowed to go back to school or seek higher learning in any capacity because James said there was no point in her doing so. She was resigned to managing the household and raising their children.

About ten years into her marriage, Beverly wanted a divorce, but James wouldn't hear it. He was in control of what took place in their family. Five years later when the kids were teenagers, she asked him again but James again refused. Over time, Beverly became bitter. She was fed up with her husband's need to control her.

Emancipation day, as she put it, came a week after Justin graduated from high school. Beverly mustered up the courage one day, while James was at work, packed up her clothes and personal belongings and left. She told Alexa that was the best day of her life. She also told her to live her life to the fullest before considering marriage and when she was ready, to pray long and hard for the right man.

"We've been decent to each other lately," she replied, answering Alexa's question.

"When did all of this come about?" Alexa asked, taking a seat beside her. She hadn't talked to her own father in almost a year. He was angry with both her and Justin because they supported the divorce. He told Alexa that he felt like everyone, including Beverly's family were in her mother's corner. When she brought up the control issues, he told her that he was only being protective of his family.

Beverly looked towards the ceiling and counted back the months. "We've been civil for about five months and have talked more regularly for the last two. You don't know this, but your Daddy had surgery for kidney stones and was down for almost a month. He needed somebody to take care of paying his bills and such and since I was the one most familiar with his situation, he asked me to do it."

"That was nice of you Mama, considering."

"Well, technically I *am* still his wife."

"Where does that leave your boyfriend Henry?"

Beverly laughed with a wave of her hand. "Henry's old poot-butt don't mean a thing. He just likes to spend money on me. I just call him my boyfriend when he's around."

"But Ma, you said you had sex with him," Alexa stated, uneasily.

"I know. Never said I was perfect. All I can do is repent and pray that the Lord forgives me."

"Are you saying what I think you are saying?" Alexa asked, her eyes widening.

"I'm not saying anything to incriminate myself right now!" Beverly retorted. "Who knows, I could get up to Vegas and find Mr. Right on Time!"

Alexa rolled her eyes. She wasn't really upset with her mother because she knew in all things she was sincere. Throughout their growing up, Beverly had given up a lot for others. It was nice to see her enjoying herself for once.

*   *   *

"I can't wait to see you," Darius whispered.

"I can't wait either," Alexa agreed. "I just hope that my mother won't drain me too much. We've been out partying like twenty year olds."

"I'm sure if that happens, I can revive you," Darius murmured suggestively.

Alexa and her mother had just returned from The Atrium Dinner Club where a hot reggae band performed. The music was great and the atmosphere was lively, but Alexa was tired the minute they walked into the club. Her mother, however, was a different story. Beverly partied like it was New Year's Eve. She danced the rumba around the room sipping on Tropical Teasers with the rest of the party animals. Alexa watched in awe at the energy her mother possessed, while batting away pesky men begging her for dances.

"I guess I'm getting too old. My head aches, my feet hurt," she proceeded to give him a list of her ailments.

"I wish I was there to remove the pain," Darius contended. "I'd give you a nice massage with some warm oil."

"Hmm," Alexa cooed from the image she created in her head.

"I would rub your naked body until you're nice and relaxed."

"I'd like that," she murmured as she lay back in the bed, closing her eyes. She could almost feel his hands gliding down her body and felt herself getting slightly aroused.

"Then, I'd turn you over and kiss you from head to toe."

"Yeah, go on, go on," she urged him.

"Then, I'd make slow love to you."

"Hmm, that's what I'm talking about."

Darius laughed deep in his throat. "You like that now, don't you?"

"Yes, I do," she calmly admitted. Alexa rolled onto her back in her bed and gazed at the ceiling. The long distance thing was harder than she had imagined. Talking to Darius on the phone was not like having him within reach. She wanted to be able to stroke his face, hold his hand or snuggle her nose against his neck. Yes, they talked for a few hours about four times a week, but Alexa was beginning to realize that she wanted more.

A knock on her bedroom door diverted her attention. "Hold on Darry," she said and held the phone away from her face. "Yes?"

The door opened and her mother poked her head inside. "Can we talk?"

"Are you okay?" Alexa inquired.

The older woman nodded, "I just want to talk to you before I go to bed."

"Okay." She turned and put the receiver back up to her mouth. "Darius, my mother needs me. Can I call you tomorrow?"

"I'll be out late tomorrow setting up a new system for a new client. So, how about if I call you?"

"That's fine."

After professing their love, they hung up. Alexa went into the guest bedroom to find her mother seated on the side of the bed.

"Is something wrong, Mama?" she asked upon entering the room. She leaned up against the dresser.

"No. I just wanted to talk to you before I hit the sack."

"You mean like we used to?" Alexa asked as a sense of warmth came over her. She recalled the mother-daughter talks as if they were just yesterday. Yet, it had been years since they committed to one.

"I guess you could say that." She patted the edge of the bed motioning for Alexa to sit down who immediately followed suit.

"I just wanted to say I had a really good time tonight. Thanks for letting me come down."

"Oh, Ma," Alexa sighed. "You don't have to thank me. I'm just glad you had a nice time because I know I was being a party pooper."

Rather than respond to Alexa's comment, Beverly surprised her by asking a question of her own. "You miss him don't you?"

"Who?"

"The young man you were talking on the telephone with. I overheard your conversation. You said the name Darius. Is that the same young man who wanted to marry you after college?"

Alexa nodded.

"When did he come back into the picture?"

Alexa explained how they had run into one another while at Maya and Bryant's wedding. Again, she purposely left out the marriage proposal. Somehow it was something that she wanted to keep between the two of them. Revealing it would bring about all sorts of complications that she was not ready to deal with.

"It's like the nine years between us had never existed. We both love one another as much today as we did back then. I know you can't understand that, given what you have been through with Daddy, but Mama, he is different. Our love is different."

"Daughter, there is a lot to consider. He's in one state and you are in another," Beverly pointed out.

"We'll cross that bridge when we come to it. Right now, we are just getting to know one another again."

"One last thing and then I am done. I just want to say, don't give up too much of yourself too soon, or you'll be setting yourself up for disappointment. Now, I know you are a grown woman, and whatever decisions you make in your life are yours to live with. I just want you to do what is right for you and that's all I'm going to say." With that, she held up her hands as if releasing her involvement in the situation.

"Thank you." Alexa replied. She was glad that her mother wasn't about to give her a lecture on men.

As she lay in bed that night, her mother's words kept haunting her mind. She loved Darius. She just hoped that this time, she was doing the right thing.

CHAPTER 13

Alexa glanced at the executive timepiece located before her on her desk. The titanium clock, which was a gift from Teressa, was made up of a propped up open book with the face coming out in the center. She loved it as it reflected one of her favorite past times.

According to the clock, it was time for her to hit the road. Her flight to Cleveland was expected to leave in an hour and a half and she was still punching away at the keyboard to her dismay. When she came to a stopping point, Alexa seized the mouse on her computer and began to save and close the several documents she had been working on.

She was so excited about her trip that she had to fight the urge to press the power button rather than go through the normal procedures of shutting down the system. Thoughts of losing the important documents caused her to refrain from doing so.

It was a sunny Thursday morning. The skies were clear and the snow was practically all melted. It was the perfect day to travel. According to Darius, the weather was about the same in Cleveland. Alexa was looking forward to her four-day vacation especially since it would be spent with the man she loved.

This would be her first visit to Cleveland. She eagerly anticipated seeing Darius' handsome face and holding him in her arms again. In preparation for her trip, she had gone shopping. She found an alluring dress to wear to the Ball that she was sure would knock Darius to his knees. Her next stop was at Victoria's Secret where she found some eye-catching pieces for Darius' viewing pleasure.

She had arranged for a cab to pick her up in five minutes. After turning off the computer, she went over to her closet and pulled out her pullman and garment bag. She placed both items near the door and turned back to see if she forgot anything when she realized she hadn't forwarded her calls to voice mail. Scurrying around to the other side of her desk, she reached to pick up the telephone when Sharon the secretary buzzed in.

"Alexa, you have a call," the woman announced.

"I'm on my way out, Sharon," Alexa informed her slightly irritated by the interruption. "Can you take a message?"

"It's a gentleman. It sounds kind of personal."

Thinking that it was probably Darius calling to make sure she was getting off okay, Alexa accepted the call. "Thanks Sharon. I'll take the call."

She sat down on the edge of her desk and waited for Sharon to transfer the call into her office and snatched it up mid ring. "This is Alexa."

"Well, well, well," a familiar male voice said. "You must really be moving up if you have a secretary."

"Who is this?" Alexa asked, not wanting to believe it was who it sounded like.

"Ouch. You sure know how to hurt a brother," the man pretended to be wounded.

"Who is this?" she repeated. The voice sounded vaguely familiar. A voice from her past that she did not particularly want to hear.

"You tell me," he replied. His response registered one person to mind. "Sean?"

"The one and only. How are you today, Ms. Alexa?"

Alexa rolled her eyes in her head yet was determined to not let him spoil her mood. If she acted snotty towards him, she was sure that he would conclude that she was still angry over the break up, which wasn't the case. Besides she knew it would hurt him more if she reacted nonchalantly about everything, including him.

"I'm doing fine and yourself?" she duly replied.

Sean paused for a moment before answering. "Good, good. So, what are your plans for lunch?"

Alexa caught her breath. "Why, are you in town?"

"Yes, I'm staying over at the Wyndham Hotel. I thought maybe we could get together for lunch, maybe talk about old times."

She shook her head with a sigh. "I'm sorry, that won't be possible. See I'm on my way out of town."

"Oh really? Where to, if you don't mind me asking?" Alexa felt like he was getting too personal.

"Actually, I do mind," she quickly replied. "So, I guess I'm going to have to pass on your offer." Even if she weren't going out of town, going anywhere with Sean was out of the question.

"Same old Alexa," Sean said, chuckling lightly.

"And you're still the same old Sean," she sarcastically replied.

"Well, I guess I'll have to sit here and wait for you."

"Don't stop your life on my account. You didn't before." She couldn't help her from commenting.

Alexa's patience was wearing thin. Sean had a lot of nerve calling her as if they were good buddies. Since fleeing weeks before their wedding, this was the first time she had heard from him in two years. She thought back to the position he had left her in. Not only was she a total wreck mentally, but financially as well. In some cases it was too late to cancel with vendors, resulting in Alexa bearing the expenses. Thank goodness Maya was there to help. She contacted all of the respective parties and pleaded for the release of her friend's responsibility from the debts incurred given the situation in which Sean left her.

"I deserved that," he admitted. "Actually, I am calling because I was hoping that we could talk about what happened."

Alexa glanced at her watch. It was already 11:45. "I'm sorry Sean I can't talk now. I have got to run. Have a nice life!"

"I'm back in Denver to stay this time, Alexa!" he shouted before she could hang up.

"Why?" she asked with a hint of disgust.

"I got a good job offer."

"Just because you are back in Denver doesn't mean you can call me up whenever you want to. You made the choice Sean, not me, to run off before our wedding. But you know, that was two years ago and I am *very* over you. So, don't try to get any ideas. I have a new life and it doesn't include playing games with you."

She hoped that Sean would get the picture, but when he laughed that same laugh that said "you're so cute," she wanted to scream. "I'm serious Sean!" she promised and slammed down the receiver. She was angry with herself for blowing her cool. She glanced at her watch again and prayed the cab driver hadn't taken off.

Forgetting all about her voice mail, she grabbed her things and marched out of her office and down the hall to the elevator, blind to those who watched with dismay in the trail of her dust.

*　　　　　*　　　　　*

The first face Alexa saw when she exited the airplane was Darius'. She ran over to him, dropping her bags at his feet. Then she threw her arms around his neck and planted an anxious kiss on his waiting mouth. After a few moments, she pulled back breathless.

"I'm so happy to see you."

"You don't *even* know how happy I am to see you," he answered.

Alexa could see a mixture of love, passion and elation swirling around in Darius' face. Their eyes locked, mesmerized by the other's presence. He touched his hands to her cheeks and kissed her softly.

Alexa's breathing stopped as her man branded her with a kiss that stirred up her insides like a tornado that trailed all the way down to the pit of her stomach. Her legs began to shake and she felt herself sinking into a sea of no return.

Darius pulled back, leaving her standing there swooning, heated from head to toe. Then without a word he picked up her bags and led her out of the airport by the hand to his warm vehicle.

Waiting for her in the passenger seat of his car was a single red rose and a mesh bag filled with candy kisses. Attached to it was a note. *"A symbol of love and some sweet chocolate kisses await you, my Queen."*

The brazen kiss coupled by Darius' small gesture made the earlier encounter with Sean fade into nothingness. She smiled at him sweetly. "Thank you, babe."

As they drove away from the airport, Alexa snuggled up against his shoulder.

Darius placed his hand possessively on her knee. "We are going to have a nice weekend, I promise."

His promise for a nice weekend began the moment Alexa entered the house. Waiting for her was a romantic and relaxing retreat. Her eyes had to adjust to the fire lit room. She waited for Darius to set her bags down before following him inside.

His taste in décor surprised her as she was expecting a typical bachelor pad—pieces of odds and ends furniture with the centerpiece of the room being a big screen television surrounded by a monstrous entertainment center containing tons of cds, movies and the latest video game equipment.

Although the house was not characteristic of these things, Darius' personal style was lacking. The house basically looked like it was suspended in a holding place as if he didn't want to put forth the effort for fear that it might not be permanent. Alexa took note of this when she peeked in the living room, which was empty with the exception of a pair of cranberry colored channel-back accent chairs placed before the fireplace. The dining room which was opposite of the living room held a mahogany Chippendale style dinette set with a matching buffet and hutch. The only accent in the room was an oil painting of the *Buffalo Soldiers Retreat Home.*

The kitchen was modern yet simple with a breakfast bar and an unoccupied alcove large enough for a good sized table. Glancing down towards the sunken den, Alexa found the source of Darius' living. There sat a man's paradise. Alexa could almost picture Darius stretched out in the recliner before the 61-inch big screen television. There he had a custom made home theater wall unit, which surrounded the large television, stereo, DVD/VHS player. Along one wall was a fireplace surrounded by built in book shelves and to the other side a chocolate brown leather sofa with a beige and brick red chenille throw draped across it.

When she turned around, she was surprised to find Darius standing there with a huge bouquet of dark red long-stemmed roses. Alexa smiled as she brought the bunch to her nose and inhaled deeply. "Baby, they are so beautiful."

"Ssh," he said. "There's more." He gently took her by the hand and led her up the stairs and into the master bathroom. Alexa's mouth fell open at the sight of the candles placed throughout the room. The oversized garden tub was filled with the aromatic rose petals. It reminded her of another night the two had shared. She turned to him to say such, but again, he quieted her with a finger to his mouth. Instead, he reached up and began to remove her clothing.

When she stood before him totally naked, he took her hand and helped her to step into the steamy water.

Once she was seated, Darius kissed her tenderly on the mouth and turned on the slow jets. Alexa eased back against the pillow that Darius had provided and closed her eyes. She gasped when she felt his hands caressing her body. Just as she began to respond to his touch, he pulled back and began to wash her body with a soft sea sponge. Alexa leaned forward, giving Darius access to her back. He dipped the sponge into the water and raised it, letting the scented bubbles run down her back and over her slick skin as he massaged her neck and shoulders in the process. Alexa shivered with pleasure when she felt his lips press against the nape of her neck. When he was done, Darius eased her back so that her neck rested comfortably against the shell shaped bath pillow once again and began to wash her front in the same gentle manner.

It took a lot out of him to concentrate on keeping his hands from roaming over her delicious body the way he wanted to but he remained the perfect gentleman. He wanted the experience to be relaxing and special rather than sexual. He turned his attention from her full breast, which were heaving in and out of the soapy water with each breath, to her legs and feet. Lifting Alexa's leg in the air, Darius delicately washed her feet, concentrating on her well-manicured toes. When he was done, he kissed each one.

Slowly opening her eyes, Alexa gazed at him with a lazy smile, enjoying the treatment.

Darius smiled in return and reached for the large, plush bath towel. He stood up and held the towel for her so that she could wrap her self inside. When she had done so, Darius scooped her up in his arms and carried her into the bedroom where he had a small setup waiting for them. He placed her down on the bed and began drying her body. When she was completely dry, he removed a small bottle of amber colored oil from a container of warm water and began to pour the contents into his hands before massaging it onto her waiting body. She moaned with each stroke of his large masculine hands. Darius proceeded to rub her body from head to toe until her moans subsided. Everything was so nice, so perfect, to Alexa that it wasn't long before she fell fast asleep.

*　　　　　　*　　　　　　*

It was dark out when Alexa awakened to find herself in Darius' bed. A smile spread across her face as she realized that she was in Ohio with her man. She stretched languidly across the king-sized bed and rolled onto her stomach to turn on the lamp on the nightstand. After her eyes adjusted to the light, she looked around, again absorbing Darius' domain.

The king-sized, cherry wood bedroom suite immediately confirmed that he was traditional. The matching chest, dresser with mirror and armoire said that he was orderly. The abstract painting, stretching the length of the headboard had the same colors that matched the comforter set. This told Alexa that he was consistent.

Easing off of the edge of the bed, Alexa's curiosities lead her over to Darius' dresser. She couldn't believe how neat it was. The items were perfectly arranged as if in expectation for her arrival. She picked up his hairbrush and gently fingered the sharp bristles. The faint smell of Dax pomade greeted her. Next to the brush were two bottles of Alexa's favorite male scents: Cool Water and Hugo Boss. She picked up the Cool Water and placed the nozzle to her nose. She loved the smell of the cologne especially when sampling it in the crook of Darius' neck.

The open closet door seemed to call out to her and she went over to explore its contents. Unlike the Darius she used to know, the closet was surprisingly neat. She smiled, convinced that Darius had gone out of his way to have the place neat as a pen just for her. The Darius she knew was tidy, but not impeccable. Not seeing a suit of his strewn across a chair or shoes scattered carelessly about the floor was odd. Being around his personal items made her miss their owner so she slipped into one of his button down shirts from a hanger in the closet and went out to find him.

Alexa could hear Darius' strong voice coming from somewhere near the living room. Probably his office, she thought. She tiptoed downstairs to find him seated before his computer, wearing a telephone headset while he plugged away on his laptop.

"What we need is a networked system," he was saying. "One that would allow each staff access to the records."

Alexa stood behind him and wrapped her arms around his neck for a hug. Darius barely jumped and turned to her with a smile. "Did you sleep well?" he mouthed while covering the mouthpiece with his hand.

"Very well, thank you." she replied and began to massage his broad shoulders.

She could feel the tension ease from his neck and shoulders as if her hands worked magic. He continued to talk shop even as Alexa swung her leg over his lap and eased down on top of him. Although a smile of surprise washed over his face when he realized that she was totally naked underneath the shirt, it wasn't enough to make him end his call.

"I was thinking about developing an affordable system for them with all of the options of our full-blown package, along with a life time service contract."

Alexa proceeded to test his resolve by kissing him all over his face and neck. Although he seemed to enjoy her advances, he continued his conversation without missing a beat.

"Right, right," he responded to the caller.

Motivated by his ability to remain calm, Alexa unbuttoned his shirt and ran her hands over the contours of his sculpted chest. He closed his eyes and laid his head back, yet still the discussion did not stop. Alexa smiled from the challenge he had proposed and knew exactly what to do to gain a response from him.

One by one, she undid the buttons on her shirt, exposing her naked body. She captured his hand and boldly placed it on one of her breasts. Darius' eyes immediately shot open and his focus slowly transferred from his phone call onto her.

"Look Braxton, I have some urgent business to attend to. Can I give you a call after I finish working it out?"

Alexa waited for him to remove the headpiece from his head. He tossed it on the desk top and rubbed his palms over her bare hips. "Gotcha!" she teased with a mischievous grin.

"Yeah you did," Darius replied as he proceeded to love every inch of her body.

CHAPTER 14

"Hey sleepy head," Darius addressed Alexa the next morning. He slid the covers from her body and gently shook her shoulder. "Get up, lazy bones."

Without opening her eyes, Alexa pulled the covers back over her and went back to sleep.

Darius chuckled and removed the covers again.

"Sto-op!" Alexa whined, reaching out for them again.

This time Darius pulled them completely off of the bed so that when Alexa searched for them again, she did so in vain. When she discovered that the blankets were not within her reach, she rolled onto her stomach and buried her head under a pillow.

Darius' eyes lit up at the sight of her round bottom totally exposed at his mercy. His playful nature wanted to smack it hard so that she would sit up hollering, but his gentler side preferred caressing the smooth skin in a loving gesture. He opted for the latter of the two by smoothing his palm over her soft flesh.

His actions brought Alexa to life and poked her head out from under the pillow this time. "I'm sleep!" she announced.

He slid up beside her. "I know babe, but I have some errands to run for the Ball. I thought you'd want to come with me. But, if you don't, I understand. You can stay here and I'll check in with you later."

His announcement brought Alexa out of her slumber. "How long before you'll be ready to go?" she asked groggily.

Darius glanced at the digital alarm clock on the nightstand. "About an hour, I have a lot to do."

"Give me thirty minutes and I'll be ready," she replied.

"Okay," he agreed, planting a kiss on her forehead. He backed off of the bed and went downstairs picking up discarded clothing along the way. A smile curved at the corners of his mouth as he reached for his shirt which somehow made its way into the living room.

Last night was truly something else. Alexa was bold coming on to him and he responded to her with much enthusiasm. He resolved that he would never look at his office chair the same again. They had loved each other so intensely that the chair had almost rolled out of the room.

Each time he looked at her he wondered what the next level of their relationship would entail. Although he promised to not press the issue of marriage again, he was getting restless from waiting. It was getting harder to say good-bye at the end of each visit. He yearned for the moment when he could just pull her into his arms when he wanted or call her from work knowing that he would see her at home later in the evening. Their planned couplings were hard because his heart couldn't love on a schedule. Yet, he tried to make the best of their time while they were together.

As he got dressed, Darius moved around the room like a kid on his way to Disney World. He couldn't wait for everybody to meet the woman who made his heart sing. It took nine years to get to this point and if he had to he could wait a while longer because Alexa was worth waiting for.

He frowned as he opened the refrigerator and noticed the empty contents. In his attempt to have the place spotless in preparation for her arrival, he had forgotten to go to the grocery store. He normally would have made breakfast if he had any food. Then Chandler's Place came to mind. Chandler's Place was a quaint, home-style café that he frequently patronized for their famous Belgian waffles. Just thinking about the thick, buttery pastry made his mouth water.

At Last!

While Alexa got ready, Darius picked up his attaché and searched through its contents for some paperwork that he needed to take with him to the school. Ordinarily when handling business for the school, he preferred to represent by wearing a suit, but this time, he was placing comfort over style. The baggy black carpenter jeans, and chocolate-brown, turtleneck sweater looked good on him.

The bedroom door opened and Alexa's foot falls could be heard exiting the room. In a few moments, she was standing there before him. Darius wondered if his eyes were playing tricks on him. In the baggy overalls and sweater, Alexa reminded him of the shy, beauty he fell head over heels in love with nine years ago. However, the woman before him held only the physical image as it was clear that she had blossomed into a content and confident woman. He admired a woman who could wear a pair of jeans and tennis shoes with as much poise as a business suit. More and more each day, Alexa was showing him how much he had missed.

"You look good, shawty," he hummed, circling around her with appreciative eyes.

"You look pretty fine yourself, big daddy." she retorted, fingering his sweater. The two paused for a moment to exchange a kiss.

"Are you ready?" He pulled their coats from the closet. "I thought we could pick up some breakfast first."

He held up Alexa's coat while she slipped into it.

"I am starving."

"Then let's go. I can't have you starving out here in Cleveland." He held out his arm for her and the two exited the house.

Alexa enjoyed the atmosphere at Chandler's as much as she enjoyed the food. The café put her in the mind of her grandmother's kitchen. The strong scent of freshly brewed Columbian gourmet coffee, along with the cinnamon and vanilla flavoring in the fresh pecan rolls made her mouth water. She enjoyed a hearty breakfast of coffee, fresh fruit, pecan waffles and country ham.

After breakfast, the first place they went was the ballroom where the festivities were to take place. Darius had to pass the setup instructions on to the Food Service Director. He also had to meet the decorator there to ensure that she had everything she needed to create the setting for their perfect evening.

Their next stop was the school. Darius had to hand over his money from the ticket sales to Reg. He also wanted Alexa to see the driving force behind the Ball—Frederick Douglas Academy.

Darius allowed Alexa to enter first before approaching the reception desk. As usual, Tamala and Chester were out front gossiping.

"Good morning, Ms. Harper, Mr. White," Darius greeted cheerfully. He reached for Alexa's hand, causing both Tamala's and Chester's brows to lift simultaneously. "I'd like you both to meet someone special." He turned to Alexa with a proud smile lighting his face as if he were about to introduce her to his parents. "Tamala Harper, Chester White I'd like you to meet Alexa Kirkwood. Alexa this is Tamala, Frederick Douglas's receptionist, and the Head of Security Chester White."

"Pleased to meet you both," Alexa said pleasantly as she shook both of their hands.

"Are you from around here?" Tamala asked.

"Well, I actually used to live in Detroit when I was younger, but my folks moved away while I was in college. Now I live in Denver."

"Alexa and I go way back," Darius announced, admiration glowing obviously in his eyes. "We attended the same college."

Alexa nodded with a gaze as tender as a caress. Both Tamala and Chester noticed their exchange and gave each other curious glances.

Darius quickly regained his composure. "Is Mr. Thornton in today?" he asked, keeping with formalities.

"Yes, he is," Tamala said, leaning over to press the security button to allow them inside.

Darius held the door for Alexa and recaptured her hand once he entered.

"Why the security door?" Alexa asked, glancing back at the metal door as it clicked shut behind them.

"Many of the students expressed concern about not feeling safe from the streets when people could just walk inside and peddle drugs, start fights or worse start shooting. The door was actually there when the place was first constructed as a YMCA. When the church purchased the building, they decided to leave it as it was."

"I guess that makes sense."

The facility was quiet as classes were in session. Darius played tour guide by pointing out the different classrooms in the facility. They continued down the seemingly remote hallway until they came to the office. The office was a buzz with the noisy hum of a copy machine. Gwen Taylor, Reggie's secretary looked up as they entered and a large smile curved her mouth. Gwen was a petite woman in her early 50's with salt and pepper hair and a pair of studious wire-framed glasses perched on her nose. Although she had no children of her own, Gwen had a motherly spirit who made all visitors feel right at home.

"Why hello, stranger!" she greeted with a smile as she stepped around her desk and gave Darius a hug.

"Good morning, Mrs. Taylor." Darius greeted, squeezing her tightly.

"I suppose you're looking for Mr. Thornton?"

Darius nodded. "But first, let me introduce you to my friend Alexa Kirkwood." He went through the proper introductions.

Gwen gave Alexa a hug. She smiled brightly, "You must be pretty special," she said with a wink. "This man has never brought a woman up here."

Darius stole a glance in Alexa's direction to find her awed by the older woman's findings. He was relieved when Reg opened the door and interrupted the conversation.

"I thought I heard you out here," Reggie announced.

"Alexa, this is the esteemed principal of this fine establishment Reginald Thornton," Hc turned to Reggie. "Reg, this is the lovely, the charming Alexa."

Alexa pushed herself into Darius' chest playfully. "It's nice to meet you, Reggie."

"Nice to meet you as well." Reg casually replied. He gestured for them to have a seat. Darius noticed how Reggie's eyes skeptically following Alexa as she past him to take a seat. His brow rose curiously as he observed Reggie's behavior, wondering what brought that on. Normally, Reg openly flirted with his women friends. So it was to his surprise that his friend didn't go out of his way to show him up with his charm. However, that wasn't the case with Alexa. It was obvious to him that he was being more reserved than usual.

He pulled the envelope full of checks and cash from his pocket and handed it to Reg. "I sold all of the tickets."

"Great. We need all the money we can get."

"How much have we collected so far?"

Reggie opened up his desk drawer and removed a bank deposit bag. He unlocked it and pulled out a stack of bills and checks along with a mini register. "So far, we've collected more than five thousand. This doesn't include your money. I'm also expecting some last minute donations."

"That's great!" Darius exclaimed.

"I know. Now we can concentrate on launching our sports program and expanding our science and computer labs."

Darius rose from his seat. "Well, we better get going. We have a few more stops."

Reggie glanced at his watch. "Yeah, class will be dismissing in a couple of minutes and if I were you, I would get going before it lets out."

Darius immediately picked up on what his friend was saying. He didn't want to chance running into Tricia Herndon. Although it had been some time since they dated, she seemed to be hanging on to the possibility of the two of them reuniting. Darius planned to share the situation with Alexa but preferred to do it at the right time.

After they made their runs to pick up a few last minute things and pay the deposit for the band, they went back to Darius' place. With four hours left before they had to go to the Ball, the two decided to lie down and watch a movie. Darius grabbed a blanket and pillow from the front hall closet and stretched out on the sofa. He reached out for Alexa to join him. Without a word, she claimed the spot before him and squirmed around until she found a comfortable spot. The two never made it to through the first five minutes of the movie. Once they were spooned together, they fell fast asleep in each other's arms.

*   *   *

"You look so fine, I don't think I want to share you with anyone tonight," Darius announced as they walked up the stairs leading to the ballroom of the Crowne Plaza Hotel.

Alexa lovingly cupped his jaw in the palm of her hand. "If you stay on your toes Riverside you won't have to share me with anybody."

Darius grabbed her up in his arms. "Trust me, I won't skip a beat."

On the way over, Darius could barely keep his hands to himself. The black floor length dress was definitely a good choice. The sleeveless dress with a simple jeweled neckline complemented her toned arms and shapely figure.

Alexa had her hair styled in mass of curly ringlets, which framed her face perfectly. The only piece of jewelry she wore was a pair of pear shaped diamond earrings, which were a gift to her self when she got her bonus last Christmas. She topped the outfit off with an elegant black velvet duster. Darius' black velvet single breasted suit jacket with black trousers and a stark white shirt made him look dashingly handsome. The suit fit him as if were made to grace his frame.

Darius handed over the keys to his truck to the valet attendant then ran around to the passenger side to capture Alexa's hand. There were all sorts of people milling about in the lobby. A large sign placed on a stand in they foyer directed them to the ballroom where the festivities were located. As they approached the room, Darius spied two men sitting outside the door.

As he got closer, he recognized one of the men as O'dell Lymon, a dedicated volunteer, and father of four active boys who attended the Academy. Having been born in the rural south to sharecropper parents, O'dell's own education was limited because he was needed at home to help bring in the harvest. At the birth of their first child, he made a vow to his wife Delilah that he would work hard to provide their children with the best education possible. Three boys later, he was disappointed when it began to appear like he wouldn't be able to make good on his promise. Then Reggie Thornton came knocking on his door one evening, talking to him about a new school opening in the area. The school was an answer to their prayers. O'dell ran out and picked up two more jobs to pay half of their tuition. Because of his determination, Reggie worked with him and was able to get partial scholarships for the boys. All the Lymons had to do was put in some sweat equity through volunteering at the school or chaperoning special school sponsored events. As far as Darius was concerned, the two had put in so much time that he believed the boys' tuition was paid in full for next year as well. Now the couple anxiously awaited the opening of Mary McLeod-Bethune's Academy for Young Ladies so that they could send their two younger daughters.

"Good evening Mr. Lymon!" Darius greeted.

At Last!

The older man jumped to his feet, "How ya doing, son?" He shook Darius' hand. He acknowledged Alexa with a hand shake as well. "Good evening, ma'am."

"You're sure looking dapper in that suit," Darius complimented the older gentleman.

O'Dell smiled, embarrassed by the attention. "You know if these monkey suits weren't required for these affairs, I would be in my overalls."

Darius laughed and turned to Alexa. "Mr. Lymon here is one of Douglas' most committed advocates. He has four sons who attend the school."

"Wow, four sons?" Alexa exclaimed. She couldn't imagine putting one child through private school let alone four.

The older gentleman rocked on his heels with a proud smile. "Yes ma'am. All but one is on the honor roll. He's too busy daydreaming about girls. Told him he has the rest of his life to do that. Right now his education is more important."

"I don't know Mr. Lymon," Darius teased, nodding his head in Alexa's direction. "Sometimes a man can't help himself."

Alexa blushed from his comment.

"I see," Mr. Lymon's brow raised. "Looks to me like you daydream quite a bit."

Darius burst out laughing, and the older man joined him. The line started to get long, so Darius and Alexa said their good-byes and went inside to join the festivities.

The ballroom was fabulously decorated in the school colors of black and gold. There was a live band playing popular R & B as well as old Motown hits, an elaborate spread of finger foods, and lighted champagne fountains placed throughout the room.

Folks went all out for the evening dressed in designer tuxedos and ball gowns dripping with sequins and rhinestones. Many came out for the celebrated event. The attendees' ages ranged from college students to senior citizens all gathered together in the name of education.

As they made their way through the thick crowd, Darius stopped several times to greet people. Alexa noticed that practically everyone present was representing a well known organization. Representation from all nine of the black fraternities and sororities, the NAACP, Urban League, and HBCU were present not to mention Ebony Magazine and Black Enterprise. Alexa was surprised to meet a broad spectrum of people from the school's maintenance team to the city's mayor.

After exchanging small talk, the two continued moving around the room leaving Alexa feeling more like she was hosting the gala rather than giving her support. Each time they approached someone who played an important part in the success of the school; Darius would lean over and whisper their title and affiliation into Alexa's ear. She sighed with relief when they moved away from their last group to a clearing. While she enjoyed special events, sometimes they could be tiresome. She had to do a lot of networking in her position in similar settings and often grew tired of putting on the business face.

"The turnout is great," Darius announced, surveying the room. "Do you want me to find our table?"

Alexa sensed that Darius wanted to remain in her company while on the other hand he wanted to continue working the crowd. She placed a gentle hand on his cheek. "Baby, I know this is a fund-raiser and you have to network. Go on and do what you have to do. I'm not going anywhere."

"Are you sure?" Darius asked, "Because, I can stay here with you." And then lower so that only she could hear, "You know I would love that."

Alexa grinned and placed a kiss on his cheek. "Go."

When he turned to leave, Alexa couldn't resist and quickly patted him on the rear. He turned around with a gentle warning. "You'll pay for that one later, woman."

His threat made her warm with anticipation and she retreated for something cool to drink.

Just as she approached the bar, she spotted Reg arriving with his date. Alexa took her drink and went over to greet them. Reggie was immaculately dressed in an expensive, tailored tux. The woman on his arm looked equally flawless in a cranberry sheath, which complimented her caramel brown complexion.

"Hi Reggie!" she called out approaching the two. It was nice seeing a familiar face.

Reggie half smiled with a nod. "Hello Alexa." He placed his palm on the small of the woman's back. "Honey, this is Darius' friend, Alexa Kirkwood. Alexa this is my fiancée, Crystal Rawlings."

"Hi, Alexa," Crystal drawled. "It's very nice to meet you."

Crystal and Reg reminded Alexa of Maya and Bryant in appearance as they were an equally attractive couple. She wondered if she and Darius looked as good together. Crystal put Alexa in the mind of Halle Berry. She was a petite woman, standing an inch above five feet, slender yet shapely. She wore her honey brown hair short, tapered in the back and on the sides with feathery bangs grazing her brow. Crystal's most captivating feature was her eyes, which were a striking gray as well as her long, curly eye lashes, which seemed to touch her prominent cheekbones when she batted them.

"It's nice to meet you, too," Alexa replied.

"Place is filling up," Reg announced, straightening his tie.

"Yes, it is," Alexa, agreed.

"So, where's Darius?" Reg asked, his eyes scanning the room.

Alexa turned and pointed him out near the middle of the room. "He wanted to stick with me, but I released him to get out and mingle. I know how important it is for him to get out and schmooze, after all, that is why we came."

Reg's eyes widened in response to her comment, making Alexa wonder why he would show so much surprise.

He then turned to Crystal, "Honey, do you mind if…" he began, but Crystal cut him off before he could finish his question.

"Go on." She assured him. "I'll be fine right here with Alexa."

Reggie planted a kiss on her cheek before departing.

Crystal shook her head with a smile. "They act like we need to have them waiting on us hand and foot."

"I know." Alexa added. "I learned long ago that it is best to not sweat the small stuff especially if no one is getting hurt."

"You are right. Besides, when you hold them back it only makes them rebel and I for one cannot stand a rebellious man."

The women decided to find their reserved table. They found their table located near the front of the room and took their seats. After ordering drinks, they began talking about everything from their jobs to their personal tastes as well as their relationships. Alexa learned that Crystal was a flight attendant and had traveled abroad to exciting locations such as Accra, Kenya and Egypt in Africa, Paris, London, Rome, Greece in Europe, Tokyo and Bangkok in the Orient and Trinidad, Aruba and Belize in the Caribbean. She and Reg met on a flight to Japan two years ago and have been dating ever since. Although she thought him to be self-absorbed at times with his various career and community responsibilities, she didn't mind their arrangement for now. But she stressed that once they were married, she was determined that most of his energy would be spent at home.

At first, Alexa was hesitant about sharing her and Darius' story, but somehow she felt she could trust Crystal. She proceeded to tell her the story of when and how they met and what they had been through, up to how they reunited at their friends' wedding.

"We have been through a lot, but I really love him." She looked up from her place at the table and searched for Darius. When she located him, she was surprised to find his eyes resting on her. He winked and she smiled sticking out her tongue playfully. Darius gripped his heart in response and the two laughed silently.

She turned her attention back to Crystal who sat there watching the whole interaction. Crystal shook her head with a smile. "You two *are* in love."

*   *   *

After cocktail hour ended, there was a short welcome and introductions over dinner followed by the party portion where the band began to play. The couples got out of their seats. Darius was egging Alexa on to join him in doing some dances from the past. After his poor attempt at doing the Prep, Snake, and Freddie Krueger, Alexa jumped in to help him out. However the surprise of the evening was seeing the ever reserved Reggie doing the Whop.

Out of breath from dancing to several songs and laughing at each other, the foursome exited the floor. Reg and Darius ran off to get cool drinks while Crystal and Alexa reclaimed their table. Minutes later, the men returned with glasses of White Zinfandel for the ladies and cold beer for themselves. Darius placed the glass before Alexa and sat down, placing his chair so that her chair was positioned at a sideways angle, putting her possessively between his legs.

"So, what kind of notes have you two been exchanging about us?" Reggie asked, sitting beside Crystal in the same possessive manner.

"Who? Us?" Crystal replied with mocked innocence.

"Yeah, I know you, Crys," he chided. "Alexa probably knows everything about me and then some."

"Are you having a good time?" Darius asked, draping his arm across the back of her chair.

"Yes I am. Thank you for inviting me."

The four sat there for a while conversing and listening to the good music when the band started to play another upbeat tune. Darius immediately held out his hand for her and the two stepped onto the dance floor with several other couples.

Darius led Alexa away from their friends, preferring to concentrate only on each other. Alexa moved sensually to the beat while Darius watched in a trance.

With a playful glint in her eye, Alexa broke the spell by whipping around so that her back was to him. She rested her head against his broad chest and he wrapped her body in his embrace. He snuggled his face into the crook of her neck and kissed her smooth skin making her tingle.

Their playfulness so reminded her of the dance shared at Maya and Bryant's wedding reception. It took a few minutes before Alexa realized that she was not at the reception but at the Benefit Ball and under the watchful eyes of some very important people. Without hesitation, she pulled away from Darius and turned around with a glance about the room. She silently prayed that no one was watching her and one of the Board members carrying on like some wild teenagers. To her relief, the others around them were into their own dancing to even notice them. With a sigh of relief, she stepped back into Darius' arms, but kept her tempestuous moves to a minimum.

Just as she grew relaxed enough to dance again, the music faded and the melody of a familiar song began to play. Alexa's heart began to race for she immediately recognized the song as the one which Darius sang to her at the reception.

"Come on baby," Darius urged, as he pulled her against his chest. "I got some words for you girl."

Before she knew it, Darius was singing to her again. She searched his eyes only to see the love he had for her and her alone, making her heart sing.

When the song ended, they walked back to their table hand-in-hand.

At Last!

"I think I'll go to the restroom," Alexa announced. She needed to refresh herself from their heated dance.

Crystal excused herself along with Alexa, to escape to the ladies room. To their surprise, the restroom wasn't crowded, which was unheard of when black women were in the house. Usually women would be lined up outside the door and the inside would be a haze of perfumes and hair spray.

Alexa stood before the mirror dabbing away the perspiration on her brow, while Crystal touched up her makeup.

"Alexa, I know that we've just met a couple hours ago, but I think you are good people."

"Thanks, Crystal; you're pretty nice too and that's not something I can say to a lot of women that I've just met."

Crystal turned from the mirror to face Alexa. "What you and Darius have is a good thing. I've known Darius as long as I've known Reggie, and I have never witnessed the connection that he has with you with any other woman he's dated."

Alexa was at a loss for words. She had no idea that they were wearing their admiration for each other on their sleeves for all to see.

Crystal continued. "Out there, I saw two people who complement one another, who need each other. After you told me about you all's past, things just made sense to me. I'm not one to get all in somebody's business; I just want you to know what you have."

Alexa wasn't sure what brought Crystal to say those words, but she agreed with her fully. Since his proposal, she had begun to wonder what it would be like to be married to Darius. The thought alone sounded so enticing that she sometimes couldn't think straight.

As they exited the restroom, Alexa spotted a woman standing at their table. She was dressed in a body-hugging dress and high-heeled sandals. Judging by her stance, it was obvious that her attention was directed at Darius.

Darius and Reggie immediately stood as the Alexa and Crystal approached. The woman whirled around to see who captured the men's attention. When she saw that it was Crystal, she smiled broadly.

"Crystal! Hey girl, how you doing?" she asked, leaning in for a hug.

"Hey, Tricia," Crystal returned, pleasantly. Tricia Herndon was not one of her favorite people, but because she worked with Reggie and her work was so important to the school, she had learned to tolerate her.

Tricia turned back to Darius with her hands on her hips. "I was just trying to get Mr. Darius here to take a spin on the dance floor, but he's acting like a spoiled sport. He knows how good we used to be together."

Alexa's brow raised curiously at the words *used to be together*. She didn't know who this Tricia was, but she didn't like the way she was acting before her man.

Instead of replying to Tricia's complaint, Crystal graciously interrupted to prevent a situation from ensuing. "Tricia, have you met Alexa?"

Tricia turned to face Alexa with a smile.

"Tricia, this is our friend Alexa Kirkwood, Alexa this is Tricia Herndon."

Tricia extended her hand. "Pleased to meet you."

"And you, as well." Alexa coolly replied. She could see right through Tricia's falseness and tried to keep her cool although Tricia had gripped her hand tightly. Tricia's reference to Darius as well as her kung fu grip brought up warning signs. Alexa's eyebrow rose as if to prepare for another assault when Darius came around to where she stood, and placed his palm intimately on the small of her back.

Tricia noticed the gesture, but tried to play it off. "So, what brings you to the event? Searching for a good man? Cuz, girlfriend you know there's plenty of money in the house. If you need me to make the introductions, let me know."

Silence followed Tricia's snide comment and Alexa steadied herself before responding. However, before she could reply, Darius stepped in. Up until that point, he felt like Alexa was handling herself very well, considering the situation. He didn't find it necessary to intrude up until that point when Tricia crossed the line with her crass comment.

"Actually Tricia, Alexa isn't here to find a man," He pulled her closer to him in confirmation. "I'm all the man she needs."

Tricia's eyes narrowed as they bore into Darius' before traveling down to their entwined hands and coldly settling on Alexa. "I'm sorry, I didn't know. I was just asking for a dance between old friends."

Alexa almost felt sorry for the embarrassing position Tricia placed herself in but when she caught Tricia's glare cutting in her direction, she knew the woman's feelings implied something more than a simple friendship.

"Its okay, Tricia," Darius replied. "You didn't know."

Alexa, however, was less forgiving. She didn't even acknowledge Tricia's apology, but had turned to Darius and hugged his arm possessively. "This has been an exhausting day sweetie and I am ready to go home."

Darius couldn't agree with her more. They excused themselves with a promise to Crystal and Reggie to get together before Alexa returned to Denver.

Despite the encounter with Tricia, the evening was a success. The school raised more than $35,000.

Darius was quiet as he opened the car door for Alexa.

She attributed his conduct to the incident with Tricia. She watched as he walked around the front of the truck to open his door. Once inside, he started the engine to let it warm up. As they waited, Darius turned on the jazz station before settling back in his seat.

"Alexa, please accept my apology for Tricia's behavior."

"Why should you apologize for her?" Alexa asked. "Her lack of professionalism has nothing to do with you."

"I feel responsible because I didn't tell you that Tricia and I used to date a while back. It didn't last more than a month or so because I didn't want to pursue the relationship. Although I told her explicitly that I wasn't ready for a relationship, she wouldn't let it go. Believe me when I say we did nothing more than share a kiss."

"I believe you," Alexa replied, squeezing his hand tightly.

"Tricia Herndon is an asset to Douglas. She is a very intelligent woman who has the children's best interest at heart, but I knew early on that she wasn't the woman for me."

"Why not?" Alexa asked. She didn't know why she asked because she didn't want to even think about the possibility of Darius being with another woman. However, his answer was worth more than gold.

Peering into Alexa's eyes, he replied, "Because she wasn't you."

A sense of warmth overcame Alexa and tears formed in her eyes from his endearing words. She inched closer to him and rested her head on his shoulder.

"I want to do it," she whispered softly.

"Excuse me?" Darius replied, taken aback by her request, his mind clearly venturing on a different subject altogether. He checked their surroundings before glancing into the back seat, thinking about how he could let them down.

Alexa reared up her head and rested her chin on his shoulder. "Get your mind out of the gutter, Riverside," she chortled. "I was referring to us getting married, that is if your proposal still stands."

Darius was so stunned he had to pull the truck to the side of the road. After turning off the ignition, he turned to her. "Are you serious?"

Alexa nodded. "I'll admit that I am nervous as all get out, but I know it's something that I want to do. I can't imagine going back to my world without you to share it with."

"What about your job?" Darius asked. "One of us is going to have to move."

"Like you said before, let's not worry about that now," Alexa quieted him with a kiss. "I just want to focus on us being together."

"You're right," he replied, elation building. Then an idea struck him. "I know. Let's fly to Vegas. We can catch the redeye."

"Well," Alexa paused. "I never imagined getting married in Las Vegas." Instead, she dreamed of a large wedding with beautiful flowers, and violin music and a long white dress. She envisioned their families being there to be witnesses as they shared their sacred vows.

Their eyes locked as they realized the time had come. Nine years couldn't extinguish the love they shared. Now they had an opportunity to seal it forever despite the distance, despite what their family and friends would think, despite everything, just like Crystal said, they needed each other.

"But, with such short notice, I know we don't have many options." Alexa placed her palm on Darius' cheek, stroking it lovingly. "Anything to be with you my love."

CHAPTER 15

Darius found it hard to sleep while Alexa, on the other hand, snored peacefully in his arms. It was official; they were now man and wife.

His eyes traveled down to the simple gold band that she had chosen at the wedding chapel gift shop. It wasn't something he would have selected for her, but she convinced him that it wasn't the style of ring but the commitment behind it that mattered.

Her words nearly brought tears to his eyes. She was a lady with a heart of gold who had captured his heart with her lasso of love. He couldn't have asked for a better woman to be his wife.

Their ceremony took place at a tiny all night, but tasteful, wedding chapel. Alexa looked beautiful in the knee-length, off white slip dress. She adorned her hair with a decorative ivory comb with tiny white pearls. Darius, on the other hand, looked quite dapper in his black suit with a cream shirt underneath.

After the exchange of rings and vows, when the Reverend Albert Crawley pronounced them man and wife, they turned to each other and embraced with a deep kiss, sealing their love. Afterwards, the two gazed lovingly into each other's eyes across the table, barely touched dinner before retiring to their hotel room. They didn't get to see much of Vegas that evening. Before they knew it, they were on the plane headed back to Ohio.

He glanced down at his slumbering bride and kissed her on the forehead, causing her to stir awake.

"Hello, Mrs. Riverside," he whispered.

At Last!

Alexa stretched, "Hello husband."

"How do you feel?" he asked.

She smiled sweetly. "Great. And you?"

"Like I'm the king of the world!" he exclaimed.

They both laughed at his reply.

Alexa snuggled closer to him and held his large hand up to her smaller one gazing at their matching bands. "So, what do we do now?"

His fingers slid down between each of hers, joining their hands. "What do you mean, dear wife?"

"By this time tomorrow, I will be on a plane back to Denver. We haven't even discussed our living arrangements."

"Well, you know that is something to consider given that Bryant and I are looking to go into business together."

Panic began to seep in and she sat up in her seat. Now it was her turn to agonize over their decision and Darius had to calm her down. "Oh my goodness, how could we have made such a rash move? What are we going to do? We should have considered your business before we did this."

Darius reached for her and pulled her back in his embrace. "We will worry about that when we get back home."

"But," Alexa exclaimed, her voice rising to the anxiety growing inside.

Darius cut her off with a kiss before her frantic emotions got too carried away. "Babe, there is nothing we can do about it in the plane. I promise when we get back to Ohio, we will talk about things."

The worry slowly erased when Alexa looked at her husband. Her handsome, strong, confident man was in charge. She had to believe that everything was going to be okay as long as he was there.

*　　　　　　　*　　　　　　　*

Darius and Alexa awoke simultaneously to the ringing of the telephone at 9:15, on Monday morning. The newlyweds were curled securely in a spooned position, with his arm draped possessively around her waist.

Darius scowled at the alarm clock, which failed to go off at the appropriate time when he realized that he was the one to blame. It was his honeymoon and he didn't think to set the alarm. He planned to call in to work first thing to let them know that he would be taking the whole week off, but apparently someone had beat him to the punch.

"Should I answer it, Mrs. Riverside?" Darius asked, burying his face into the tangles of her hair.

"Whatever you decide, husband," she sultrily replied.

After six rings, the phone was silent. Darius rose up on one elbow and gazed down with adoring eyes at his sleeping bride.

Alexa felt him staring at her and opened her eyes. "What are you doing?" she asked and reached up, cupping his bearded cheek with her palm.

"Checking out my wife."

Alexa stretched with a satiated grin. "Can you believe it? I is married now!" she exclaimed, sounding like Sofia off of *The Color Purple.*

"I believe last night." His hand slid up the planes of her curvaceous hip.

"So, husband, what's on the agenda for today?" She loved the way Darius' new title rolled off her tongue. It made her feel delicious inside.

"I have something special planned."

"Such as?"

"It's a surprise."

"Okay, I like surprises." Ordinarily, she would be filled with anxiety about the whole situation. She couldn't believe how at ease she was. Upon their return, she made a vow to herself that she would not focus on anything except being a newlywed. It was hard, but her love for him made it easy.

Darius leaned over her, reaching for the telephone. "I better call the office, I can't have them wondering where I am."

Alexa listened as he informed the appropriate person that he would be taking a few vacation days to take care of some "very important business." He smiled down at her as he said those three words.

This time, when he leaned over her to hang up the receiver, on the way down, he pulled her against his chest and eased back onto his side of the bed. "Your man's hungry. How about a little breakfast?" He began kissing her over her neck and face.

With a mischievous giggle Alexa readied herself to oblige him.

*   *   *

"Baby, where are we going?" Alexa nervously asked. It was quite difficult not to mention embarrassing being out in public wearing a blind fold.

"Don't worry, my lady," he assured her. "We're almost there."

If not for his hold on her arm guiding her along the way, Alexa was sure that she would not have gone along with the surprise. A blast of cold wind greeted them like a slap in the face and Alexa shrank against his chest.

"It's freezing!" she shrieked.

"I'm sorry," he apologized with a kiss to her forehead. As if to make up for the discomfort, he attempted to shield her from the cold by covering her in the folds of his goose down coat.

Alexa wanted to end the game by pulling off the dark scarf, but decided to be a good sport. She didn't want to ruin things by complaining. As they continued further, she noticed the walk beneath their feet change from a flat concrete to a sloping wooden plank.

At that moment, Darius came to a stop. He grasped her hands and Alexa could feel him step around her so that he was standing in front of her.

"Okay, carefully now, lift your leg high and step down," he said, his breath warming her face.

"Darry, this is scary," she moaned uneasily.

"I promise, there is nothing to be scared about," he said with a gentle tone. "Besides you're safe with me."

Alexa knew Darius wouldn't lead her into danger and did as she was told. The minute her feet touched the surface below, she felt the foundation sway slightly. A moment later, she heard a door open and Darius guided her through the narrow passageway, where the cool winds were replaced by enveloping warmth. A delicious aroma of vanilla and cinnamon filled her nostrils, causing her curiosity to peak.

"Can I take it off now?" she asked, reaching for the blindfold. She was growing increasingly inpatient.

"Give me a sec," he said moving away from her.

Alexa could hear him fiddling with something as he whistled merrily to himself. Within minutes, soft music filled the air.

"Okay, now you can take it off." Darius yelled from across the room.

Alexa didn't waste time to untie the scarf, and pulled it from her face. She immediately gasped at what she saw. From what she could tell, they were on a small houseboat. Across the small room stood Darius by a bistro sized table set for two. Near the table was a window with the curtains drawn and the most magnificent view of Lake Michigan and the Canadian Coast in the distance. The scene immediately brought back memories of one of their favorite pastimes.

"Darry, it's beautiful!" she cried, rushing over to him. She wrapped her arms around his neck and kissed him tenderly.

A grin spread across Darius' face. "Mm, girl I should surprise you like this more often."

"You do and you just might get anything you want."

At Last!

He inhaled the feminine scent of perfume in the crook of her neck as he lifted her in his arms and proceeded, without words but loving caresses, to ask her to make good on his first request.

CHAPTER 16

The bridal department at Macy's did nothing but remind Alexa how much she missed Darius. Two weeks had passed since their wedding and she missed her husband desperately. Darius' absence left her feeling on edge. When they were together, she felt like their love could conquer all. Apart, she felt alone and insecure.

On her way to work that morning, she reluctantly slipped the platinum band from her finger and placed it on the gold chain around her neck. Both of them agreed to keep their nuptials private from friends and family alike. It was a hard decision to make, but their history was still fresh in everyone's minds. They also knew that the knowledge of their elopement would not settle well, especially with the mothers. They would get around to telling them in their own time and in their own way, and did not need nor welcome any nagging regardless of the intent, from well meaning loved ones. After everyone was told, the couple would have a reception.

Keeping their wedding a secret proved to be difficult. With Darius being her only co-conspirator, she looked forward to the opportunity to be able to love him openly in the presence of friends and family without worrying about being judged.

The previous night, they spent two and a half hours on the telephone with Darius making plans for him to fly back to Denver for a weekend. He tried toiling over his schedule with her on the telephone, but realized that he had to check his current commitments as well as his own personal workload. The conversation then shifted from them onto the Ball. Thanks to committed community leaders and business men and women, the school was able to raise more than $200,000 in contributions from the fund-raiser alone. Thoughts of the affair brought Tricia Herndon to mind and Alexa couldn't help but gloat to herself at the thought of picturing Tricia's face once she learned that she and Darius were married.

Although the encounter with Tricia Herndon had left a bad taste in her mouth, she knew she didn't have to worry. She trusted Darius and knew that if Tricia tried to proposition him in any way, he would definitely put her in her proper place.

A smile curved Alexa's lips as she replayed the word "husband" in her head. She was so engrossed in her thoughts that she didn't notice Teressa holding up the ice blue slip dress before her.

"You don't like it," Teressa groaned with disappointment clouding her face.

"What?" Alexa asked, looking from the dress to Teressa.

"The dress," Teressa replied, waving it before Alexa's face. "I said you don't like it do you?"

Alex gazed back at the dress. It was cute, but not her style. "Is that the bridesmaid dress that you picked out?"

Teressa nodded with hesitation. "Do you like it?"

"Well, the color is different." How could she tell her friend without hurting her feelings that the dress just wasn't right?

"It's ice blue. I thought it would be cute for a summer wedding," Teressa explained.

Alexa didn't want to break Teressa's spirit, but she was there as a friend and she wasn't about to keep her mouth shut on matters that needed a second opinion like the dress she held in her hand.

"You want me to be honest with you right?"

Teressa nodded.

"This color is pretty, but I think you could find a color that would better complement our complexions. For instance, your cousin Grace could wear it because she is lighter skinned and the blue would compliment her undertones. But your sisters Tawnya and Taleah are darker than me and this color is not right for me."

To prove her point, she held the garment up to her face.

Teressa wrinkled her nose at the contrast. She thought the blue would be perfect because, according to all of the magazines, the color was hot for the season, but she wanted a look that would be talked about in a good way.

"You're right." She took the dress and placed it back on the rack. "I'm glad I brought you with me. I knew I would need someone who would be honest with me."

A beautiful sage color caught Alexa's eye and she scurried over to the rack to find four floor length dresses with spaghetti straps and rhinestone beadwork across the bust line. The dresses came with matching sheer wraps.

"Teressa, what do you think of these?" she asked, holding one up for her friend to see.

Teressa screamed as she ran over and took the dress from Alexa. "These are gorgeous!"

"Aren't they nice?" Alexa agreed. "Plus you could do a lot with this color."

Teressa nodded. "I like, I like." In her excitement, she let out a scream for joy and gave Alexa a hug. "Thank you for your help Alex. I'm going to charge these right now."

Alexa took a size ten from Teressa's hands and headed for the registers. "I will pay for my own."

Having accomplished one of the most difficult items on Teressa's list of things to do, the women exited the store feeling triumphant and extremely satisfied with their purchases.

"Now let's go find some shoes." Teressa suggested.

"What kind of style are you looking for?" Alexa asked as they headed in the direction of the nearest shoe store. As Teressa began to describe the shoes, Alexa noticed a familiar figure out of the corner of her eye. It couldn't be, she said to herself as she got closer, but the regal features and copper complexion told her that her conjecture was true.

At a watch stand 10 feet away from her was Sean Hardaway. At the sight of him, a sick feeling immediately came over her. She was about to steer Teressa into another direction, when Sean glanced up.

"Alexa!" He shouted and hurried over to where they stood. He surprised her with a tight hug.

The hug caught Alexa off guard. Instinctively, she pushed him away hard and slapped him squarely across the cheek.

Sean stood there astonished, holding his cheek and looking around to see if anyone witnessed the blow. "Why did you do that?"

"Who do you think you are grabbing me like that?" she lashed out angrily.

"Damn woman, it was just a hug!" he grimaced.

"Don't you ever walk up on me like that again!" she huffed. Seeing Sean brought back a mixture of emotions that she had repressed over the years. The way she felt, she could have slapped him back to Africa.

"Alexa, please lower your voice," Teressa suggested from the sidelines. People around them were beginning to stop and stare. "You're causing a scene."

"Yes, you're causing a scene, Alexa," Sean added, looking around at the curious spectators embarrassed by what had just occurred.

"I don't care," she retorted, glaring in Sean's direction. "I told you to stay away from me Sean."

"Why can't you let bygones be bygones?" he asked sternly.

"What you did was wrong. It didn't matter that you didn't want to marry me, but the way you went about it was humiliating. You just skipped town and left me to deal with everything."

"Would it have made you happier if I married you anyway, knowing that I wasn't in love with you?" he threw back in her face.

Alexa's eyes watered and she mustered everything that she had to prevent herself from lashing out at him again. "Screw you, Sean!" she cried and marched away.

Teressa caught up with her just as she stormed into the women's restroom. She pushed through the door so hard that it hit the wall with a loud bang.

"Alexa, what in the heck is wrong with you?" Teressa shouted from behind.

Alexa headed straight for an open stall and stood there shaking from anger.

Snatching a piece of tissue off of the roll, she blew her nose. Suddenly she wished she were in Ohio, with Darius. *Why am I even here?* She thought. *I should be with my husband.* Thinking about him and the distance between them caused the tears to fall.

The two weeks seemed more like two months. April was fast approaching. The end of the week would mark month four of their reunion and two weeks of marriage. With each passing day, she felt like she was getting emotionally worse without him.

After blowing her nose again, she exited the stall to find Teressa standing there with a sympathetic look on her face. Alex couldn't help but smile at her misguided friend and she knew that she had to explain her tears. The need to talk to somebody was eating at her and as far as she could see, Teressa was the best candidate as she was far removed from the situation as anyone and would be unbiased.

"Can we talk?"

"Are you okay?" Teressa asked.

Alexa nodded. "I think I will be fine," she replied with a sigh. "Let's go find a place to sit."

They gathered the dresses and exited the restroom in silence. Thank goodness there was a restaurant located in the mall where they could sit down in privacy. The two went inside and found a secluded table. After placing their order, Alexa began to talk.

"I'm sure you know that was Sean, my ex-fiancé."

"I gathered that."

"Today was my first time seeing him since he bailed out days before our wedding. I guess that little display you just witnessed was a result of pinned up frustrations." She pointed to her tear-filled eyes. "But these tears are not because of him."

"Then why were you crying?" Teressa asked, confused at why her friend would not be crying after seeing her ex.

"Because, there is someone else. Someone who I love and miss very much," Alexa replied with a remote look in her eye. "And who I also married two weeks ago."

"What?" Teressa shrieked her mouth and eyes opened wide in awe. "You, you're married? When? Who and why didn't you tell me before now?"

"It's a long, complicated story and so far you are the only one who knows and that includes both of our families, so please keep it under wraps," Only when Alexa got Teressa to make a verbal promise that she wouldn't tell a soul, did she began to fill her in on the details surrounding her relationship with Darius ending with her recent trip to Ohio.

"We didn't want to tell others because we wanted to give ourselves some time to get to know one another again. Plus, with everybody in our business the first time around, we wanted to ward off outside influences."

Teressa took a deep sigh. "Believe me when I say that I am honored that you shared this with me Alexa, but marriage is a serious commitment. I can't believe that you eloped."

"I know it sounds so unlike me to make a rash decision but I do love him very much and I felt like this was a decision I didn't have a whole lot of time to ponder over."

A pause stretched between them as Teressa searched for something to say. Finally, she just shook her head. "The only thing that matters is that the two of you are happy."

Alexa nodded with a smile. "We are."

"Then all I need to say is congratulations girlfriend!" Teressa stood from her seat and leaned over to give Alexa a hug.

For the first time in months, Alexa felt free with someone other than Darius. It was a relief to have the weight of her secret removed from her shoulders for that brief moment.

She reached inside her blouse and withdrew her necklace where her wedding band had hung between her breast against her heart and she showed it to Teressa. Alex felt bad for being too cautious with her friend. She hadn't taken their friendship as seriously as Teressa did and that made her feel bad.

Teressa resumed her seat with a chuckle.

"What is so funny?" Alexa asked.

"That poor Sean. He probably thinks you are on your way to an asylum or something."

Embarrassed by her behavior, Alexa managed a smile. "I do feel kind of stupid getting all out of control like that but you had to understand where I was coming from. Do you think I went overboard?"

The pensive look on Teressa's face told it all. "I think you could have handled it better."

"Is damage control in order?"

"I wouldn't go out of my way to clean it up. However, if you just happen to see him again, it wouldn't hurt to be a little more composed. You could also drop a line about Mr. Darius. He sounds so nice. I can't wait to meet him. When is he coming to town again?"

Alex shrugged, "I'm not sure, but when he does, maybe we can get together with you and Lewis so that you can meet him."

"Sounds cool," Teressa replied, and then added, "I can't believe that you are married. You never struck me as being the spontaneous type."

"I guess love will do it to you," Alexa retorted, relieved that she finally got the chance to get it off her chest. Suddenly she wanted to soar to the rooftops exclaiming her love for Darius to the whole world.

*   *   *

"What's up, boo?"

Alexa immediately smiled at the sound of Darius' voice.

"Hi Darry," she greeted cheerfully. She pushed her chair away from the computer.

"Um," Darius groaned. "I haven't heard you call me Darry in a long time."

"Oh yeah? When was the last time?" she replied, fully remembering calling out his name in the heat of passion.

"Let me see, you were in a compromising but very enticing position."

"Okay, okay you remember!" She shouted, cutting him off.

Darius laughed. "So how's my baby?"

"Tired. I need a vacation already. Do you want to run away with me?"

"My dear, I will run where ever you want me to," his response surprised her as he sounded very serious.

"I have some vacation time coming up and I thought maybe we could meet somewhere between Denver and Ohio. Maybe have a real honeymoon." Her voice trailed off.

"Oh yeah like where? Nebraska?" he quipped.

"I was thinking some place more interesting like Kansas City. I heard they have some nice jazz clubs, delicious barbecue and romantic bed and breakfast inns."

"Hmm, I've been to KC a few times and it was pretty nice. When were you thinking about going?"

"You tell me. You said you had to check your schedule."

Darius paused for a moment as he leafed through his planner. Either his personal business or the school took almost every weekend. The only weekend he had available was close to the end of the month. "Sorry baby, I can't get away for awhile."

Alex whined. "What's awhile?"

"Try three weeks."

"Darry, no!" she whined, again.

"I'm sorry, baby, but I have meetings every weekend. Bryant and I have this big deal in Detroit this Saturday. I have two new contracts to pick up the following weekend in addition to coordinating a youth retreat for the school."

"I guess business comes first," Alexa muttered, in obvious disappointment.

"No, you come first," he quickly interjected. "I'm just a man of my word. I don't break commitments. Just like if I had an arrangement with you, I wouldn't allow anybody to interfere with our time. I would turn anyone down in a heartbeat so I could be with my lady."

Alexa smiled with pride, grateful to have an honorable man. A lot of men would bail out of all responsibility for a chance to spend a week in bed with their women. But Darius was not like a lot of men, which is why she loved him so.

"You're right," she sighed. "How about I make all of the plans and call you with the details. All you need to do is show up."

"Ooh, I think I like this already," he replied in a low husky voice. He liked the sound of her being in total control.

"Don't worry, you will," she assured him.

Just as Alexa was about to set the receiver back on its base, Sharon popped her head inside her office. "Mrs. Holland called down. She wants to see you in her office at your earliest convenience."

Alexa's heart began to pound. It wasn't often that the Publication Director called her for an unscheduled meeting.

"Thank you, Sharon," Alexa said, reaching for her planner. She wanted to make sure that she did not over look an appointment or scheduled meeting. However, when she checked her daily agenda, there was nothing scheduled.

She prayed that a situation did not arise that called for an emergency meeting, which she did not know about. In addition to her spontaneous vacations, Alexa knew that her mind had been focused on other things lately and that sort of thing could happen. The last time an unplanned meeting was called occurred because of a controversial article submitted by a freelance writer named Trent Darwin. The feature story was about little Tammy Holliston, a homeless six year old with AIDS. The story was gripping and the magazine received tons of mail including checks from people who wanted to help the Holliston family's plight.

However, after much investigation, it turned out neither Tammy nor the Holliston family could be found. The shelter's referenced in the articles turned out to be abandoned buildings. Later, while under much pressure, Darwin admitted that the story had been fabricated. Apparently, he was experiencing writer's block and had created Tammy in a desperate attempt to finance his $500-a-week crack habit.

Alexa shuddered when she recalled the bad press the magazine and Marks-St. Claire had received. Since the incident, she made it a point to thoroughly check all credits before accepting a story.

The ride up the ten flights to the executive floor was a breeze. Before Alexa knew it, she was approaching the executive receptionist, Ramona Tinsley, an older jovial woman who reminded her of Mrs. Claus with a bushel of white hair tied back in a bun.

"Good afternoon, Ramona," Alexa greeted.

The older woman raised a hand and mouthed "hello." She pointed to the headset notifying her that she was in the middle of a call.

Alexa nodded and continued past her until she came to Mrs. Holland's executive assistant Cheryl. Cheryl was a young, very astute woman who took her job very seriously. Upon Alexa's approach, she plastered on a smile. "Mrs. Holland is waiting for you," she said almost invitingly, which only made Alexa uneasy. Cheryl was never that friendly towards anyone.

Alexa slipped through the partly open door to find Mrs. Holland seated at her small round table sipping tea and reading the morning newspaper. She knocked on the tall oak door, announcing her presence.

The older woman glanced up over the rim of her eyeglasses at the sound of Alexa's approach.

"Hello, Alexa dear. Come in and have a seat," she beckoned.

Alexa smiled and entered the room, taking the first available seat at the table. "Good afternoon, Mrs. Holland."

Bettye Holland's fair complexion and chiseled features put Alexa in the mind of Lena Horne. Her ageless beauty and sophisticated demeanor were the envy of her white female counterparts who longed to pull off the age game as successfully.

"How are you today?" she asked, refolding the paper.

"I am fine and you?"

"Great!" the older woman exclaimed.

Alexa could not help but feel a little uncomfortable with Mrs. Holland's sudden exuberance as she was used to seeing her more reserved.

The older woman removed her glasses and crossed her arms on the table before her. "I suppose you are wondering why I called this meeting."

Alexa nodded. "I admit I am curious. It's not often that I come here without an appointment."

Mrs. Holland chuckled and eased into a more comfortable position, crossing her legs and moving her folded hands to her lap. "No sense beating around the bush then. As you know the company has been doing very well these past few quarters. If you've been keeping up with our stock, you will see that it has steadily increased and split twice in the last year and a half. One of the company's future objectives was to expand our readership into emerging markets provided that we met our financial goals which we most definitely have."

She leaned forward as she prepared to deliver her pitch. "Based on some other sources in the industry, women of color are subscribing to mainstream magazines geared toward professional women at an increasing rate. They are making more money, more decisions and are more complex than the woman of the 80's. What we want to do is offer women of color between 25 and 45 a magazine that focuses on issues that are of a concern to the Millennium Woman."

Alexa's eyes widened, pleased with the direction that the company was trying to go, while wondering where she fit into the plan.

"The magazine will be launched out of our home office in New York and we need a young, committed, professional woman with fresh ideas to run it." With that she paused. "So what do you think about being Editor-in-Chief of your own magazine?"

Alexa gasped, totally astounded by what was proposed to her. Words could not come easy to her, as she was caught off guard and speechless. She brought one hand to her heart and held the edge of the table with the other as if to steady her self.

"So is this a yes or a no?" Mrs. Holland asked with a smile.

Alexa nodded emphatically. "Definitely, a yes!"

"Great! I'll inform Gregory and the Board that it's a go."

"Mrs. H," Alexa began, breathlessly. "I don't know what to say."

"You don't have to say anything, Alexa. You have already demonstrated your capability, as well as your dedication to the company. You are very intelligent, sharp and understand the direction this company wants to head in the new millennium. We believe in rewarding and advancing those who excel in their positions."

If Alexa didn't know it would be considered unprofessional to give her boss a hug in such celebrated situations, she would have. Instead, she thanked her with a firm handshake. She exited with a smile as big as Christmas on her face.

As Alexa stepped onto the empty elevator Mrs. Holland's words struck her. She considered it a blessing from God that she ended up working under her tutelage. Bettye Holland started out as a part-time receptionist with the company and worked her way up to Executive Editor and Vice President.

It was Mrs. Holland who prompted her on how to conduct herself in business meetings with the predominantly white male board. When Alexa wanted to skip the company picnics and Christmas parties like many of the black employees who preferred more of an atmosphere that reflected their culture, Mrs. Holland discouraged her. She taught her how to network and when to do it. So Alexa took up golfing and any other activity that would place her side by side with the corporate big shots. Over time, Alexa appreciated her attentiveness, especially now.

Once she got into her office, the first person she phoned was Teressa. She explained the new developments, ending with Mrs. Holland's kind words.

Teressa shrieked. "Congratulations!"

"Thank you," Alexa replied.

"Now how are you going to break the news to Darius?" Teressa added. "You're married now and have to consider him."

"I know," Alex replied again. This time Darius' name radiated through her head. How would he take her accepting a job that would take her away from him again? Would he be willing to forgo his business plans to move to New York? The excitement she felt moments before slowly melted into a pool of trepidation.

"I better go Teressa. I have a lot of work to get to."

"Do you have lunch plans?" Teressa quickly asked before Alexa could hang up.

"Yeah, I have some calls to make," she hesitantly, replied.

"Well, good luck to ya girlfriend, whatever you decide."

As she hung up the telephone, Alexa immediately felt like going home. She didn't know what to do. Her head pounded like a bass drum and she felt a wave of nausea and prayed the feeling would go away.

What would Darius say? Would he be happy for her? Or, would he look at this, as another attempt of Marks-St. Claire to shape her future without him. The last thing she wanted was for him to put up another wall of defense. She didn't want to lose him again. Yet at the same time, she didn't want to lose such a wonderful opportunity that could change her career as well as her life—their lives. Closing her eyes, Alexa lay her head down on her desk. She was caught between a serious rock and a hard place and she had nowhere to run.

CHAPTER 17

Darius spotted Reg sitting in a booth by the window of the End Zone, their favorite sports bar and eatery. Whenever they wanted to kick it and watch a big game after work, they would swing by the place for a platter of 'Da Bomb' hot wings, dinner fries, and beer.

Because of their busy schedules, the two had been trying to catch a game together every chance they could get. On this particular night, Darius was rooting for the Detroit Pistons while Reg favored the New York Knicks.

"What's up Midget," he called out to the waitress as he entered the building.

"Hi, Darius," the woman returned with a smile. Midget got her nickname from the regulars because of her petite size. Melina Fuentes or Midget, as, she was known by the folks at the End Zone, was a fiery blend of African and Cuban ancestry. Her short stature didn't fool those that knew her, especially Darius and Reg who had experienced her hot-tempered impatience and somehow lived to tell about it.

Reg glanced up from his play sheet at the sound of Darius' name. "What's up, playa!" he shouted out from across the room.

Darius waved and shouted hello to several of the regulars before addressing Reg. He was glad that he took his casual gear with him to work. He changed into his Piston's gear before leaving the office to show support for his team. The Piston's emblem was printed boldly across the front of his Grant Hill Jersey. Reg, who hadn't changed from his work clothing, wore a Knicks sweatshirt over his dress shirt.

"The Piston's bro and you know it!" Darius laughed, taking his seat. The two slapped each other's hand.

"Yo, we will see about that!" Reg retorted, as he returned to his playing sheet.

Darius removed his own play sheet from his jacket pocket. He had highlighted every team he thought would eliminate its opposition. At the very end, he had Detroit coming out on top. So far, he wasn't doing too badly.

"What y'all having fellas?" Midget greeted them, "The usual?"

"You know it," Reg replied.

She took their orders and returned with a pitcher of beer and two mugs.

"So, are you going to try and check out some games before the season ends?" Reg asked. "You know William can get us some seats a couple rows behind Spike."

"Well, you know my company has center court seats as well," Darius teased, trying not to be out done.

"Yeah, right. Seriously, William says he can get a pair of tickets for the game on the 1st."

"That won't work," Darius replied as he took a swig of his beer.

"What's up?"

"I'm meeting Alexa in Kansas City."

Reg shook his head with a laugh. "Man you are more whipped than I thought"

Darius immediately grew irritated by his friend's reactions. He was getting tired of his outward disapproval of their reunion. "What's up with that comment bro?"

"What comment?" Reg asked, not bothering to tone down his voice.

"Why do you keep coming down on Alexa?" Darius asked. "What has she done to you?"

"Bro, its more like what has she done to *you*?" Reg said with cynicism lining his voice. "I'm just looking out for you is all."

"Well, thanks, but no thanks," Darius interjected. "I can look out for myself. Besides, there is nothing to look out for."

Reg snorted. "Are you sure?"

"What is that crack supposed to mean?" Darius asked, narrowing his eyes. He was trying hard not to knock Reggie's head off, but his patience was wearing thin.

"I mean, I was the one who was there when you came back from Detroit and man you were tore up. You looked busted wearing them old jeans and shit barely taking showers. You lost so much weight you looked like you had AIDS or something."

"Screw you, man. I ain't tryin' to hear that." He remembered clearly how he stumbled around like a zombie for months thinking of nothing but the situation and how grateful he was when the clouds finally broke and the sunshine poured through. It was then that he realized that he could live with his past. Now that he was back with Alexa, he wanted to forget the past and concentrate on their future.

Reggie held up his hand and shook his head. "Nah, nah, you want to know why I feel the way I do. Like I was saying, I have never seen a man so strung out like you were over a female. Looking at you made me realize that I could wait a long time for Mrs. Right. You never told me more than the fact that you loved her and you didn't understand why she didn't accept your proposal, but that was enough for me. I care about you like a brother and I don't want to see you hurt again."

"It's all different now."

"Is it? How do you know if she won't up and go away again without a glance back at your feelings? Are you *that* sure about your relationship."

Darius nodded. "Very. I know what we have is strong, and from this point on if you can't come correct with your comments, then don't come at all," he added in a firm tone.

Reggie held up his hands as if absolving himself from the situation. "Cool."

Someone had turned up the volume on the 61-inch television as the players from both teams headed onto the court for tip off. Midget arrived at that moment with a steamy platter of hot wings and spicy fries. She laid the bill between the two of them. "Enjoy," she cooed before strolling away.

Darius squared up with Reg who appeared not to back down as well. He appreciated Reg for his insight and his faithfulness as a friend, but he didn't want him to try to come between him and Alexa. He loved her and if Reg couldn't accept that then too damn bad because one day soon he was going to make a decision that will change both of their lives.

Reg spoke up first as he dug into the wings. "Like I said, Knicks gonna whip that Piston ass!"

CHAPTER 18

"I'll talk to you later," Alexa called back to Tia Perez, her new Executive Editor of Radiance magazine.

It was a gray Wednesday afternoon and by now the word was out about Alexa's promotion. It was getting hard to keep smiling at the steady stream of well wishers, from Board members to the mailroom clerk.

The place was still buzzing about the launch of the new magazine and Alexa's promotion. She smiled as she recalled her mother's excitement upon hearing the news.

"I'm so proud of you, daughter. That Mrs. Holland must truly think highly of you. I knew no matter what if you maintained your focus you could achieve anything because you are so bright and intelligent."

Hearing such words of praise from her mother partially diminished her anxieties over taking the position. She held her chin high as she replayed her mother's words in her head while rounding the corner to her department.

"Hi Sharon," she greeted the receptionist as she entered her department. "Did I get any calls while I was out?"

Sharon smiled and nudged her head towards her office. "Maybe you should see for yourself."

Not quite understanding what she meant, Alex cautiously approached her office. Seated in one of the chairs holding a bouquet of yellow roses was Sean.

Her mouth dropped. "Sean, what are you doing here?" After their last encounter she couldn't believe that he would have the gall to come to her job.

Sean immediately stood up. "I came to apologize." He handed her the flowers. "Here these are for you. Yellow roses mean friendship. I hope that we can make amends, as friends of course."

Alexa stared between the roses and Sean's nervous smile and relinquished her anger. "You didn't have to."

"I know," he interjected. "I deserved that slap." He rubbed the spot where Alexa's hand landed more than a week ago, as if the stinging pain was still present. "What happened between us has really been on my mind, and I was hoping to get a chance to give you the explanation that you deserved."

"Forget it, Sean," she replied. "It's not necessary."

"Yes, it is," he insisted. Alexa noticed how he took a couple steps towards her then stepped back as to not offend her again by invading her personal space. "Can we go someplace where we can talk?"

Her first response was to say 'no' when she remembered Teressa's words concerning her last encounter with Sean. Their meeting could bring closure to the whole situation. She could also do as Teressa suggested by dropping Darius' name so that he'd know she was not spending her night agonizing the loss of their relationship.

"Sure." She placed the flowers in an empty vase that she found in her credenza and grabbed her things.

Alexa noticed Sharon's eyebrow rise as they passed her desk. She didn't want any office gossip floating around. "I'm going to a *business* lunch," she informed her. "I'll return in an hour."

As if on a timer, the elevator doors opened with a spot for the two of them. Without a word, they stepped on and rode to the parking garage where Sean's BMW was parked.

"Where would you like to go?" he asked as he disarmed the vehicle and opened her door.

She shrugged her shoulders. "It doesn't matter to me," she casually replied as she slipped inside.

Sean decided on a nearby cafe that wasn't quite as busy during the noon hour. The place was quiet. Most of the patrons were senior citizens out on their daily lunch excursion. They immediately found a secluded booth and placed their orders.

"So what's up?" she asked after the waitress departed.

"I thought about what you said and had to agree. The way I left things was wrong. I was a jerk for treating you the way I did and I am sorry."

"Hmm," she snorted. "That's putting it a little mildly."

An uneasy laugh escaped him. "I don't know what to say other than I wasn't ready for marriage."

"Then why did you ask me to marry you?" she charged. "I didn't twist your arm. Why did you have to go there with me?"

"Because it seemed like the right thing to do. We both were settled in our careers. We got the chance to do everything we wanted to do like travel and buy things we wanted. We lived comfortably. It seemed like the natural order of things."

It had never occurred to her that men planned their lives in the same manner as women. She assumed they simply went with the flow of things. If they were dating then they continued to date until they were either handed an ultimatum or another woman came along.

Sean continued. "You and I had been dating for a while. You were intelligent, sexy, and fun to be around. I loved you for who you were, but while you had it going on in every imaginable way, I was still empty inside."

Alexa nodded. "I understand, because after I got past all of the glitter and glamour of having a wedding, I realized the same thing. There was something missing for me too. Something that marrying you could not cure."

Sean leaned forward; his face lit up like a Christmas tree from her own confession. "Did you feel it? Did you feel that way too Alexa?"

She nodded. "It took me a while to see that I loved you too, but I wasn't in love with you because, my heart belonged to someone else. It always had."

Sean's mouth dropped opened. "What?" Apparently those were not the words he expected to hear.

Alexa immediately noticed his surprise and quickly cleared any mis-understanding. "Don't worry, it wasn't when you and I were together. It was way before us." She proceeded to unfold her history with Darius.

"Do you still love him?"

Alexa smiled with a look of love in her eyes that told Sean all he needed to know.

He reached inside his jacket pocket and pulled out a slip of paper and handed it to her. Alexa noticed that it was a signed blank check payable to her.

"What is this for?"

"My half of the cost for the wedding. It's the least I can do."

She placed the check on the table and pushed it back across the table to him. "I don't need it." She smiled with nothing but Darius in mind. "I have everything I need."

＊　　　　　　　＊　　　　　　　＊

Darius re-read the card attached to the tiny pitchfork tucked in the stem of roses. *"Give me another chance. Love, Sean."* He took a deep breath to maintain his composure. Who was this Sean and why in the hell was he sending flowers to his wife?

That old sinking feeling dared to re-enter the pit of his stomach, but he was determined not to go there. He wasn't about to go through that personal hell again. An old saying that his mother used to say came to mind. "If you're catching hell don't hold it. If you're going through hell don't stop!" As far as he was concerned, hell wasn't his destination in their relationship.

He claimed the nearest chair and leaned back, waiting for Alexa's return. Reg's words came to mind and he fought to keep them at bay. He didn't want to doubt her love for him or the new relationship that they had built.

Darius decided a walk was what he needed to clear his mind. He remembered passing a Coke machine in the lobby on his way upstairs. Maybe he could get one and chill before broaching the subject. He was about to leave the office when he heard Alexa returning.

"Did I get any calls?" he heard her ask the receptionist.

"You got something," the woman replied, nudging her head towards the door of Alexa's office.

"Oh really? What now?" Alexa asked, somewhat irritated by all of the surprises over the course of a few days.

At that moment, Darius stepped around the corner. "Me."

Alexa's eyes immediately lit up, and a smile spread easily across her face. "Darry!" she gasped and ran into his arms. Her eyes watered up as she pressed her face against his chest.

Darius wrapped her up protectively in his embrace. "Hey, lady," he murmured against her hair. He caught the surprised expression on the secretary's face and briefly wondered if her look had anything to do with the roses on Alexa's desk.

Alexa pulled back taking both of his hands into her own. "You tricked me. I thought I wouldn't see you for weeks."

Darius shrugged, staring into her face and momentarily forgot the roses because of her beautiful smile. "I managed to pull some strings here and there."

"How long are you going to be here?" she asked, cuddling back into his embrace.

"Only for two days. So, can you take the rest of the day off?"

She smiled slyly. "I'll see what I can do." So as not to be rude, she quickly introduced him to Sharon before leading him into her office. Once inside, she closed the door and fell against him smothering him with kisses.

"Whoa now," he teased as he took a seat in the chair, pulling her down on his lap.

"I'm sorry, I just missed you, baby" she replied with a soft sigh.

"Seems like you're not the only one full of apologies," he retorted, pointing to the bouquet of flowers.

Alexa rolled her eyes. "It's not what you think," she began. "I got those from an ex-fiancé."

"Your ex-fiancé?" he exclaimed, dropping his arms from around her waist. "I don't get it Alex."

"Then let me explain."

She proceeded to tell him about her relationship with Sean, including how he backed out of the wedding up to when she ran into him at the mall.

"I was upset with him for acting like everything was okay. He sent the flowers to apologize for being forward with me. I only agreed to go out to lunch with him so I could tell him that he need not contact me any further because I am involved with someone."

"And you think he accepted that?" he asked, disgruntled by the simplicity of her statement. He knew how men, particularly brothers were when it came to a taken women. They loved challenges. Trying to regain the affections of an old flame posed the best challenges especially when what they had was good. He ought to know, because the challenge was before him just a few months earlier.

In addition, he found it hard to believe that this brother who was about to marry his woman, would back away just because she said she had a man. As a young man, Darius remembered challenging a woman's faithfulness to her man by making a pass at her anyway just to see if he could accomplish something. Those days were long gone now as his energies were set on one woman. But there were still many men out there who provoked the challenge.

She nodded. "He told me to tell you that you are a lucky man," she repeated Sean's words.

Darius nodded in agreement. "Yes, I am."

"And I am one lucky woman," she added with a kiss.

The two got lost for a moment in a passionate kiss when Darius pulled back. He looked at his watch. "I have exactly 52 hours and I don't want to waste one damn minute."

Alexa laughed. "Aye, aye." She hopped off his lap and disappeared for a few minutes. When she returned, she quickly grabbed her coat and purse. "Ready when you are."

*   *   *

Darius brought a bowl of hot buttered popcorn into the living room while Alexa followed with two glasses of Pepsi. He sat the bowl on the coffee table and went upstairs to retrieve the stadium blanket Alexa told him he would find in the guest room closet. Just as he bounded up the stairs, the telephone rang.

Alexa placed the drinks down and answered on the second ring. "Hello?"

"I hope you aren't doing anything you shouldn't be doing." The caller said.

Alexa sat up from the sound of Maya's voice.

"Hey girl!" she exclaimed. "Long time no talk to."

"I know, what's up with you?"

"Nothing."

"Nothing my behind. I heard you and Darry are back together."

She hesitated, not knowing exactly all that Maya knew "Who told you that?"

"Bry, who else? He picked up on you two at the reception and confirmed with Darius a couple weeks ago that you two were trying to make it a go again."

"I'm sorry May," she began. "I intended to call and tell you, but time got away from me." Alexa wanted to tell her friend the real good news about them tying the knot, but declined, wanting the announcement to come from both of them at the right time.

"Yeah, I know how it is when things are going so well that you're bogged down enjoying the moment."

Alexa laughed at her friend's comment. "I guess you could say that."

"Are you happy?"

Alexa sighed dreamily. "Yes."

"Who would have known this would happen?" Maya asked out loud. "It was just four months ago that the two of you were at each other's throats. I knew when I got you two together sparks would fly."

"Whatever," Alexa moaned. Leave it to Maya to think she had something to do with everything involving the two of them.

"So have you told Darius the good news about your promotion?" Maya asked, referring to Alexa's promotion. Maya was one of the first to know.

"Not as yet," Alexa whispered, so Darius wouldn't overhear.

"Alex you have to tell him. You're supposed to be in New York by June and May is almost here."

"I know, I know," Alexa groaned. "Don't you think I know that? I'm just waiting for the right time."

"I think the right time is now," Maya shot back. "How are you going to try to rebuild a relationship based on secrets? You really need to approach this delicately. You both have experienced a great deal of pain from what happened in the past. You of all people, Alexa, should know the challenge you have before you with Darius."

Alexa knew that Maya was right. Had she known that they had gone against all advice and eloped, she would be devastated.

"I can only pray that you are taking things slow," Maya continued. "Trust me, when I tell you to hold off getting involved physically right now."

"Why do you say that?"

"Because when two people who have a past such as you and Darius get involved sexually, you are placing yourselves in a dangerous position. When you share yourself with someone, you are creating a soul tie. After being apart for so long and getting back together physically you're essentially taking on more baggage than what you left behind."

"Darius and I are adults Maya. I think we would be mature enough to leave the baggage in the past."

"But you thought you left your heart in the past too, now where did that get you?"

Alexa couldn't reply because Darius had returned to the room carrying two pillows and the large blanket she requested. He flung the blanket out in the air so that it floated down perfectly over her, then fluffed up one of the pillows and placed it behind her back.

"Thanks, baby." she whispered.

"Who you talking to?" he asked as he snuggled up beside her. He began licking playfully at her neck with his tongue.

"Maya," she whispered.

"Hi May!" Darius shouted, smiling mischievously in Alexa's face as he began to undo the buttons on her blouse.

"What's up Captain D?" Maya shouted back.

"Maya says hi."

Darius nodded and opened his mouth to reply when Alexa pressed her palm against his face. Darius poked out his lip in response making her smile.

"Well, I don't want to hold you two lovebirds up. If I know you and Darius like I know I do, I know you two are probably naked now."

Alexa laughed as she thought about some of their escapades. "Forget you."

Before hanging up, Maya made a heart felt plea that pulled at Alexa's conscience. "Please, hon, trust Darius and your love for one another enough to do the right thing. Don't do anything rash. Take your time and allow the healing process to begin." Alexa let Maya's words marinade in her mind. If there was one thing Maya knew about her was her fear of confronting people. The thought of telling Darius, made her so nervous that she felt faint.

"I will," she promised.

"I'm only saying this because I love you and I hope you know that."

"I know and I love you too," Alexa returned.

"Good, now call me if you need me."

Alexa placed the handset on the hook with a sigh.

"Are you sure that was Maya?" Darius asked with a strange look on his face.

"Yes that was Maya," Alexa said. "Who else could it be?"

"Sean." He flatly replied.

She immediately pushed Darius away with irritation and sat up. "I can't believe you said that."

"I know. I'm sorry," he quickly apologized. "I just can't believe that brother."

"I told you he didn't know about us baby. I had to tell him."

"I know." He pulled her into his arms again. "I just can't stand knowing that I am so far away from you when there are brothers here pushing up on you."

"Darius. I could say the same about you, but I don't."

He nodded slowly from her response. "I know. I trust you." He kissed her sweetly on the neck. "I'm just feeling a little out of it. I miss you like crazy. It's hard being married and not living with your wife, especially when I think about you practically every moment every day. Then there's my job. I am so ready to get out on my own that I can't stand going to work sometimes. Plus, I'm still trying to keep up with my responsibilities at the school. I just need there to be some stability in one area in my life." He took her hand into his. "We need to talk about what we are going to do."

His words did not come as a surprise. She knew that it was inevitable that decisions had to be made.

"You know, I'm glad I decided to come." Darius sighed with a squeeze of her hand. "You have this way of making me relax."

He reached up and traced her jaw line with his forefinger. "I love you," he whispered.

"I love you too," she returned.

*　　　*　　　*

Darius' visit was exactly what Alexa needed to get her through the week. The two spent most of the weekend in the house watching rented videos and eating take out. Darius wasn't up for sight seeing or a night out on the town. All he wanted to do was sit around her place, relax and enjoy his wife.

"Do you ever feel guilty?" Alexa sultrily asked one evening as the two were curled up on the sofa. Alexa, who was pulling up the rear, pressed her face against the baby soft skin of Darius' bare back. She kissed him tenderly, loving the feel of his flesh against her mouth. Her arm was possessively draped around his hip.

"About what?" Darius asked as he turned onto his back, giving her full access to him.

"About lying to our family and friends."

"We aren't lying," he replied.

"The only reason why you say that is because nobody suspects anything, so you don't have to make something up."

He laughed lightly, knowing full well she was telling the truth.

"If you want to know the truth, I'm not ready to share you with the world yet. Call me selfish if you want, but I'm not eager to deal with the questions or comments." He rolled onto his side and propped his bearded chin in his palm. "I want to give us the chance we missed nine years ago. I want you to feel good about me being your husband and you being my wife. I know that the distance makes it hard, but when we are together, it's like the first time all over again. You make me want to love you harder and all I want to focus on is doing just that."

Tears welled in Alexa's eyes from his touching confession. She wanted the same, more than anything else as well. Leaning over, she planted a sweet, love filled kiss on his mouth. For the first time, the anxiety that she had felt days before slowly evaporated as her whole being blossomed like a flower ready to receive love.

Alexa promised that she would make their trip to Kansas City worthwhile. She had just received a package from the Visitor's Bureau in the mail and had made a mental note to preview the contents at lunchtime.

Once they were together, on fair territory, she would bring up the announcement about her new job. In fact, maybe moving to New York could be an answer to their prayers as far as the new business was concerned. Not only would it provide them with a fresh start, but it would also eliminate argument over their future living arrangements.

All Darius had to do was discuss the possibility with Bryant. It would be exciting starting their new lives together in a new city. She had to come up with a plan to sell New York City to him and present the idea to him the right way. Reaching into her desk drawer, Alexa removed a note pad. She drew a line down the center of the page and wrote pros on one side and cons on the other.

In the business she was in, she always found it beneficial to weigh the possibilities of a project before taking it on. Under the word pros, her hand lit across the page in fervor. After acquiring a good number of points, she turned to the opposing side. It was as if reflecting on the negative. Sometimes one negative point could be so detrimental that it could outweigh all positive potential. She closed her eyes and said a silent prayer that Darius would understand.

CHAPTER 19

Alexa had been so engrossed in her work that by the time she stopped to take a break, it was lunchtime. The office was quiet as most of the employees were out on lunch or at meetings with clients. Hunger pangs confirmed that it was time to eat. A hot pastrami and Swiss sandwich from Pizzazz's Deli down the street sounded appetizing. She grabbed her coat and was about to transfer her calls to her voice mail when the telephone rang.

With a sigh she picked it up. "Thank you for calling Marks-St. Claire, this is Alexa."

"Hey Alexa, this is Crystal." Alexa recognized the familiar southern drawl right away.

"Hi, Crystal!" she greeted cheerfully. "How are you?"

"I'm fine and you?"

"Good."

"I was just calling to say that I'll be in Denver in exactly two hours. I wanted to know if you want to get together."

"Sure. Just give me your flight information and I'll meet you at the airport."

Crystal recited the information while Alexa scribbled it down on a notepad.

"I'll just leave from here and meet you at your gate. So how long are you here for?"

"Until tomorrow morning," Crystal replied.

"Then you have to stay with me," Alexa insisted.

"I don't want to intrude.

"Girl, please. I won't take no for an answer. I have plenty of room. Plus, it would be nice having some company."

"Are you sure?" Crystal asked.

"Yes!" Alexa exclaimed with a smile. It would be nice to have another human voice around. The place was lonely without Darius' presence.

"Thanks, Alexa."

"No problem. I'll see you at 3:30."

Alexa smiled as she hung up the telephone. Crystal was a really, nice person. She had good vibes about her the moment they met. Crystal must have felt the same or she was sure she wouldn't be calling.

The remaining two hours went by fast. Before Alexa knew it, she was at the airport waiting for Crystal to exit the jet way. Crystal was one of the four flight attendants exiting the plane with their Pullman's in tow.

"See ya!" she called out to the others as she spotted Alexa.

"Hey, girlfriend!" Crystal cried. She looked professional in her tailored navy blue dress, the company's uniform, and a colorful red and gold scarf tied around her neck.

The two exchanged hugs.

"My feet are killing me," she groaned. "I had three flights already this morning. Thank goodness I have the next few days off after tomorrow morning's flight."

Later the two settled down before a take out dinner of chicken Florentine, garlic toast, and salad from Camille's, one of Alexa's favorite restaurants in her neighborhood.

"Do you like your line of work?" Alexa asked.

Crystal took a sip of water and nodded, "Yes, I love it. It will be hard getting used to not traveling so much once Reg and I get married, which is why I'm trying to visit all of the places I can. I know I am going to have to settle down once that happens because family is more important to me than my career."

Alexa toyed with the idea of bringing up her promotion, but Crystal's strong comment regarding family made her think twice about it. She wanted to get a feel for the situation through someone's eyes that saw Darius on a regular basis.

"Can't you work part-time rather than totally give up your career?" Alexa asked trying to fit her situation into the conversation.

Crystal shook her head adamantly. "I'll just have to find a new line of work."

"Why if you love it so much?" She couldn't understand why Crystal should have to sacrifice her passion in order to be with the man she loved. It sounded so one-sided, so conditional.

"Because Reg wouldn't have it any other way. We've discussed what we want for our family, especially when we have children. He told me that he never wants us to spend a night away from one another unless it was absolutely necessary. He even wants us to eat dinner together every night. With my job that would be impossible. I understand where he's coming from though. Both of my parents were home for breakfast in the morning and dinner at night."

She sighed, thoughtfully. "And because I come from a long line of traditional, southern black women who regardless of their education or careers they had before they met their husbands, they set it all aside to take care of home once they got married."

"Does that bother you?" Alexa asked. She couldn't understand that way of thinking. "I mean just giving up your career like that to be a house wife?"

Crystal nodded sadly. "Part of it does, but I know its something I have to do. All of the marriages in my family are successful because of the tone the women set."

Crystal's last words reverberated in Alexa's head. It was hard for her to come up with such a cut and dry resolution for their situation. On the one hand, she loved Darius and having him back into her life. But on the other, she had put in some time with Marks-St. Claire and felt obligated to fulfill her position to the fullest.

"So, what's with all the questions?" Crystal asked. "Are you thinking about leaving your job?"

Alexa shook her head. "Actually, it's just the opposite." She proceeded to fill Crystal in on her promotion followed by Mrs. Holland's glowing evaluation of her.

"You go girl!" Crystal shouted, enthusiastically. She reached up for a high-five.

"Thank you, thank you," Alexa replied, taking a bow from side to side. "I am so excited."

"You should be. Being the Editor-in-Chief of your own magazine ain't small time. Go on head sista in charge!" Crystal teased.

"That's right," Alexa echoed her comment. She couldn't believe how at ease she felt with Crystal.

The rest of the evening was spent talking about the things to do and places to see in the Big Apple. Because of her occupation, Crystal had been to New York many times, even had friends there. She suggested that Alexa look them up the minute she got settled as they were good people. As she had imagined, Crystal was turning out to be a good friend.

CHAPTER 20

"All in favor for hiring John Sears as Athletic Director say aye," Albright Givens put to question.

"Aye." The vote was unanimous.

"All those who oppose, say nay."

Not a single person voted against the promotion.

"Great, we will induct Mr. Sears into his new position on Monday. Now is there any old business to discuss?" the older man asked as he peered over his wire-framed glasses.

One of the board members, Harold Prater, brought up the status of the CAT testing preparation, which Reg was able to effectively address. When no more concerns were brought to the table, Albright called for a motion to adjourn. Darius accepted and another second it.

As people stood to leave for the evening, Darius quickly gathered his things. His flight was scheduled to leave in exactly one hour. Reg sided up beside him as he stuffed his papers into his attaché.

"You going to Denver again?" he asked, rocking back and forth on his heels.

"No, I have to go up to Detroit. Bryant and I have to meet with the bank."

"You are really pressing forward with this, huh?"

Darius nodded. "Yes. You know that I've always wanted my own."

The two men departed the room after final calls of goodbye. Once in the hallway, Reg resumed their conversation.

"I do not doubt your business dreams," Reg stated. "I was just wondering what your intentions are."

"Meaning will I leave the school in an upheaval?" Darius asked with a sidelong glance. "The answer is no. I will handle things right. Don't sweat it."

"So, what are your plans for your business?" Reg asked as they exited the building.

Although he was his friend and knew that he could trust him completely, Darius wasn't sure if he liked discussing his plans before they were enacted. He and Bryant had tied up the final touches on their business plans recommended by their attorney. The purpose of this trip was to complete the final paperwork and get started on putting their plan into action. After careful consideration and upon the advice of their attorney, the two had dismissed the thought of setting up a second office in Ohio. They came to a conclusion that they should concentrate all efforts on a home office in Detroit before, branching out to other locations. Besides, Darius in turn wanted to discuss with Alexa about her making their home in Michigan again where their love first began. The two were finally going to reveal their secret, put an end to the long distance, address their life plans and tell the world about their union. He was sure that she would be ecstatic about being near Maya again.

"We are meeting to discuss that. But trust me, when I return, you will be the first to know where I stand."

Reg smiled and patted him on the back. "So, do you need a lift to the airport?"

Darius has planned on calling a cab, but jumped on the chance to save his money. "Yeah, I'd appreciate that."

As they approached Reg's Mercedes Coup, Darius couldn't help but notice how immaculate the car was, mirroring its owner in cleanliness and class. Reg disarmed the alarm allowing Darius access to the trunk where he placed his bag.

At Last!

After slamming the trunk shut, Darius got inside the passenger side. The car's innards were equally spotless on the inside with a hint of cherry scent. Darius smiled, as he couldn't imagine his friend using any kind of artificial scent enhancers. He thought Reg seemed more like the type who'd prefer to preserve the new leather smell.

"You know when you and Crys get married, you're going to have to give this baby up don't you?" Darius announced smoothing his hand across the glistening dashboard.

"Bullshit!" Reg quickly replied, slamming his door. He started up the engine and let it roar denoting its power.

Darius laughed, "Man, you know you're going to have to make room for them 2.5 kids and that dog Crys wants."

Reg grunted as he turned onto the expressway, shifting gears smoothly. "Yeah, well we'll cross that bridge when we get there."

"So how long are you two going to wait to have them little rug rats?"

Reg shrugged. "I don't know, man maybe two or three years."

"Damn, why are you waiting so long? Crystal is already thirty. You don't want to be going gray at the same time she has junior," Darius teased.

"First of all, the men in my family lose all of their hair before gray even sets in. Secondly, Crystal wants it that way, and third there won't be any Reginald Capehart Thornton Jr. if I have my say."

Darius burst out laughing. "Capehart? Bro I never knew that was your middle name." His laughter filled the car. "I can't say I blame you on that one, though. But seriously, you need to go on and get them babies out the way. You know you're getting old."

"Hey, at least I *am* getting married. I have a lot up on you, brother. And with Alexa's company transferring her to New York, your plans will have to be reassessed. So if anybody needs to step up their game it would be you."

The smile on Darius' face faded as he processed Reggie's words. The words Alexa and New York rang loudly in his head. A more sober

Darius turned to his friend for clarification. "What the hell you talking about, Reg?"

Reggie stopped rambling and averted his attention from the road with an utter look of surprise. "Tell me you knew that!"

"Knew what? What are you talking about Reggie?" Darius repeated calmly. He didn't want to go off on him like some mad man, but he could feel the potential rage rising from deep within.

Reggie sat there with his mouth wide open in disbelief.

Darius was getting more irritated by the second. "Dammit Reggie, what's up?"

"I hate to be the bearer of bad news, but your girl is about to move to New York."

Darius laughed uncomfortably, repeating his earlier question. "What you talking about man?" The heat rising in his collar made him feel like he was sinking in a pool of hot lava.

Reggie proceeded to fill him in on Crystal's visit to Denver and the conversation that she and Alexa shared. "According to Crys, your girl was offered a big time promotion with her company and is moving to New York sometime late May or early June."

"Yo, I don't believe that. We're supposed to be meeting in Kansas City next weekend. I just spoke to her on the telephone last night and she didn't mention anything about a promotion."

"You said she planned this trip right?"

Darius nodded.

"Maybe she was going to tell you then. Sort of like a Dear John face-to-face," Reggie offered.

Darius laughed sarcastically to keep from showing his disappointment. No, she didn't do it again, he said to himself. After what that they had been through, she was about to leave again! Darius couldn't believe this. He opened his heart and allowed himself to love her again. Hell, he even married her. What more did she want from him?

"Man, I'm sorry I have to be the one to tell you," Reggie announced. He sounded pretty sincere. Darius was grateful that despite the situation, he refrained from bad mouthing Alexa.

"Me, too." He coldly replied. He turned his focus onto the roadside. The muscles in his jaw twitched as he struggled to control the anguish within.

The two rode in total silence for the remainder of the drive. Darius was relieved when Reggie stopped the car in front of the airport entrance. The airport was more crowded than either of them would have anticipated for the evening. People milled in and out of the sliding glass doors as if it were high noon.

Darius opened the door.

"Are you going to be okay?" Reggie asked, pressing the trunk release button.

Darius avoided his friend's face and nodded. "I'll be fine." He got out retrieving his bag from the back. Stepping around to the driver's side, he shook Reggie's hand. "Thanks for the ride. I appreciate it."

"No problem," Reg replied. "And D, take it easy okay."

Darius nodded and called goodbye before disappearing into the crowd.

The flight was crowded. Darius was glad that he made reservations early enough to get a seat close to the front. He shoved his overnight bag into the compartment above and took his seat by the window. He felt like a brick had hit him. The pain throbbed at his temples and he closed his eyes, hoping the nagging feeling would go away. Yet, all he could see was Alexa smiling at him with those incredible hazel-brown eyes and sweet dimples. He tried to blink a few times to erase her image, but was unsuccessful.

"Damn!" he muttered to himself. How could she do this to me again! He didn't know what to think or how to feel as the mixed emotions fought to posses him. Pain, anger, sadness, fear, loathing all surrounding him like a billowing cloud, making him extremely down at one moment and up in a rage the next. Finally, the glare on his face melted into a sad frown and he leaned back into his seat.

"Are you going to be okay?" a voice close to him asked.

He opened his eyes to find an attractive flight attendant standing over him. She had hazel eyes like Alexa's and dimples when she smiled. "Excuse me?" he asked as he realized it wasn't her.

"I asked if you are going to be okay," she sweetly replied with a concerned expression. "You look ill."

I feel ill. "I have a slight headache. Do you have an aspirin or something?"

"I'm sorry sir, it's against company policy to distribute pharmaceuticals," she replied empathetically. "However, I can get you a pillow and a glass of water."

Darius nodded. Five minutes later, she returned with a glass of water and a pillow. She propped the pillow up against the window for him.

"Thank you," he murmured as he eased his head against it.

A sympathetic passenger overheard his request and passed over a bottle of ibuprofen. Darius shook two of the extra strength tablets into his palm and popped them into his mouth followed by the glass of water. He wished he were in first class so that he could order something hard to drink to numb the pain he was feeling. Once the plane took off, and had reached proper altitude, he unbuckled his belt and reclined back in his seat, closing his eyes determined to sleep the pain away.

*　　　　　*　　　　　*

Darius found himself asking Leon Jefferson, the attorney, to repeat his words several times throughout the meeting. No matter how hard he tried, he couldn't shake his conversation with Reggie. Because he knew he could not behave rationally, he avoided calling Alexa as he had promised. Instead, he went to bed trying to keep his focus on the purpose of his trip.

If he didn't look out for his future, no one would. As it stood, the new business was all he had. On the outside, he was doing a good job of hiding his feelings but he was a wreck inside.

Many times, he played scenario after scenario in his mind on how he would treat the situation. He thought about how he would respond to her, down to the careful words he would choose. He knew Reg was right and he was wrong for jumping into their relationship with his nose wide open. Hell, it was beyond a simple relationship, they were married. Although things may not have been handled the conventional way, they made vows.

He had to believe that she wouldn't allow anything to come between their love again. When he asked Alexa to marry him, he prayed that her love for him was strong enough that she could walk away from everything including Marks-St. Claire, who had met her needs for so long just to be with him. He knew it would be a stretch for her, but he needed her to place him first by transferring her trust from the company to him.

Knowing that she was incapable of doing this, made him very resentful and he grew increasingly disgusted with himself for not listening to Bryant's and Reggie's wise counsel by rushing things. Additionally, he failed to listen to her concerns about the relationship early on. He was so happy to have her back that he didn't want to deal with anything that would question their love for each other. All he wanted to do was relish in the fact that he had won her back into his life.

"Darius. Darius."

He came back to the present at the sound of his name being called. "You okay, man?" Bryant asked with a look of concern.

"We can wrap things up until tomorrow," Leon suggested with a worried expression.

"Yeah, uh, good, that sounds like a good idea," he stammered. "I am feeling a little under the weather."

"No problem," Leon replied, gathering his things. "I know how it is when you have a lot on your plate and you're moving full speed ahead."

"Yeah, right," Darius replied as he stacked his papers and placed them inside his brief case.

Darius and Bryant agreed to meet with Leon the next day following church. On their way to the truck, Darius heard Bryant exhale loudly in annoyance.

"What's wrong?" Darius asked, although he had some idea. He opened the passenger door and climbed inside.

"You," Bryant bluntly replied.

"What do you mean?" Darius asked, pretending as if he didn't know. He knew that it was obvious that he wasn't focused on the meeting.

"Do you want this or not?" Bryant shouted angrily as he slammed his door.

Darius whirled around to face his cousin. "Why do you say that?"

"I'm talking about you not paying attention in our meetings, canceling meetings. Basically acting like we aren't in this together. Like Leon said, you have a lot on your plate and you need to decipher what is more important. We have been talking about starting our own business for years. Now that we're getting closer to seeing our dreams realized, you want to start trippin'. This is something that I want to do. Something I intend to do whether you want to do it or not."

"I want to do it too B, it's just that I had a setback."

"Setback? What setback?" he asked without masking his irritation.

"It's nothing. Nothing at all," Darius replied not wanting to give details. "You're right. I have been screwing up. I need to prioritize my projects. I have my personal life, the school, my job, and our business all screaming for a piece of me. I'll just have to let something go."

Bryant's tone softened after Darius' outburst. "I'm sorry if I'm coming down hard, but this is very important. We are at a critical stage that can either make us or break us. We family and all, but my wife and kids are my priority!"

Darius nodded slowly because he knew exactly what he had to do. Something had to give in his life.

*   *   *

It was a sleepless night. Alexa had tossed and turned, waiting for Darius' to call to no avail. He promised to call her once he made it to Detroit. Each night, she laid in her bed, wide awake until the wee hours of the morning, hoping to hear the telephone ring. On Monday morning, she paid for it.

She had an open schedule all morning. In anticipation of a trip to New York to check out the office space, she had managed to clear away the last minute miscellaneous items on certain projects as well as forward those that did not require much work to a consultant who could fit it into her schedule. She decided it would be a good time to review the Kansas City tapes in preparation for their weekend excursion.

Alexa took the videotape, along with the information packet, and a mug of coffee into the executive conference room. The room was perfect for reviewing the video because it eliminated any interruptions because of its location away from all of the executive offices. The room was dark as Alexa entered. She quickly headed over to the tall windows and pulled back the black out curtains, letting the sun shine in. The VCR and television were located in the mahogany armoire.

After powering up everything, Alexa slipped the videotape into the VCR and eased back in one of the plush, high-back chairs just as the bars of the tune *Kansas City*, poured from the television speakers. The video opened with a beautiful sunrise stretching across the horizon of the Missouri River. The scene transitioned into an aerial shot scanning the downtown skyscrapers of Kansas City, swiftly moving frames from night to day.

"Wake up to Kansas City where the east meets the west," the narrator announced.

The video touched on the concept of the old west with images of Jesse James and other old West outlaws and heroes to the open-air markets where vendors peddled their wares, to the widely recognized summer jazz festivals and the alluring casinos occupying the night life.

Alexa flipped through the full color booklet, which illustrated the amenities of the different hotels, motels, and bed and breakfast inns. There were also descriptions of restaurants, nightclubs and theater attractions. She found the perfect little bed and breakfast located in historic part of the city surrounded by quaint restaurants and vintage shops. According to the brochure, one could *"lounge in the comforts of the fully equipped room complete with hot tub or follow the stone path of the tranquil garden perfect for meditation. If you're in the mood for more, just step outside and catch a romantic carriage ride around downtown. The shopkeepers of the quaint shops on the Plaza invite you to take a little bit of our City home with you. There are many keepsakes as well as Kansas City memorabilia for you to choose from to remember the Show Me State by."*

Alexa was sold by the time she finished reading the brochure and previewing the video. When she returned to her office, she got on the phone and made reservations. To her delight, *Bring in Da Noise* was showing that same weekend, so she quickly reserved two tickets. The next stage of her plans involved the Victoria's Secret catalogs inside her attaché. Over the weekend she had thumbed through the catalogs and folded back the pages, which displayed several sexy pieces to add to her boudoir. She was sure that each item would knock Darius off his feet.

Once she had called in her orders, she placed all items in the top desk drawer and directed her attention on delegating a stack of articles to the two interns who worked in her office. After about an hour of solid focus on the work at hand, the telephone rang. Her heart jumped thinking it was Darius calling to apologize for not calling as promised. She quickly picked up the receiver on the first ring.

"This is Alexa."

"Alexa this is Teressa. I was wondering if you could run an errand with me over the lunch hour."

Alexa's hopes deflated and she sank back into her seat, disappointed that it was not Darius. "Sure."

"Are you okay?" Teressa asked. "If you're busy, you don't have to go"

"No, no," Alexa interrupted. "I'm fine. I just thought you might be Darius. I haven't heard from him in days."

"Maybe he's busy," Teressa offered.

"Maybe so," Alexa resolved. "I sent him this custom made invitation. It was really cute with real lace and satin."

"Where did you get that?"

"Bernie in the Design department makes them on the side."

"I didn't know Bernie designed cards. I'm going to have to get with her to come up with some ideas for my invitations."

Alexa was too busy thinking about Darius to think about invitations. "I mailed it on Monday. I hope he gets it before this weekend. You know we're supposed to meet in KC."

"He will. It doesn't take mail longer than 2 days to get from Denver to Ohio. I should know because that's where I send my Visa payment and they always cash that puppy two days later."

"So, what kind of errand do you have to run?" Alexa asked, changing the subject. She didn't want to think about Darius all day. She knew his trip was going to set him back but he promised he would make it to Kansas City. She just hoped that everything was okay.

"I have to run by the bakery and taste some samples for the cake and I knew I better ask you to come or else I'd hear it all week."

"You're right!" Alexa teased. "I'll meet you in the parking garage."

She was about to hang up the phone when she decided to make another call to Darius' office. The telephone rang twice before the receptionist answered.

"I'm sorry. Mr. Riverside is out in the field. Can I leave a message for him?" the nasally-voiced woman asked.

"No, no message," Alexa replied. She had called so several times and knew the woman probably suspected that she was the repeat caller. She sighed as she returned the telephone's receiver to its base. She would just have to wait to see him in Kansas City.

*   *   *

Alexa had really outdone herself, Darius thought as he parked his rental car in front of the Sunrise Bed & Breakfast. Located on five-acre stretch of land, the inn was an intricately designed Victorian structure with a full wrap around porch complete with swing. Though the flowers had not made their grand appearance, he could tell that in full bloom they were probably a magnificent sight judging by the detailed landscaping. He took his garment bag off the seat and headed up the stone walk and rang the doorbell.

An older woman dressed gaily in a colorful muumuu with a matching scarf knotted on the side of her head and holding a miniature Maltese met them at the door. She introduced herself as Ms. Audrey Elmore, the owner of the establishment.

"Good morning, Mr. Riverside. I'm glad you could make it," she greeted in a thick island accent. She stepped aside to allow Darius to enter.

The décor on the inside of the house was an eclectic mix of B. Smith meets the Caribbean. Immediately to the left of the entrance was a picturesque sitting room dressed up beautifully in bright colors of teal, orange, fuchsia and gold. Three white sofas draped with colorful throws were strategically placed in a u-shape before a decorative marble fireplace where a fired roared to life. A wide iron framed coffee table held an assortment of hard bound picture books and a beautiful arrangement of exotic flowers. Above the mantel was a huge ornate framed mirror. There were oil paintings depicting island life hanging on the walls along with a beautiful baby grand piano. The room was definitely inviting.

She caught Darius' awed expression. "The sitting room is open to all guests at all times. Feel free to come down whenever you like. We have coffee and fresh rolls on the buffet every morning." She led him upstairs to their room at the end of the hall.

"You'll have lots of privacy back here," she announced with a knowing twinkle in her eye.

Darius wished he could share in her joke but felt the privacy would come in handy when he handled his business. Ms. Elmore entered before him and proceeded to open the curtains to give him a full view of the room. The vivid colors used in decorating immediately caught his attention. The colors gave him the feeling of being somewhere other than Kansas City. The king-sized bed was draped in a bright green, yellow and orange comforter with a delicate eyelet trim. Several colorful throw pillows of different shapes were stacked neatly against the headboard. The room also contained an armoire with television, an antique roll top desk and a small sofa. There was a small dinette set placed in an intimate alcove with a large floor to ceiling bay window overlooking the garden below. Alexa had really outdone herself when she selected this locale, he thought to himself.

He sighed. He hated for such a beautiful place to go to waste, but this trip would not be ending on a positive note.

"Breakfast is at 7:30 in the morning," Ms. Elmore announced as she breezed past. "You can have it sent up to you if you wish. Just let me know the night before."

"Thank you," he replied. He placed his bag on the floor near the door.

"Enjoy," the older woman sang as she exited the room.

Walking over to the window, he stared out, without really seeing. Not wanting to sit around and wait for what was to come; Darius grabbed the keys to his car and decided to take in Kansas City. He needed to get his mind off of Alexa.

∗ ∗ ∗

An hour after Alexa's arrival, Darius returned. The knowing smile on Ms. Elmore's face told him that she had checked in and was upstairs awaiting his arrival. Darius' heart raced as he headed up the stairs towards the end of their beginning. He took a deep breath as he produced the room key from his jacket pocket and unlocked the door.

With the exception of the evening glow from the sun peeking through the sheer curtains in the alcove, the room was pretty dark. Darius tossed his keys on the dresser and started toward the bathroom when he noticed Alexa's silhouette lying on the bed.

Alexa tried to stay awake, but fell asleep shortly after making herself comfortable. Darius looked down at her. She really looked like an angel sleeping there with her hair fanned around her head. He almost didn't want to disturb her, but he had to do what he had to do. He reached out and gently shook her on her shoulder. Her bare skin was so soft. Slowly turning down the covers, he sucked in his breath when he realized she was nude underneath. Knowing this aroused him and he considered abandoning the breakup for one last intimate encounter, but his principles won out.

"Alex," he called out her name in a firm tone.

She stirred awake, yawning and stretching before opening her eyes. "Darry?"

"Yes, it's me," he thickly replied.

She immediately sat up, allowing the sheets to fall from her body, exposing her full bare bosom. "Hi, baby!" she cooed and rose up on her knees to give him a hug.

Alexa's soft body coupled by her feminine scent almost weakened him. He kissed her on the cheek. "Hey." He stiffly replied. Alexa immediately sensed something was wrong and she sat back down on the bed. "I'm sorry for falling asleep. I was exhausted from my flight."

"It's okay," he assured her while trying not to be stirred by her mere presence.

She stepped off of the bed with her outstretched arms. "Welcome to Kansas City," she purred as she stepped to him, slipping her arms around his waist. She perched up on her tiptoes and planted a soft, passion-filled kiss on his mouth. Darius, although succumbing to her physically, turned his head away.

"What's wrong?" she asked with concern in her voice. Her question unnerved him. Something had been wrong all along and she didn't ask him then.

"Maybe I should be asking you that question," he shot back.

"Why?"

Darius looked into Alexa's eyes. There were no signs of remorse. It was as if she either did not know or did not care. He shuddered at the last thought.

"I heard some disturbing news last week," he began, pacing the floor. "What I heard involved us and I want to, need to clear things up for good today."

The tone of his voice signaled to Alexa that what he was discussing was serious and she reached for her robe.

Darius' glanced up into her eyes for they told all. He wanted a straight answer and he wanted one today. "I heard that your job is transferring you to New York. Now when I heard this, I was thinking, I know after all we've been through, Alexa wouldn't accept a job without even consulting her husband. I would just like to know if this is true. Tell me that its not."

Darius' gentle plea made her shoulders slump with guilt. Judging by her response, he knew that Reggie's words were true. He needed to know for himself.

He also wanted to hear her claim it verbally. "So, is it a lie?"

Alexa's mouth moved, but no words came out.

"Alexa?" he called out her name sternly.

"It's true," she finally whispered, lowering her head in defeat.

"Damn," he cursed under his breath, turning away from her. A barrage of emotions attacked him like bees to honey. Tears clouded his eyes, but he was not going to give her the satisfaction. Not this time.

Alexa ran to him immediately and touched her hands to his chest. "But baby, let me explain."

"Explain what Alex? I don't know what kind of game you're trying to play, but this time you won't win!" he shouted angrily, flinging her hands away from him. He stomped across the room only to turn around and rush back. "I am so damn sick of coming in second place to your job. You act like Mark's-St. Claire is your entire world!"

"Darius, no, don't do this," she pleaded, tears pooling in her eyes.

"What was this all about?" he asked, surveying the room with a sweep of his arm. "Was this an attempt to appease me? Am I worth anything to you?" Each of his words cut her like a knife. "What were you planning on doing? Seduce me silly like you did last time then get up in the middle of the night and disappear? Well guess what? I am foiling your plans. I will walk out of here with my dignity intact, which is much more than I can say for you!" Darius picked up his bags and stomped for the door.

In a flash, Alexa seized his arm, "No, Darius please let me explain."

Darius moved her to the side. "No, I'm tired of explanations. I'm tired of giving myself to you and not getting the same in return." He opened the door. For a moment he paused when he realized what was about to transform. This was the last thing he wanted to do, but he had no choice. The scenario, which took place nine years ago, could not repeat itself. Immediately, those loathsome feelings of hurt, anger and nausea swirled in his chest. He hated the feelings and had believed that they were behind him once and for all. He turned around to face Alexa with a solemn expression on his face.

"When I asked you to marry me, I thought it was because you had changed and that we deserved a second chance. Since you can't be the type of woman that I love and need in my life then I say we end this right here, right now. I'll file the papers for divorce first thing when I get back to Ohio." With that said, he opened the door and closed it quietly behind him.

CHAPTER 21

Alexa placed her Coach carry-on and purse on the conveyor belt to be scanned by airport security. She stepped through the frame of the metal detector and sighed, grateful that the small silver buckle on the belt in her jeans did not set the alarms off. The airport had a way of making people feel like criminals with those wands and she wasn't in the mood to be searched.

She picked up her purse and bag as they rolled through the dangling plastic slats on the conveyor belt and turned to meet the others at the gate. With her eyes hidden behind the dark sunglasses, she hoped she gave off the impression that she wished to be left alone. She made no sign that she was aware of anyone except herself in her little world. The ache in her heart consumed her, making her think on little else and she knew it would be a long time before the pain went away.

Once she gathered up the strength to stop crying Alexa tried to look at the situation from Darius' perspective. It was then that she realized she should have handled matters differently. Darius was right, she should have told him about the promotion right away as they were trying to bring their lives together, not tear them apart. Now, he was out of her life and to her fear, for good.

His harsh words came to mind sending her back to the scene at the bed and breakfast. Upon Darius' departure, Ms. Elmore came rushing to the door moments later to offer consolation. "Are you okay sweetie?" she asked. Alex couldn't even respond because she was broken. Although the older woman tried to convince her to stay the whole weekend, Alexa declined. She didn't think her mind would be clear and ended up checking out that evening.

After paying for the room, Ms. Elmore saw her to the door. Although Alexa had just met her, she could sense a loving and compassionate nature from the older woman, which was what she needed.

"Don't fret none honey," Ms. Elmore offered with a hug. "Although it may not look like it, but God is in control." She pointed to the sky.

"Thank you Ms. Elmore," Alexa murmured. When she pulled back, she placed the tickets to the show that she would be missing again into the older woman's palm.

Before she realized it, Alexa was approaching gate twelve where her flight was headed to Chicago and onward to New York. Had the situation with Darius not occurred and everything was in order, Alexa would be exhilarated at the thought of fulfilling her destiny with Radiance, but today she was not feeling the whole project. One minute she was on top of the world. She had a dream career and was married to the one true love of her life and the next minute, the whole life she had dreamed about was now an illusion.

"Good morning, Alexa," Tia greeted, interrupting her thoughts.

The airport was quiet at 5:30 in the morning. Alexa preferred the early flights and was accustomed to the early morning commuters shuffling along in their own worlds, trying to balance a cup of coffee while reading the Journal.

Alexa glanced up to see Tia Perez sitting there, "Hi Tia."

"Are you in disguise?" Tia asked, pointing to the dark glasses. The sun wasn't even out yet.

"I'm fine. Just tired," Alex replied. She took a moment to slip the scarf from her sleek hair. However, the glasses remained, as she wanted to hide her tear-swollen eyes.

"I know the feeling. Morning flights just aren't my thing, but I made an exception today. I'm excited about the magazine!"

"Yep, it's finally here," Alex replied, with a hint of cynicism.

Tia gave her a questioning glance, which Alexa ignored. Instead, she retrieved a book from her bag. It was a romance by a hot, new writer Kim Louise. Alexa liked Louise's style because she could identify with her resilient female antagonists. Her books typically centered on professional women with hurtful pasts where they triumphed. Her latest novel featured a character named Sabin Strong who was entwined in a delicate romantic situation. Alexa had started reading the novel the night before and was eager to pick up where she left off. She wasn't in the mood for conversation and hoped that the others would sense this and leave her alone.

One by one the remainder of their group arrived and before Alexa knew it, they were being called to board the plane.

✳   ✳   ✳

"So son, how is your love life?"

Darius paused. His mother's question was unexpected. It was just one week ago that he had shared his news of his situation with Alexa. The excitement that she displayed despite the fact that her son had eloped was surprising. She was thrilled that her son had reunited with his first love and looked forward to meeting her new daughter-in-law. Darius had planned on the two of them making a visit to Detroit for that purpose. Now he was embarrassed to tell her that the meeting would not take place after all.

"A mess," he quietly replied.

"Why?" she gasped. "What happened since we last talked?"

The two were seated at the kitchen table eating homemade apple pie and drinking coffee.

Darius gulped and began recanting the events leading up to the trip to Kansas City. "I thought this time we got things right. I thought us getting married would mean Alexa would not take our love for granted again, but I guess I was wrong.

His mother showed remarkable calm as she sat up in her seat positioning herself to lecture. "I know you are a grown man, but you can't go around treating marriage like a light switch, son."

"I love her and I wanted to prove it by going all the way. I just couldn't have her going back to Denver without some kind of connection to me."

She shook her head. "Son, it sounds like you married Alexa for selfish reasons."

"How can you say that?" he quickly replied. "She was being selfish by putting that job before us."

"I know it sounds farfetched, but trust me. I am a woman. I know these things. When a man asks a woman to marry him, it is serious. A proposal is something that all women long to hear and it's not to be taken lightly. Maybe she wasn't ready to get married and did it out of fear of losing you, who knows? I think you should have allowed things to progress naturally."

"Mom, we already knew each other. I was just picking up where we left off."

"Where you left off you were children," she pointed out. "Now you are adults who have built lives separate from each other complete with jobs and other relationships. You must take that into consideration."

Darius paused. He hadn't thought of that. Sean was a presence in Alexa's life after they were together. He remembered Alexa telling him how humiliating it was for her when Sean stood her up at the altar. That level of rejection could have long term damaging effects on anyone.

"I guess I didn't consider that."

"Do you still love her?"

"Of course," he blurted out. "But, I can't let myself open like that again. I may be a man, but my feelings run deep too."

"Give her time. If her love for you is as strong as you say, then she'll come back to you. Remember, real love doesn't stray too far or too long before it comes back home."

Darius studied the wise expression on his mother's face. "Well Mama, I'm not sitting around waiting for that to be the case. In June, I will be moving back to Detroit to start up that systems consultant business that Bryant and I have been talking about for years."

"Oh Darius, that is wonderful!" she exclaimed. She leaned over and hugged him. "I guess its time to make those plans a reality."

"Yes ma'am." He replied. "Our business angle, technological skills, and knowledge of the industry, we believe that our business can be very successful. Bryant has a proposal with the city that looks very promising."

Annie cupped his chin gently. "You know I'm proud of you, right?"

He nodded. "I know, I still can't believe that everything is falling into place, but one thing. It worries me to leave you alone in the city."

She quickly dismissed his comment with a wave of her hand. "Boy shoot, there's no need to worry. You've been a good son staying here in town with me for all these years. It's time for you to get your own life get together."

"I know, but with Deidra moving to Texas I can stand the idea of you here all by yourself."

"You won't have to worry about me. I've actually been thinking about checking out Texas myself. Deidra asked me to move with her." With a sigh, her eyes scanned the four corners of the room. "Since your Daddy passed and now that you'll be leaving, it couldn't have come at the right time. Besides, it's not like I will be leaving anyone behind."

"Are you sure that's what you want to do, Mama?" he asked. He knew how wild his younger sister could be. She was single, headstrong and loved to party.

"I know what you're thinking, but your sister has settled down quite a bit. She got approved for a transfer with her job and is looking into buying a house. She's going to need me there to help keep her on track," she said. "Plus I'm kind of looking forward to some warmer weather."

"Are you going to leave out with Deidra?"

She nodded. "I wanted to talk to you first to get your opinion. I thought maybe you'd be interested in staying in the house, but since you're moving to Detroit, maybe we could look at selling it."

Darius glanced around the tiny kitchen. Though small and lacking the conveniences of modern appliances, the room would always be remembered for the love that was poured out to all who came there. His mother was the most hospitable person he knew and showed made everyone who visited feel like they were right at home.

The old steel framed chair where his father always sat after coming home from a long day on the job remained in its regular spot behind the door. The brown vinyl covering was now cracked and chipping away. Darius could almost picture his father plopping down in it to remove his shoes like he frequently did. Although he was tired, he still found time to take on Darius' active baby brother Eric who met him at the door each evening to climb into their father's lap and fall asleep.

With a thoughtful sigh, Darius cleared his throat. He would miss the little house that his dad bought for his growing family back in the 70's. The three-bedroom ranch home provided the perfect shelter for his wife and their five children. When the neighborhood began to change in the 70s and most of their neighbors headed for the suburbs, the Riverside family stayed true to their community. Initially, he couldn't understand. But as he got older he respected his father for his decision to keep his family put. He owed his love for community activism to his father who would have been proud of the legacy that he passed on.

"I'll contact a Realtor first thing tomorrow, Mama."

Annie held her head slightly towards the ceiling with tear-filled eyes. "Jack, it's time for us all to move on. This house has brought us so much joy, watching the children grow up and all. But now it's gotten to be too much for me and I believe it's time to pass this blessing onto another family."

Darius reached across the table and gripped her hand in his. Although they didn't have much, his parents provided a stable, secure and loving environment for their children. Their teaching prepared them for the rough road of life that was ahead. Darius felt like he learned well. The only area he struggled in was relationships. Sure they talked about the birds and the bees and how Darius was expected to treat a woman, but he never really discussed with his father about how much love could hurt. Yet, when he glanced over at his mother, he immediately understood why the subject never came up. His Dad had an angel and he didn't know of any other way.

CHAPTER 22

The New York evening air was chilly. Alexa shivered as she scurried across the room to close the partially ajar window. Her head hurt from the pressure of the day and she was looking forward to collapsing in her bed. She had just returned from another strategy meeting with the team Marks-St. Claire had assembled as the new staff for Radiance Magazine.

Her stress was attributed to having to learn the new staff coupled by the expectation from the home office to have the Radiance office fully functioning in less than two months. Alexa was anxious by all that was on her plate because she also had pressing personal matters that she had ignored due to her hectic schedule. For one, she was still on the hunt for an apartment. Teressa and Lewis had expressed an interest in buying her house and they were in the process of sealing the deal. While she was grateful for that weight being lifted from her shoulders, she still had her own housing to deal with.

Although the company was gracious enough to pay for temporary housing in a classy Manhattan hotel near the office, there was nothing like being in your own place. Judging by her busy calendar, Alexa really couldn't see when she could arrange an appointment with the realtor. She was too busy traveling back and forth from Denver to New York every other week. Her hours were long and absorbing leaving little time for anything afterwards except a small dinner and a bath before collapsing into bed.

She actually preferred the long working hours to having her evenings free. Being preoccupied helped to keep her mind off of Darius. Tonight however, she wouldn't be as lucky. The team was given the evening off as a reward for staying on the set time line.

Alexa found her self able to enjoy being at home for the first time in weeks. To her chagrin, much had been neglected back in Denver since stepping into her new position. There were projects to complete, an office to clear out and positions to fill. At home, there were plants to tend to, loads of laundry to wash and several past due bills to pay.

"How did I get so behind?" she asked herself as she flopped down on the side of the bed with an exasperated groan. She had gone from a fairly relaxed job that didn't require much attention outside of her forty-hour work week to a very intense position that held in the horizon long hours and many late nights. She was in for calls made to her home at inconvenient hours, not to mention early morning meetings at the spur of the moment.

Up until now, her promotional transitions were a breeze, but this position was like no other that she had ever held. She prayed that she could adjust to the spontaneous and tedious schedule with a pleasant attitude. While her daily duties consumed her days, thoughts of Darius invaded her nights. It was hard swallowing the fact that their relationship was over. She truly missed curling up against him in bed while they read the morning paper over coffee as well as enjoying each other's conversation via the telephone every night.

She missed Darius' strong arms holding her protectively through the night and hearing his soothing, baritone voice as they talked late into the night on the phone. She had grown accustomed to his outright admiration of her and his adoring glances and warm caresses. No man had ever made her feel like he only had eyes for her regardless of the many beautiful women around them.

"No, I can't think about him!" she shouted out in the empty room. She needed to occupy herself with something to do. Reaching for the remote, she turned on the television just as the telephone rang.

"Hello."

"Hey, Alexa." It was Maya.

"Hey, girl."

"Long time no talk to. I'm surprised I caught you in your room."

"You and me both," Alexa sarcastically replied.

"You don't sound so good. What's eating you?"

"Just tired, I guess."

"So how is your new job coming along Ms. Editor-in-Chief?"

"Besides the long hours, trips back and forth to New York and the never ending meetings, it's all good."

"Wow, is it what you thought it would be?"

Alexa didn't have the heart to admit the truth to her or anyone for that matter. She didn't want to confess that this time she was second-guessing her decision.

"I knew that being in charge of a magazine would have a lot of responsibility with few allowances for distractions."

"I bet you were prepared for that loot too, huh?" Maya teased. "So, are you making good?"

"Let's put it this way. I think I might retire the old Honda and get uptown like you!" Alexa quipped. She had to admit that the monetary benefit was definitely a reward.

"All right now," Maya replied, with a chuckle. "For real, do yourself a favor. I know you're in the throws of your greatest career move ever and sometimes when things work out in such a way, we have a tendency to believe that you are on the right track. I implore you to pray about what's going on. Ask God if you are in His will because that is where we find peace in the end."

"Why do you say that?" Alexa asked, surprised by Maya's examination. In her opinion, the position must have been meant for her because she was filling it.

"I just don't want you to get into the habit of making decisions based on your emotions. In all that we do, we should ask the Lord for guidance."

"You wouldn't happen to be referring to Darius, would you?" She knew that he had to be some way affiliated with her comments.

"Well, yes. But I'm thinking of you as well."

Alexa exhaled loudly. She knew the conversation was going to go there.

"Maya, you know writing has been my dream since I was in fourth grade. I always wanted to reach and inspire people through my writing. Now that I have the chance to influence possibly millions of women, you're telling me I need to pray about being here because of Darius?" Confusion mapped her mind. If there was one thing Alexa always believed was that Maya was in her corner. "This is my destiny."

"Alexa, I know that writing is your passion, and I am confident in your abilities, but I am also aware of the fact that marriage is a very serious matter. You made a vow to Darius and you just can't say 'I do' one minute and 'I don't' the next. It just isn't right."

Alexa silently pondered Maya's words over in her head. Things had happened fast for her. A week after accepting the new position, she was on a plane to New York for their first official meeting. Everything was a blur. So much so, that all she could do was ride the wave. She had every intention of including Darius in her plans but had waited a little too long before the chips fell to her dismay.

"I appreciate your advice Maya, but I think this position wouldn't have been offered to me if I wasn't supposed to fill it. As for me marrying Darius, it was something that I thought was the right thing to do at the time. If Darius loved me like he said, then he wouldn't have handled me the way he did. He should have given me the chance to explain myself. All I did was try to protect him from a potentially painful situation. I was thinking about a way to approach the subject in a delicate manner that he could deal with, but he didn't want to hear it. Right now, he could be in running his business successfully in New York with me!"

Maya sighed in exasperation. "Alexa, I think you're missing the point."

"What point?"

"The one thing that is needed in a relationship is honesty. Honesty coupled by a sincere apology can heal a wound. If you want to repair the damage done, mix those together and go back to your husband."

"It takes two to fix this mess," Alexa stated.

"And I think you should be the catalyst. I just want you and Darius to be happy." She knew Alexa could be stubborn especially when she thought she was right.

"I *am* happy," Alexa confirmed with emphasis.

Although Maya was skeptical about her answer, she left it alone. She knew that Alexa comprehended where she was coming from, but she was being stubborn. She just hoped her obstinacy would not prevent her from doing the right thing.

Maya sighed. "The Lord just put it on my heart to call you. I'll let you go so you can get some rest."

"Thanks, I'll talk to you later."

After Alexa replaced the cordless phone back on its base, she lay gazing at the ceiling, trying to make sense of the confusion. It had been awhile since she spent some time with God. Her schedule made her sleepy by the end of the day and in the morning she rolled out of bed at the last minute. Plus, when Darius was around, she couldn't find a convenient time to set aside time for prayer. She was lucky if she got in a thank you while in the car on her way to work.

Just as Maya had suggested, she rolled off the side of the bed and knelt with her hands clasped tightly together.

*   *   *

"So, you've decided to set up in Detroit?" Reginald asked.

"Yeah," Darius confirmed. "We have our office space selected and the plan is to open the doors in August." The plans were finalized. It was a long time coming, but was definitely worth the wait.

The two were seated at their usual table at the End Zone eating their usual meal of five-alarm chicken wings, barbecue ribs and spicy fries with beer.

Reg took a long swig of his beer and placed the bottle on the table, shaking his head in disbelief. "I can't believe that you're doing your thing."

"Got to. Bryant and I have wanted to merge forces for a long time," Darius replied, picking up his napkin to wipe his sauce covered fingers. "I'm just glad that I can see the light at the end of the tunnel."

"Why move to Detroit? I thought you were going to open up shop here? Besides, is the market for your business big there?" Reg tossed out one question after another.

"No, we scrapped the idea of having an office here. Detroit is rebuilding man. The mayor is committed to revitalizing the city. He's caught the attention of several big named corporations as well as minority-owned businesses in an effort to attract them into investing in the city. Bryant said his goal is to create an Atlanta of the North."

"I don't know if I can imagine the Olympics there," Reg joked.

Darius laughed. "No, maybe not for awhile, but they're getting it together. Besides, you know me; I'm a grass roots kind of guy. I like to get in on the ground level where I can get my feet wet."

Reg nodded. He could attest to Darius' commitment to the inner city, especially the black community. When he first mentioned the school's concept to him, that was all Darius wanted to talk about. It was as if he had made the school his own personal project and like his own, he saw it through to fruition.

"You know there are going to be some disappointed folks around here."

Darius chuckled. "I'll miss everybody." He glanced at the food on the platter. "You don't suppose I can get some wings and fries like these in Detroit?"

"You damn sure won't get them served to you by someone like our Midget."

The two laughed, giving each other five.

"Seriously now, I'll wrap up everything tight before I jet." Darius held out his balled fist.

"Cool," Reg replied.

Darius felt compelled to say more but he knew it wasn't necessary. Reg was just that kind of guy. He appreciated his friend for having his back over the years. Although his style was sometimes a little too direct, Darius knew his heart. Over the years Reg had proven to be a good friend.

Reg looked up as if he had just read Darius' mind. "Hey, I know you probably don't want to talk about this, but I want to say I'm real sorry about what happened with you and Alexa."

"Thanks man, but that's behind me now," he lied. He didn't want to discuss his feelings for Alexa. The humiliation of having been duped a second time was unbearable.

"Are you guys getting a divorce?"

Hearing the word *divorce* stunned him. He never really ingested the term let alone the fact that he would be going through one. Darius couldn't believe that he had been married for three months.

He recalled the astounded look on Reg's face when he told him that he and Alexa were married. He sat there with his mouth wide open like he was trying to catch flies. Bryant and Maya were just as shocked. Darius was surprised that Alexa actually kept their secret from her best friend. He assumed that if there was one person she would tell it would be Maya. The encounter was painful when he learned that wasn't the case. Within an hour's time, Maya went through emotions from disbelief, to anger and finally giving way to tears of sadness. Both she and Bryant were hurt to learn that their best friends got married behind their backs.

"Didn't you trust us enough to tell us?" Maya cried.

It hurt him to see her cry as well as the obvious disappointment lining Bryant's brow. He regretted that he handled things in the haphazard manner and wished he could have done things differently. It was then that he realized that he set the tone for the secrecy in their marriage. Maybe if he wasn't so bent on keeping their marriage a secret, Alexa would have felt comfortable enough to talk to him about her promotion. But then again, she did predict correctly that he wouldn't be amicable about her accepting the new position. He was determined not to play second fiddle again.

"Darius!"

Hearing his name brought Darius back to the present. He had been drifting off a lot lately.

"I'm sorry, what did you say?"

"I asked if you thought you two could work things out or are you going to file for divorce."

"Alexa has moved on to New York and I'm having my attorney draw up the papers now."

"You sure this is what you want dog?"

"I'm surprised to hear you say this Reg. I know that Alexa wasn't your favorite person."

"She was pretty cool. Besides, I know that you two are crazy about each other."

Darius reached for his beer and took a swig. "I guess good things must come to an end at some time."

"Crys feels bad about her part in the whole thing. She feels partially responsible."

At Last!

"Tell her I said not to worry. Deception has a way of coming out sooner or later. You two just concentrate on setting a wedding date and let me know so I can fit you into my schedule."

Later as Darius lay in bed, he succumbed to the image of the cinnamon-hued beauty with the layers of glossy hair and sexy smile gazing at him through amber, passion-filled eyes.

He inhaled deeply, trying to recall the sweet feminine scent of her perfume. He envisioned himself kissing her sweetly and filling his hands with her womanly curves.

"Damn," he muttered. He missed her more than ever. He had to fight the feelings as Alexa made it quite clear where her loyalty lied.

As he had told his mother, he didn't have time for indecisive women who couldn't appreciate his goodness. He felt that the whole situation could have been avoided had Alexa come to him in the beginning and allowed him the opportunity to give his input on her taking the job. But, like the headstrong woman she was, she handled matters without him.

The thoughts of them together that had so captured him quickly diminished by Alexa's defection. Just when their relationship looked promising, the scales became unbalanced because of her ardent desire to succeed.

Groaning in disappointment, Darius rolled onto his side. In a few months, he would be starting a new life. Once he moved into his own place and the business was up and running he would find himself one day not reflecting on what could have been. Maybe one day he would finally leave Alexa Kirkwood in his past. The thought of this future date lifted his spirits. Maybe one day, the sorrow he felt today would no longer be his partner. There would be a day when he can look back at this situation and view it as a lesson learned.

CHAPTER 23

"Oh, Darius!" Alexa cried out in her sleep.

The sounds of her own voice made her bolt upright in bed. She was surprised to find her breathing ragged and beads of perspiration lining her brow. The tender spot between her thighs was pulsating in sync with the rapid thudding of her heart.

She hugged her knees to her chest and prayed that the urges would go away on their own. But each time she closed her eyes all she could see was Darius' dark image standing tall before her. His penetrating eyes pulled her into those deep dark pools as if communicating with her without words.

In an attempt to erase his image from her mind, she jumped up from the bed and stomped into the kitchen. If there was one thing that would calm her anxiety was ice cream. She was getting tired of these dreams of Darius coming to her every night. Recollections of the two of them flooded her mind: making love, wrestling in play or sometimes just holding one another without words as if communing with their minds. The dreams had grown stronger over the last couple of weeks particularly since she received the divorce papers from Darius' attorney.

She remembered when they arrived by certified mail to her office. She was in a foul mood and receiving the papers hadn't helped any. According to the document, Darius' only request was that Alexa take back her maiden name. His request hurt her because he knew how much it meant to her to have his name. She cried in her office, not sure how she had made such a mess of her life.

In a daze Alexa was surprised to find her self standing in the kitchen before the refrigerator. She opened the freezer door and pulled out the half gallon tub of Moose Tracks ice cream. The only thing that eased the need burning inside was a large bowl of her favorite ice cream and a good movie.

After scooping out a heaping serving, she wandered into the great room and plopped down on the sofa. She picked up the remote and began to channel surf. Usually if nothing caught her eye on one of the many movie channels she would turn on music videos.

Flipping through the channels Alexa couldn't find anything that she wanted to watch and settled for *Midnight Love* on BET. A video was just starting. She pulled a throw over her legs and settled back in her seat as the music started to play. The ballad sounded faintly familiar, she thought as she ate a spoonful. When the artist began to sing, she immediately recognized the lyrics of the song that Darius belted out to her when they were dancing in each other's arms.

She closed her eyes remembering how special she felt in his arms. Then all the memories came flooding back into her mind. She visualized scenes of the two of them together both past and present. In each image they were happy. She could almost feel a veil of exuberance coming over her. Her final image was of the two of them standing before one another in the church in Las Vegas, sharing their wedding vows.

She had been nervous when the Minister asked if she took Darius to be her husband. However when she looked up into his eyes, there was nothing that could make her say no.

A strong sense of longing and emptiness immediately enveloped her. The pull was so unforgiving that she could not think to do anything else but try to soothe the ache. Regardless of the possible repercussions her actions would cause, Alexa knew that she would be abandoning her sensibilities once again.

      *   *   *

The doorbell rang with urgency as if the person was deliberately trying to hurry him along. Darius swore aloud as he stepped from the shower. He wrapped a towel around his waist and almost slipped on the wet floor trying to exit the room. He rushed into the living room to the front door. The irritation he felt prevented him from checking the peephole as he normally would. Rather, he simply turned the dead bolt and flung open the door prepared to give the perpetrator a piece of his mind when his jaw dropped open at the sight of Alexa.

She looked different. Her face was free of makeup and her eyes were slightly swollen and red. The playful glint that they were known for was gone replaced by a look of desperation, which gave away to her vulnerability. His eyes traveled down the full length of her. She looked like she lost weight. The tan leather jacket seemed to swallow her up and the jeans she wore, which were meant to fit slim, seemed to hang from her hips. Her hair was combed off of her face and smoothed down her back in no particular style.

"What are you doing here?" he asked. If it weren't for the cool breeze hitting his wet skin, he would have thought he was dreaming.

"Darry, I don't know…I mean, I'm not sure why…" she stammered nervously. "I came because I miss you…I mean I miss us." Finally with an exasperated sigh she blurted out, "I need you."

His brow rose skeptically at her confession. It was their first encounter since the Kansas City incident.

His heart thudded rapidly in his chest and his mind replayed her words, trying to decipher the true meaning. He had longed for the opportunity to place all care in the back of his mind and take her words the way he wanted. Yet there were the conflicting thoughts that controlled him. 'Make her leave' 'Take her right there in the entrance' he didn't know which suggestion was right. It was Alexa who made up his mind for him when she kicked the door shut and shrugged out of her coat, letting it fall to the floor.

With a smoldering gaze, seemingly hot enough to dry his wet body, she stepped towards him and slipped her arms around his thick torso. She pressed her nose against his damp flesh, inhaling his musky, masculine scent. A soft moan escaped her throat as she paused for a few seconds remembering the smell of him. She gazed up from her stupor, her eyes settling into his dark pools.

Darius' wanted to push her away, but she was doing something to him. The arousing moans rising from her throat and her warm body pressed against him began weakening his resolve.

It came as no surprise when Alexa wrapped her arms around his neck and pulled his head towards hers. Her tongue pushed through his lips as she claimed him with authority, beckoning him back home. The kiss was a mix of attitude, frustration and fear, along with a deep down desire to give into the soulful reunion.

Darius tried to fight his emotions by keeping his arms to his sides. But Alexa wouldn't have it. She molded her body against him so until he had no choice but to succumb, and he did. He groaned with defeat and pulled her against his hardness, cupping her healthy bottom in his palms.

Neither had the desire to think about where they were going nor the clarity to rationale what they were about to do. Instead, they relished in the console of being in each other's arms again. With a sweep of his arm, Darius scooped Alexa into his arms. He carried her into the living room where he eased her down on the sofa. With nimble fingers, he proceeded to remove her clothing until she lay nude before him.

Then as if trying to make up for the lost time between them, they made earnest love. She came first muffling cries of joy against his broad shoulder. Darius was on her heels, shouting out his release. Finally when normal breathing resumed for them both, Darius rolled onto his back and shielded his face with his forearm.

Alexa propped up on her elbow and studied him for a moment. She teasingly ran a swirled pattern down his torso with the tip of her finger and was surprised that it garnered no response from him. Initially she thought he was still coming down from the high that their powerful lovemaking had taken them, but when he still hadn't uttered a word after a few minutes she suspected something was wrong.

Sitting up slowly, Alexa pulled her clothing to her bosom. The buttons from her blouse were scattered everywhere on the floor. She retrieved each one within reaching distance. After doing so, she glanced back to notice that Darius still had yet to move.

"Alexa," he finally called her name.

Her eyes brightened with hope in her heart. The scenario hadn't developed the way she had planned, but she never claimed to be good at these things. She just did what she wanted to do. And at the present time the urgency was to be with her man. The moment she made the plane reservations hours earlier seemed like a flash of light. She went from eating ice cream and watching videos to boarding a plane to Ohio six hours later.

"I think you better go," he choked out the words.

At first Alexa thought she did not hear him correctly and leaned in closer to him.

"What?" she asked incredulously.

"I said I think you should leave," he repeated more firmly.

Alexa felt like she was slammed into a brick wall. How could he tell her to leave after she came so far just to see him?

"This doesn't change things between us," he continued as he rose from his place on the floor. She watched him saunter across the room towards the bathroom, his muscles flexing with the slightest movement.

At Last!

"I'm going to take a shower now," he announced over his shoulder, "When I come back, I want you gone."

CHAPTER 24

One Month Later

"Penny for your thoughts?"

Maya's soft voice interrupted Darius' quiet reflection. Bryant had to run to the office to pick up some paper work and Maya had just put the girls to bed.

"I'm sorry May, did you say something?" Darius asked, looking down at her. He was standing in the Bryant's grand living room watching the magnificent view of the setting sun.

Maya placed a hand on the middle of his back and gave him a nurturing pat. "You seemed so distracted this evening. I just wanted to make sure you were okay."

He nodded, not sure of the answer but not wanting Maya to worry. He also did not wish to bring Alexa's name up. "Just thinking about the move and trippin' off the fact that Bryant and I are finally going to do this."

Maya sighed with eyes aglow. "I know. Can you believe it! My baby's wanted this for a long time. It's nice to finally see his dreams come true."

Darius always admired the endearments Maya and Bryant shared. The two never seemed too shy to share their feelings for one another in front of anyone. Alexa used to call him baby too, especially when she wanted something. In fact, Maya kind of sounded like her when she said it. He could picture Alexa with her head cocked to the side and her bright eyes shining against the glow of her smooth brown skin as she called him her baby in the same soft voice Maya had just used.

"Damn," he seethed, cursing himself for relating everything back to the woman.

"What?" Maya asked with caution.

"I'm sorry. I'm just thinking about all of the things I have to take care of before the big move." He lied. Although he knew Maya was one of the few women he could trust with his feelings, he wasn't ready to share them just yet.

"Darius, I'm not trying to get in your business, but in case you need someone to talk to, know that both Bryant and I are willing to listen."

Darius' heart melted from the sincerity of the woman before him. Feelings of guilt washed over him from the episode that brought tears to her eyes when he revealed his marital status. "Thank you, Maya. That means a lot," he replied giving her a hug.

Maya smiled broadly. "Now with that said, what do you have to take care of?"

"Well, first of all, I have to look for a place to stay."

"A place!" she shrieked. "You can stay here with us."

"Maya, I don't want to burden you guys."

"Darius, please. You know, Bryant wouldn't have it any other way." She replied. "It would be like old times."

With the exception of Alexa, he thought.

"And don't tell me you wouldn't like to come home to a decent hot meal every once in awhile?" Maya said, temptingly.

Darius' eyes lit up. Now that thought was inviting. "Well, now that you mention it."

"Sold!" she exclaimed, raising her fist in victory.

"But I promise it will only be for a month," he assured her.

Maya gave him a hug. "Sure, whatever you say."

When Darius pulled back, Maya couldn't help but notice the sad look that remained in his eyes. Through his smile she could see the pain. She knew that eyes never lied. She learned that skill when interviewing people for a news story. As she left the room, she said a silent prayer for him and Alexa. Only time, and the love she knew filled their hearts, would present the results that they were meant to be.

*   *   *

The telephone rang three times before Alexa answered. "Hello," She growled huskily into the receiver. It was snowing again. Her voice started fading the night before and when she woke up that morning, she didn't have the energy to get out of bed.

The long hours at work and the commutes to New York were taking toll on her mentally and physically. When she awakened earlier, her head was pounding and she was running a fever. She sought relief with sleep-inducing painkillers, and was on her way to sleep when the telephone rang.

After calling her job, she meant to turn the telephone's ringer off so that her machine would pick up, but she had fallen asleep before she could do so.

"Alexa?"

"Yeah?" she asked wearily. It was a deep male voice. One that was very familiar. But for the life of her, she couldn't think of whom it belonged to.

"Are you okay?"

"I don't know," she wearily replied with a shiver. The thermal pajamas and flannel robe did little to stop the chill running through her body. One minute she was freezing and the next she was burning hot. It was also getting difficult to breath. She raised her hand to her forehead to check her temperature and was surprised to find her flesh to be warmer than normal.

What's going on? She thought. She tried to focus her eyes on the digital numbers on her alarm clock but the numbers were blurred. A sudden pain shot through her and she cried out. The room suddenly started to spin wildly and her heart thudded rapidly out of control.

"Alexa! Alexa!" the caller shouted her name. "Are you okay?"

"No. I'm not feeling well at all. Please, help me," she whispered in delirium before the room went totally black.

When she came to, she found a man standing over her trying to remove her clothes. She tried to scream, but nothing came out. Another man appeared and another as she struggled to fight them off, but she was too weak and she blacked out again.

*   *   *

The next time she tried to open her eyes; she couldn't because her lids were heavy. She attempted to sit up, but it was like straining against a 300 pound weight. She moaned with all the strength she could muster and sank back against the pillows, crying softly.

"Just relax honey," a soft voice gently urged. "I'm going to give you something that will help you to relax."

Alexa moaned when she felt a prick in her arm but she did as she was told and gave in to the exhaustion that consumed her.

*   *   *

A warm sensation on Alexa's arm awakened her. This time it was easier to open her eyes. At first, the images before her appeared dim, but after several blinks, she began to make out the smiling face of her parents.

"Praise the Lord!" Beverly cried and began stroking the back of Alexa's hand.

"Ma? Daddy?" Alexa whispered before coughing several times. Her father came to her aid with a squeeze bottle of water. Supporting Alexa's head, he held the straw to her mouth, allowing her to take a sip. When she had enough to drink, Alexa held up her hand and allowed him to ease her back against the pillow.

Seconds later, Beverly returned with a doctor and a nurse who began asking Alexa questions as they checked her vitals. After much examination and only when it appeared that she was stable, the two left. Shortly after, her father announced that he was going down to the cafeteria to grab a cup of coffee as well as give Justin a call to let him know that she had regained consciousness. Once the room was quiet again, Alexa turned to her mother with a questioning look.

"Mama, what am I doing in the hospital?"

Several large vases of every kind of flower imaginable filled the room, making her wonder if her condition had been fatal.

"Baby, you are sick. If it wasn't for Sean, who knows what could have happened."

"Sean?" she asked confused. What did he have to do with her condition? She didn't even remember talking to him.

"Yes. He heard about your promotion and called to congratulate you. He said you sounded ill and asked him to call a doctor before passing out on the phone."

The word promotion stood out like a sore.

"Oh my goodness!" Alexa exclaimed, thinking of Radiance and the many meetings she had ahead of her. "I'm supposed to be in New York." One of the meetings was to plan the publicity details. As Editor in Chief, she knew it was vital that she be present through the entire process.

Beverly stopped her by gently pressing down on her shoulders. "Baby, you aren't going anywhere. Besides you were supposed to be in New York four days ago."

"Four days!" Alexa exclaimed. "I've been in here that long?"

"You were pretty sick. The doctor said that your healing depended a lot on plenty of rest and since you were in a lot of pain, he kept you sedated."

"I got to get out of here!" she cried and pulled back the covers in an effort to sit up again. However, after days of lying still, the blood rushed to her head, making her lightheaded. She moaned and fell back against the pillow. Tears of defeat filled her, eyes and she began to sob softly.

"No you don't," her mother retorted as she replaced the covers, tucking them neatly into place. "All you have to do is get better. Your job will just have to understand."

"No Ma, you don't understand. Marks-St. Claire is all I got!" The tears rolled like little waterfalls down her cheeks but she was too exhausted to wipe them away.

"No baby, *you* don't understand," Beverly gently replied as she wiped away Alexa's tears with a crumpled tissue. "You have made that job your life to the point that you don't have a life of your own. The only time I think I've ever seen you so happy was a few month back. Now you are a mere shell of what you used to be. Since you got that promotion all you've been doing is eating, sleeping and breathing that company. You're hardly home. It's obvious that you haven't had a decent meal, you're so thin. It's like you're going through the motions without any heart. Money and prestige have never been major issues in our family. I don't like seeing you like this. I want you smiling and happy again. If it means you leaving that company then let it be. There are more important things in life."

More important things. Those words rang in her head. Like what? Darius? She couldn't even hold onto that belief. The last they were together, he told her in certain terms that it was over between them. Her mother didn't understand that the happiness that was there was now gone and she had to make the best of what was left in her life.

"But I have a house and bills to pay. Remember you said a woman has to be independent and establish her own to be successful. Isn't that important?"

Beverly shook her head with a pitiful expression. "That is not all there is to life. I want to apologize to you and your brother for every thought I planted in your heads. I was going through my own personal problems that I didn't have sense enough to see what I was creating in you two. I wasn't woman enough to challenge your Daddy's ways because I believed it wasn't my place. I was raised to believe that the man was the head of the household, and he made the decisions benefiting the family. Even if I thought it was wrong, I was too afraid to speak my own mind. Now that we have separated, I see that it's not hard to do. In fact, men actually respect that more than anything else." She sighed with a sad look on her face.

"I wish I had known that before now," Alexa admitted, wiping her tears away. "I tried so hard, Mama, to be what everybody thought I should be. I tried to make the right decisions so that everyone could be happy but it didn't work. Then the one time I tried to do something that I wanted to do it blew up in my face. Now look at me. I'm damn near crazy because I can't make up my mind about what I want in my life. I feel like such a failure."

"You are not a failure." Beverly said with authority. She embraced Alexa with a tight hug. "You're only human. We all make mistakes. Look at me," she took Alexa's face in her hands. "I almost cut off my blessings by nearly destroying my marriage. I could have and should have done things differently, but I've asked for forgiveness from your daddy and the Lord and I am willing to do whatever it takes to make things right again. I just needed to say that because I want the curse of broken marriages to be broken before they get started."

"Mama, I need to apologize because I haven't been completely honest with you either."

Alexa proceeded to share the painful details concerning her short-lived marriage. "So I'm not perfect either. The trouble is that I don't think I can fix mine."

Alexa was relieved when Beverly refrained from negative comment.

"Anything is fixable if you want it bad enough." she said instead. Her words reminded Alexa of Maya's statement.

Alexa reached for Beverly's hand and squeezed it tightly. "Thanks Ma for not judging me and for listening as a friend."

Beverly smiled through her tears and gave her daughter a hug. As she pulled back, she reached up and brushed aside Alexa's bangs lovingly.

"I'm going to stay here with you until you get better," she announced.

Alexa welcomed her proposal, because she knew that she needed personal care for awhile. Besides, she really wanted the company.

"I have to call the company to let them know that I will be out."

"It's done. Sean contacted them for you. Your boss called this morning to say that your medical leave was approved." Beverly promptly replied.

Alexa sighed. "I guess I can forget about being Editor-in-Chief of Radiance. We had a deadline and I don't' think that they will stop the presses on my account."

"If that is what happens then it was meant to be," Beverly plainly stated. "I've learned over the past few months that when we are not focused on the right things, the Lord allows for situations to come into our lives to bring us back to him. If it were meant for you to keep your position then time will tell, but for now we are on His time."

Alexa wondered when her mother got to be so prophetic. She couldn't recall her ever making such bold statements before. Looking at the older woman standing before her, she could sense a difference. She saw an aura about her that she had never seen before as though she was finally at peace with herself. Their conversation, along with the drugs the nurse gave her, made Alexa exhausted once more and she found herself yawning.

She watched as Beverly retrieved a bible from her bag. After a quick prayer, she flipped through the pages and began to recite the 23rd Psalms.

"The Lord is my shepherd, I shall not want. He makes me lie down in green pastures; He leads me beside quiet waters. He restores my soul."

Alexa did not hear the rest for she fell right to sleep.

CHAPTER 25

Restoration was exactly what Alexa needed. Her doctor couldn't understand how she had managed to keep her crazy schedule as long as she had. She had a good amount of fluid in her lungs that had it remained undetected another week, the results could have been fatal.

In addition to an antibiotic, her prescription included lots of rest, nutritious meals and reduced stress at all costs until her body was completely functioning at an optimal level.

As Alexa suspected, the magazine had to move forward. Regretfully so, she was informed by Mrs. Holland that she was replaced in her position as Editor-in-Chief. She tried consoling her, stating that it had nothing to do with her but was a business decision. She promised that there would be more opportunities for Alexa in the future and advised that she not be too disheartened. Despite her loss, Alexa was happy to learn that her successor was Tia Perez. Tia was a hard worker and most deserving than anyone else she could think of.

It took awhile, before Alexa could stop viewing her illness as a setback but as the beginning of change in her life. Her lifestyle was consuming her. The long hours and neglecting herself as well as the important things in life were becoming too much like the norm. She hadn't even taken time to keep in touch with her family or her friends. Subconsciously, she felt that those who were not related to Marks-St. Claire were viewed as time wasters.

As promised, Alexa's mother stayed in Denver to help out during her recuperation period. Alexa knew that God had ordained the time for them because they were both able to spend quality time together where they talked about some personal issues.

On one particular evening, mother and daughter sat down to share a heartfelt discussion. All along, Alexa thought she lived a life that was on the opposite side of the female spectrum than her mother. She believed she was more driven because she chose to pursue her career goals and actually attained most of them at an early age.

It had been all about her career and she placed everything, including love and having children on the back burner for success. While Alexa's definition of success was making a mark in the corporate arena, Beverly's was creating a comfortable home life for her husband and children.

In the early years of their marriage, all Beverly wanted to do was succeed at being a good wife by pleasing her husband. She also wanted to be the picture perfect mother, baking the cookies, helping with the homework, ensuring that Alexa and Justin were properly dressed and well fed. She placed so much energy in her home and family that one day she woke up and felt drained.

Alexa vividly remembered this period because her mother started behaving differently.

"I guess our lives mirrored each other's more than we thought," Alexa said with a sigh.

Beverly nodded. "But that doesn't mean we have to dwell on our past mistakes or beat ourselves up for the choices we made."

"What do we do then?" Alexa asked. "How do we stop beating ourselves up? When do the feelings go away? I feel like a fish out of water." Tears pooled in her eyes and streamed down her cheeks. Never had she felt so out of control. She cried so much in the past few months that she thought she couldn't cry anymore. When her relationship with Darius ended the first time, she had Marks-St. Claire. Now she had nothing.

Beverly leaned over and handed Alexa a worn, leather bound book, which she immediately recognized as her mother's bible.

"Ma, I don't know," she began. Although she had attended church, she had never really absorbed the scripture in her mind and heart. She couldn't even apply the passages to her own life.

Beverly shook her head. "What don't you know?" She asked smoothing her hand over her daughter's hair. "The only reason why you don't know is because your attention has been focused on all of the wrong things." She placed the bible in Alexa's hand. "Give it a chance, baby. Give God a chance to make a difference in your life. I know I am."

Alexa traced the gold lettering with the tip of her finger. The pain she felt from a life of uncertainty seemed so strong as if someone had died. Beverly called out the scripture Isaiah 41:10. Alexa thumbed through the bended pages. When she found it, she read it to herself. *"Do not fear, for I am with you; do not anxiously look about you for I am your God. I will strengthen you, surely I will help you, and surely I will uphold you with my righteous right hand."*

After she was done reading, Alexa looked up at her mother and knew that she was going to have to change her perspective. It was going to be hard, but she was determined to move ahead to the fulfilling life that God had promised for her.

Each night mother and daughter studied and discussed the meanings of passages. When they had questions, they called Alexa's pastor. For the first time Alexa felt peace as she filled her spirit with the gospel. She was hungry to find her life purpose. Together the pair fasted for 21 days, prayed and meditated on scripture.

To help stay focused, Alexa typed up some scriptures on the computer and posted them in noticeable places throughout the house. The positive tone of the words helped to ease the anxiety when it tried to get the best of her. As a result of her studying, Alexa learned some life-changing lessons. No matter what, despite all of her shortcomings, God loved her totally and completely; He presides over all things and only with Him were all things possible; every moment with the one you love is precious and should be treated so and lastly; life is too short to wait until tomorrow to do things.

Immediately following the fast Alexa felt strong enough to move around the house. She and Beverly got to do activities that they used to enjoy together like cooking and gardening. Alexa was meaning to landscape her yard but never had the time to do it. So the pair went to Home Depot and bought materials, flowers and shrubbery. They also made time to take in a few cultural events around the town. One being the second run of *Bring in the Noise*.

Alexa could not agree with the reviews more, the performance was excellent! While leaving the theater, she was surprised to run into Sean accompanied by a date. She immediately ran over and greeted him with a hug. Both Sean and his date were taken by surprise by her actions.

"What brought that on?" Sean asked with a surprised look on his face.

"For saving my life. I learned that it was you who called the ambulance. I appreciate your looking out for me like that." She told him, and then extended her hand to his date so as not to exclude her from the conversation. "Hi, my name is Alexa. I'm a friend of Sean's. I hope you realize what a good man you have. Treat him well."

"Thank you," the woman meekly replied.

With a parting wave, Alexa entwined her arm with her mother and the two walked away. Suddenly a feeling of elation came over that she had never felt before. If she could, she felt like going back to everybody she had ever unknowingly mistreated and ask for their forgiveness. Even those who she thought did not deserve it. However, she knew that though the number was small, it may not be possible. What she did know was that the Lord knew her heart and there was one person that she had to contend with whether she liked it or not.

She reflected on this alone in her den as she sat in the glider reading one Sunday afternoon. I will be strong enough to face him, she told herself as she closed the book. She knew the day was coming soon because in a few short weeks Darius would be moving to Detroit to start his business. She had to catch him while his mind was free.

Monday would be her first day back at work on a full-time basis. Most of the work she had been doing was done at home and involved nothing more than editing articles. She was somewhat apprehensive about getting back to her old routine. It would be strange confronting her peers knowing that she would not do so in the same capacity. She prayed that the transition would be a smooth one.

*   *   *

A month's absence at Marks-St. Claire seemed more like a year. Much had changed. With the onset of the new magazine, some major restructuring took place that affected the home office. One of the affects hurt Alexa deeply. The elimination of the Design Department meant that her good friend Bernie was out of a job. The company couldn't offer her a position comparable to what she had been doing or making for that matter and ended up letting her go with a severance package.

In addition, Jesse was promoted to Cover Editor when the former abruptly resigned. Rumor had it that he accepted a VP position with a publishing company in New York. However, no one could be too sure because it had not been formally announced.

Alexa was glad when lunch time rolled around. As usual, she agreed to meet Teressa in the cafeteria. Standing in the entrance, Alexa scanned the room for her friend when she spotted her at the registers paying for a salad and a bottle of water. She smiled, shaking her head; Teressa was still determined to get into her size 8 dress. She didn't have the heart to tell her that her crash diet wasn't serving her well.

"Hey girl!" Teressa greeted as Alexa approached. After placing her tray on the table she gave Alexa a big hug.

"Hey," Alexa said with a smile. It felt good to see her friend. She had been receiving hugs, cards and calls from well wishers welcoming her back all day. She was rendered speechless when her coworkers surprised her with a huge basket of flowers, a card and a gift certificate for lunch at her favorite restaurant.

The two sat down and Alexa began to remove the contents of her lunch. Before leaving, Beverly prepared, packed and stored what seemed like a ton of entrees in Alexa's freezer. Alexa smiled with appreciation at the tasty home cooked meals each time she removed the cover. Lunch today was Shepherd's Pie.

"You look good, girl," Teressa commented on Alexa's appearance. "Very well rested."

"Thanks," Alexa replied. She too noticed how healthy she looked as she got ready that morning.

"I guess taking time out to pamper yourself after a nervous break-down will do that for you,"

Alexa's eyes widened and her mouth dropped at Teressa's comment. "What did you say?"

"I'm sorry. I shouldn't have brought it up," Teressa said, shrinking back into her chair with a guilty look on her face.

Alexa laughed more out of astonishment than humor. "No, you said it now. You think I had a nervous breakdown?"

Teressa shrugged. "That's what I heard."

"But you know I was sick, Teressa. I told you I had a severe case of Mono on top of a respiratory infection."

Teressa lowered her eyes in shame. "I know that is what you told me, but you wouldn't call me or return my calls. You wouldn't even accept visitors. I just assumed you were too embarrassed to tell me the truth."

"Teressa, I had to work through some personal issues involving both my marriage and my mother. She was here to help me work through them. We spent a lot of well needed time together."

Teressa pushed her tray away as if losing her appetite. "I'm sorry, Alexa. I should have been more sensitive. Please forgive me."

Alexa peered around the crowded lunch room. "Is this why people are walking around looking at me all pitiful?"

Teressa shrugged her shoulders. "I can't speak for them, but that is what was going around."

Alexa's natural impulse was to tell Teressa off but she knew deep down that she couldn't. Doing so would only validate in people's minds what they assumed was true. Although she didn't care what people thought, she was determined to end the gossip right then and there.

"I forgive you Teressa, but please as my friend, understand that I would not lie to you about anything. If we are going to remain friends, we have to respect each other. That means if I tell you something, I need you to trust that I am telling the truth okay?"

Teressa nodded with downcast eyes like a child who had been scolded by her mother.

"Now, that we've squared that away, how are you coming along with your wedding plans?"

Teressa glanced up nervously into Alexa's eyes and knew that she had been forgiven. She vowed from then on to be the best friend that she could be.

*   *   *

Alexa's anxieties regarding her position at Marks-St. Claire did not diminish by the end of the week. In fact with each day, her restlessness grew. Although her prayer life was steady she prayed, she still felt like something wasn't right. She reached for the phone to call her mother for support, but abandoned the idea and quickly hung up.

"*I've got to work this thing out on my own,*" she came to a silent conclusion.

Now here she stood in her old office feeling like a trespasser. Yes, she had given Marks-St. Claire her all and they rewarded her for every bit of her dedication. But there was a persistent nagging inside that would not go away.

Her eyes lifted towards the ceiling. "Lord I can't take another step without you. Whatever your will for my life, please, please show me the way."

She sank into her chair and buried her face into her hands and surrendered her future. She prayed for strength, the ability to trust, and guidance. About an hour following her prayer while in meditation, the turmoil that had settled in her stomach had slowly diminished and was replaced by a sense of peace. She began praising the Lord at her desk as tears of joy streamed down her face. Then she got up, fixed her makeup and went to go do what she had to do.

CHAPTER 26

Alexa smiled at the sight of the sun rising across the horizon. The picturesque view was symbolic and paralleled the latest chapter in her novel of life.

As the sky transformed from black velvet to a myriad of deep purple and lavender ending at magnificent shades of oranges and yellows, her heart lifted with hope that she too would have a ray of hope, another moment to shine; another chance.

Her car was packed with enough personal belongings to carry her through a couple of weeks. Handing in her resignation was the hardest, yet easiest thing to do. The fact that the obligation she felt she owed the company was so strong saddened her, but the idea of walking away on her terms was freeing. Not only had Marks-St. Claire been good to her, but Mrs. Holland as well.

She led the path for her as well as many other ambitious women at the company. She set the standard and the others followed with much respect. Alexa was glad that she took her resignation well. It was no secret that Alexa was well respected by the older woman. Alexa, however, was now determined to stop others from influencing her into making decisions that were not good for her. No matter how much money they offered or the title they put before her name, it all would not matter if she had to sacrifice herself or the ones she loved in the process.

She only wished she had adopted this philosophy before her break up with Darius. It seemed like after her spiritual encounter, she saw with new eyes. For the first time, she could actually understand Darius' position on what happened. The first time she recognized that, she cried.

Darius was a wonderful presence in her life. He had taught her so many things that she would cherish forever. Whereas before, she was consumed by her own issues, Darius helped her to acknowledge the needs of others who were not as fortunate. She actually began to see those around her: homeless people, blue collar workers; people who were not as fortunate as her to be blessed with a good education or career. From that point on, she adopted the belief that success was nothing without the one you love.

As she turned onto I-80 headed towards Gary, Indiana she prayed that she wasn't too late. By her calculations, if she continued to drive non-stop she would be through Indiana and into Cleveland in about five hours. She planned on going straight to his place of employment, hoping to catch him before leaving for the day.

She turned up the volume on her radio and listened to the morning talk show hosts discuss the topic of relationships. She smiled at the advice that a local family psychologist gave to some of the callers. Some of the advice she could relate to, others she could not. For the most part, it was entertaining and helped to kill the time.

About an hour outside of Cleveland, Alexa stopped to fill up her tank at a clean little rest stop. She took the time to freshen up after her long drive. After pumping the gas, she parked the car off to the side. Then searching through her duffel bag, she pulled out a little bag containing her toiletries. She also pulled out a fresh set of clothing. The last thing she wanted to do was try to ask for a second chance looking and smelling like she had been out rolling with pigs.

With the items in hand, she practically bounced into the restroom with a spring in her step. The closer she got to Cleveland, the anticipation of seeing Darius again grew. When she finished freshening up, she emerged from the facilities clean and comfortably dressed in a sporty running suit and a pair of tennis shoes.

The glint in her eye was slightly marred by the distant possibility that she was moving forth in vain. She quickly pushed the negative thoughts to the side. She wasn't about to be dissuaded now. She had nothing but herself and her love to give. Even if Darius told her it was over for good, at least she wouldn't regret for the rest of her life that she did not even try to win him back.

Patting the divorce papers in the pocket of her jacket, Alexa slipped on her shades and hopped into her car. As far as she knew Darius didn't know anything about her illness, which is why she didn't get around to returning them to him. She was glad that she didn't give up by signing her name and sending them back. With them in hand, she was going to speak her peace. If he wanted her to sign she would, but not without him knowing the mistake he was about to make.

Before pulling off, Alexa took a moment to pray. "Dear Lord, I know I am not perfect and neither is Darius, but I know that he is a good man and I know that I love him. If he doesn't want a relationship with me, please let me be respectful and understanding. And, let this be a lesson to learn. Please guide me in my words and actions. Amen."

*   *   *

"You have a meeting in ten minutes with Dustin and Carlton," Donna, Darius' secretary, reminded him.

Darius nodded. "Thank you, Donna."

The woman half smiled before exiting the room. It was plain to see that he was not the same man. He went from being a nice guy to being exceptionally nice by giving her Friday afternoons off or an extra half hour for lunch, to being gloomy all in a matter of a few months.

Her heart reached out to him as if he were her own son. She knew the change in his behavior had to do with Alexa. Anyone could see that he cared for her deeply. She noticed the admirable glances he stole in her direction in addition to the way he hung on to her every word. Donna just prayed that his broken heart would heal. It was just two weeks ago that he formally announced that he was relocating to Detroit to start his own computer consulting business. Her prayer was also that his new journey would be approached with confidence and excitement as she knew his life was taking a new turn.

           *   *   *

Darius glanced at his daily planner and frowned. He had an appointment with his barber after his 1:00 meeting. Later that evening he had a fraternity dinner cruise to attend. Although he had purchased two tickets, he was going alone. The tickets had been purchased in advance for him and Alexa.

The thought of arriving on the boat without Alexa changed his mind and he made a mental note to give them to his barber Sam. At least someone could enjoy the festivities because he wasn't up for it. With a groan, he grabbed his notes for his meeting and headed to the conference room.

           *   *   *

Alexa's heart fluttered as she parked her car in the parking lot at the company, where Darius worked. She lowered the mirror above her head. Without any make up, she looked like the fresh faced 22-year-old Darius had fallen in love with nine years ago. She felt like it too, given her current employment situation and her casual attire combined with her unfaltering love for him.

With a hopeful mindset, she exited the car and walked towards the building prepared for whatever the outcome.

Donna glanced up at the sound of the elevator doors opening and was surprised to find Alexa stepping out. A frown immediately lined her face when she saw who it was.

Despite Donna's reaction, Alexa smiled. She knew it would not be easy. Nothing worth something came easy. She knew she was going to have to fight to keep her man.

"Hi, Donna." she cheerily greeted.

"Hello," the woman replied with disdain. She peered over her glasses at Alexa with a look of disapproval.

"Is Darius available?"

"I'm sorry, but he's in an important meeting right now," she retorted, as she crossed her arms guard-like before her ample bosom. "Even if he was available, I'm not sure he would want to see *you.*"

Alexa's eyes lowered from the cut of the woman's words. "Donna, your loyalty to Darius is commendable and I respect you for that very much."

Donna remained unmoved. "Like you said, I am loyal to Mr. Riverside, and I look out for his well being *only.*" Alexa was all too familiar with the formidable woman who thought of Darius as a son as well as her employer. She remembered Darius mentioning how he trusted the older woman completely. She was sure that Donna was aware of the situation and was protecting Darius like any person who felt for someone as she did for Darius.

"I understand your position, but I really need to talk to him." Tears formed in Alexa's eyes, but she blinked them back determined not to let them fall. "Donna, if I am correct about your relationship with Darius, then I know that you are aware of what occurred between Darius and I. Being a young, career woman, I focused more of my attention on advancing my career and less on my relationship. I hurt Darius, not once but twice, and I hate myself for it. But I can't keep wallowing in what I did wrong. I strongly believe that the important thing now is to concentrate on what I can do to make things right." Before she finished, a tear rolled down her cheek and she quickly swiped it away. "I need to tell him that I'm sorry. I need to tell him that nothing is more important to me than telling him, no, showing him how much I love him. So if you could, I'd appreciate it if you got Darius for me please."

At first Donna appeared as if she would not budge. However, it wasn't until the older woman offered Alexa a tissue and told her to wait in Darius' office that she felt she got somewhere.

Alexa exhaled through relieved tears. She mouthed a silent, "thank you."

⋆   ⋆   ⋆

Luckily, Darius was seated near the door when Donna poked her head inside the conference room. She tapped him on the shoulder and motioned for him to step out into the hall.

With a look of irritation on his face, Darius followed Donna out into the hall. "What is it Donna?" he asked. "I asked that I not be disturbed."

"Forgive me for interrupting," she apologized. "But you have a visitor."

"Donna, I'm in the middle of a meeting with the President and Vice President of the company. Have him or her make an appointment for tomorrow," he replied and turned to go back into the conference room when Donna caught him by the arm.

"Darius, I believe this is very urgent. The party is waiting in your office."

Darius saw the serious look on Donna's face and knew he should find out who it was. He stepped back into the conference room and excused himself. With a frown, he sauntered down the hall and towards his office. As he pushed opened the large oak door, his jaw dropped at the sight of Alexa seated in a chair before his desk. At the sound of his entrance, she turned around and smiled, making his stomach jump.

Despite his initial reaction, his eyes narrowed in anger.

"What are you doing here?" he demanded to know.

"Hi Darry," She said his name so sweetly he felt like scooping her up into his arms.

Darius closed the door for privacy, to avoid anyone overhearing anything. He didn't know where their conversation was headed and didn't want anyone to be privy to the details. Once the door was closed, he leaned against it and eased his hands into his trouser pockets, spreading his strong legs defensively.

"As I said, what are you doing here?" he repeated.

Alexa stood up. "Is that any way to treat somebody who drove all the way here to see you?" she asked in a nervous voice.

Darius shrugged his broad shoulders. "What's the purpose of this visit? Did you get bored in New York? No, let me guess. This is this another seduction? What shall I do? Push my papers off of my desk this time?" He asked with a sweep of his arm.

Alexa lowered her eyes. "I deserved that."

"Whatever." Darius scoffed scathingly as he strolled past her.

Alexa closed her eyes and shook her head slowly as she mouthed a short prayer asking the Lord for the right words to say to make amends.

"Please, Darius. I know we aren't on the best terms, but you never gave me a chance to give you my side of the story. Before you make a final conclusion about us, please hear me out."

"Why should I?" he whirled around, his eyes boring into hers.

"Because I'm still your wife and you owe it to me, and yourself."

They stood there for a few seconds—his frozen glare competed with her pleading gaze. She sighed with relief when he finally nodded.

Finally she was getting somewhere with him. She walked over and stood before him. The passage about going boldly to the throne of grace ran through her mind.

"Please forgive me for not telling you about taking the job. I was wrong."

"You got that right," he interrupted in agreement.

"I know, but I want to tell you something that I have never told you before." She sat on the corner of his desk and proceeded to tell him how her mother's powerful influence had affected her. She told him about her mother's own troubled marriage and how it served as the catalyst in planting the thoughts inside her head. She hoped that by sharing her fears she had touched his heart with her words.

"My mother thought she was doing the right thing and I can't blame her because she didn't have anyone to confer with. Her own mother was dead and she didn't have any sisters. I suppose that if I didn't know any better, I would probably tell my daughter the same so that she wouldn't get hurt either."

Darius began pacing back and forth across the floor. The muscle in his jaw flexed in anger. "What I can't get over is how you just walked away from what we had, especially after all that we had been through. Alexa you were my wife, my best friend. You were the only woman I ever loved and you knew it. Hell, I wouldn't have asked you to marry me if I didn't love you." The pain in his voice was very evident.

Alexa wanted to run over and comfort him with a hug, but refrained from doing so because she did not want to stop him from sharing his feelings.

"As crazy as it sounds, I thought I was doing the honorable thing. See, although I loved you I was scared that if I gave up my career, I'd be giving up the one thing I had control over in my life. Consequently if I poured my energy into our relationship and things didn't turn out right, then I would be left with nothing."

Darius stopped pacing with a look of disappointment on his face over the wasted years. "Damn it, Alex, if you loved me and you knew how I loved you then you should have shared your fears with me and trusted that our love would have survived."

At Last!

Alexa looked into his eyes. "I know that now." She stood away from the desk and walked towards him. "But I'm not walking away anymore. Baby, I'm sorry for what I put you through. I hope you can forgive me because I love you more than anything. I've been so lonely without you and I don't think I can go another day knowing that you won't be a part of my life."

Her words caused his stance to relax and he searched her eyes for a hint of a chance for them. "You said you love me more than anything?" he asked, repeating her words.

Alexa nodded with hope-filled eyes. She had prayed for a new beginning and hoped that this was the sign that she ask the Lord for.

"More than say, Marks-St. Claire?" he asked.

She responded by pulling the letter from her pocket and placing it into his hand. Darius removed the paper from the envelope and quickly scanned the contents of the letter. Elation rose in the pit of his stomach, that he could not force back his smile upon reading her letter of resignation.

"You quit?"

Alexa nodded. "Yes, I did a week ago. I packed up as much as I could in my car and drove here praying that we could work things out." She walked up to him and placed her hand in his. "I meant it when I said I love you, Darius. I want you in my life forever. Please say yes."

Annie Riverside's words immediately came to mind: *Real love doesn't stray away too far or too long*. Darius' heart swelled with joy.

"My lady, is this a proposal?"

Alexa thought for a moment. She was proposing that she would be totally honest with him and not hold back her feelings. She was proposing that nothing, especially her career, would take precedence over her husband again. And, she was proposing that she would be the loving and supporting wife that he needed and deserved. With that said, she concluded that she was proposing that Darius give their love another try. With a broad smile, Alexa replied. "I guess it is."

Darius slowly lowered himself before her onto one knee and raised her hands to his mouth. Staring deeply into her eyes he pressed a gentle kiss on the palms of her hands. "Then, I do, *again.*"

The floodgates immediately lifted as tears of joy poured down Alexa's face. She sank down on her knees before Darius, sobbing. "I love you, and I will never let you go again," she promised, kissing him all over his face.

"I love you too," Darius confirmed. "And, I'm sorry for being so selfish. I'm sorry for not being supportive of your career. I'm sorry…"

Alexa cut him off with a kiss.

The scene was so intense that it brought tears to Darius' eyes. Alexa saw the tears brimming in his eyes and tenderly cradled his head in her arms, kissing them away before they could fall. Her touch was so gentle and poignant that Darius could not help but release his own emotions. Before he could stop himself, he was weeping along with her.

"I promise I won't make you sad again," she murmured through kisses.

A knock on the door interrupted their private moment, followed by Donna's intrusive footsteps. Her jaw dropped at the sight of her boss in a heap on the floor, crying in his lover's arms.

"I, I'm sorry Mr. Riverside," she stammered apologetically. She turned to retrace her steps when Darius called out her name.

"Donna, these are tears of joy!" he exclaimed. "I'm getting married!" he captured Alexa's face in his palms and kissed her sweet and slow. "We're getting married, again."

EPILOGUE

A gentle July breeze paired with the orange glow of the evening sun created the perfect romantic setting for a wedding. As a sign of their commitment to one another, Darius and Alexa wanted to reaffirm their vows before family and friends.

Since the pair was moving to Detroit, Maya and Bryant insisted that the wedding take place in their backyard. Maya was eager to coordinate the wedding and reception since she was now off from work on maternity leave. Her stomach protruded in the lilac empire waist dress, revealing another addition to the Renault family on the way.

Maya's skills proved to be successful, as the end results were breathtaking, revealing a strong potential for a career change in the future.

Strolling through the yard, Maya kept busy by making sure everything was in place. She had taken great care in decorating the yard into a white matrimonial dreamland. White sateen chair covers with big bows were draped over the fold-up chairs placed theater style in the back yard where the ceremony was to take place.

Maya thought it was perfect having the two exchange vows beneath a white canopy surrounded by topiary trees bearing white roses and draped with sheering.

The reception would take place near the pool beneath a white tent. Everything inside the tent, including the table and table coverings, dinnerware and white rose centerpiece were white as well. Maya finished the look by hanging white Japanese lanterns. She had tested the effect the night before and it was so beautiful that she couldn't wait for the reception to begin to see the surprised looks on everyone's faces.

Alexa was speechless when she saw the view from the rear bedroom where she was getting ready. Later when Maya came inside, she ran up to her and hugged her through tear-filled eyes.

"Maya, thank you. It is beautiful!"

"Girl, stop crying before you mess up your face," Maya teased, although tears were forming in her eyes as well.

Downstairs, Darius was in the study gazing out at the growing crowd. Whereas most men would have paced the room anxious from the fact that his bachelor life was coming to an end, Darius was the epitome of contentment.

Deep down he knew he had the girl and all of this was for everyone else's benefit. He couldn't wait for the ceremony to come and go so that he could get to the good part and that was being alone with his wife.

"You're not having second thoughts are you?" A voice from behind interrupted his reverie.

Darius turned around to find both Bryant and Reg standing with big grins on their faces.

"No, never," he replied with a smile.

"Well, potna, you beat me to the altar not once, but twice," Reg exclaimed, with a pat on the back.

"Tell me about it."

"Say, I'm sorry about my reservations concerning Alexa. I can see that she is truly a good woman who loves you very much and I know she will make you happy."

Darius was touched by his friend's words and gave the man a brotherly hug.

"So, baby boy," Bryant interrupted, stepping towards Darius. "Are you ready to do this again?" he asked as he began straightening his tie and smoothing his jacket.

"Most def," Darius quickly answered. "Most def."

*   *   *

Inside, Alexa was a vision of loveliness in a sleeveless, white, silk gown with jeweled neckline, fitted bodice and A-line skirt. Her hair was pinned up in the back causing the curly tendrils to push forward, delicately framing her face. Her look was topped off with Maya's *borrowed* tiara.

Her hands shook nervously as her mother assisted her in slipping on the white elbow length gloves.

"Don't be nervous," Beverly said gently, rubbing Alexa's hands in an attempt to calm her.

"I know. I just don't want anything to go wrong."

"Don't worry honey, everything will be fine. Maya has everything under control and I saw Darius out back and he looked like a man who was ready to make you his wife." she said squeezing Alexa's hands. "I'm sorry to have underestimated your love for one another. Now that I know what you both have been through, I couldn't think of a finer man to call son." With that, she stepped back, holding Alexa at arms length. "I can't believe that my baby girl is getting married?"

"Don't you mean our baby girl?"

The two women turned around to find Alexa's father poking his head inside the door. Beverly grinned and waved him inside. He pulled his girls into his wide arms and the three of them joined hands in a small circle bearing smiles.

Since her reunion with Darius, Alexa learned that her parents were giving their love a second chance. It seemed that Alexa's wedding announcement was the catalyst in their getting back together. According to Beverly, James called her up unexpectedly and said it wasn't proper for the two of them to be apart when their daughter had resolved her issues. So, with her permission, and on her terms, he asked to court her again. Of course, she was smitten by the whole act and quickly agreed. Alexa could see a renewed sparkle in both of their eyes that had been absent for many years. She thanked God for restoring her parents love in addition to her love with Darius.

The organist began the instrumental interlude signifying that the time had come.

"Are you ready baby girl?" her father asked as he extended his arm.

"More than you'll ever know daddy," she replied, slipping her arm into his.

The three headed downstairs to the great room where the wedding party consisting of Maya, Teressa, Crystal, Bryant, Reg, Darius' brother Eric and Justin were waiting.

Justin immediately sauntered over and took Beverly's arm. Before going outside, he paused to give Alexa a big hug and kiss. "You look gorgeous, sis."

"Thanks, Justin," she replied through tear-glistened eyes. "Remember you're next."

"We will see," he replied. Alexa smiled hopefully as she sensed newness about her brother as well. After he released her, he took their mother's arm and stepped through the threshold and down the aisle.

"You nervous, baby girl?" James asked, patting her hand.

She nodded, with a nervous smile on her lips and tears in her eyes for what was the happiest day in her life.

"Don't be. You've got a good man," he assured her with a kiss on the nose.

She smiled up at him, "Yeah, like my Dad."

The smile on her father's face was as bright as a lit up baseball field at an evening ball game. She could swear that she even saw tears form, something she had never seen before, but then again changes were taking place in everyone these days.

At Last!

At that moment, the French doors opened, and the evening sun's glow draped their bodies. The organist began to play the jazzy notes to the song Alexa was to enter on. It was the perfect depiction of their love for one another.

The melody alone caused him to gulp back his emotions for the memories, which had been sealed in his heart overwhelmed him. When Maya stepped before the microphone the spectators sighed collectively as she began to sing.

On cue, Alexa and her father began their stroll down the aisle. Her eyes looked past the crowd towards the front where her husband stood waiting. When their eyes met, her smile broadened and she blocked out everything, choosing to focus on nothing but the spot waiting beside him.

The ceremony flew by without a hitch. Before either of them knew it, Pastor Washington blessed the marriage and announced them as husband and wife. Darius turned to his bride and paused momentarily to gaze upon her with adoring eyes.

She blushed under his careful examination. He gently caressed her cheek with his palm before gliding the tip of his forefinger down her jaw line. Stepping in closer to her to fill the space between them, Darius tipped her chin so that their eyes met.

"Alexa, I know we've been through a lot, but if I had to go through this all over again, I couldn't think of a better person than you to share the experience. I promise to give you the best that I got and more." With that said he lowered his head and placed a tender kiss on her waiting mouth. Tears rolled down Alexa's cheek as she wrapped her arms around his neck, receiving him wholly against her bosom. With all her mind, body and soul, she knew that she'd feel the same eternally.

ABOUT THE AUTHOR

Lisa Harrison-Jackson's love for writing was recognized in elementary school where a fourth grade creative writing assignment turned into a passion for story telling. Although she has had several articles published in magazines and newspapers, *At Last* is her first published novel. In addition to writing, she enjoys reading, writing poetry and film study. She resides in Atlanta, Georgia with her husband and two daughters. She is currently penning her second novel to be released in 2004.

AUTHOR'S NOTE

I believe that there is a little Alexa and Darius in all of us: the desire to be loved, honored and cherished by the one you love, to have a fulfilling career or clear purpose in life and most important a desire for a personal relationship with our Creator. My goal in writing this book was to create a realistic character, facing real issues and making real decisions whether good or bad. My hope was to touch my readers' hearts and motivate them to examine their lives as well as encourage them to be strong enough to step out in faith if a situation calls for it, knowing that God is in control and He will never fail them.

Tracy L. Usher
907 Gross Lake Pkwy
Covington, Ga. 30016

0-595-20869-X

Printed in the United States
25187LVS00005B/132

9 780595 208692